BROKEN HOPE

A DARK MAFIA ROMANCE (VOLKOV BRATVA)

NICOLE FOX

Copyright © 2019 by Nicole Fox

All rights reserved.

No part of this book may be reproduced in any form or by any electronic or mechanical means, including information storage and retrieval systems, without written permission from the author, except for the use of brief quotations in a book review.

❦ Created with Vellum

MAILING LIST

Sign up to my mailing list!
New subscribers receive a FREE steamy bad boy romance novel.

Click the link below to join.
https://readerlinks.com/l/1057996

ALSO BY NICOLE FOX

Kornilov Bratva Duet

Married to the Don (Book 1)

Til Death Do Us Part (Book 2)

Heirs to the Bratva Empire

Can be read in any order

Kostya

Maksim

Andrei

Tsezar Bratva

Nightfall (Book 1)

Daybreak (Book 2)

Russian Crime Brotherhood

Can be read in any order

Owned by the Mob Boss

Unprotected with the Mob Boss

Knocked Up by the Mob Boss

Sold to the Mob Boss

Stolen by the Mob Boss

Trapped with the Mob Boss

Volkov Bratva

Broken Vows (Book 1)

Broken Hope (Book 2)

Broken Sins *(standalone)*

Box Sets

Bratva Mob Bosses

Tsezar Bratva

Other Standalones

Vin: A Mafia Romance

BROKEN HOPE

A DARK MAFIA ROMANCE (VOLKOV BRATVA)

They kidnapped my wife and baby. I'll go through hell to get them back.

Eve was a pawn in a violent game.

Until she became the queen of my world.

She saved me from my own darkness.

But now, my past is threatening to consume us both.

I tried to keep her safe.

Locked away like a princess in a tower.

Up there, she was protected from everything…

Except for me.

Now, I'm knee-deep in the underworld.

I'll do whatever it takes to rescue my family:

Lie.

Steal.

Kill.

And once this is all over…

Once my wife and baby are back in my arms…

I'll slaughter every man who laid a finger on them.

No one takes what's mine.

1

EVE

I feel the rumble beneath me before my eyes open.

It takes me a moment to process that I'm not at home in my bed. That I'm not even lying down. I'm sitting up in the back of a car, and I have the worst pain in my neck. When I roll my head on my shoulders, I wince, squeezing my eyes closed even tighter.

Then, I smell Luka.

For a moment, the familiar scent of his cologne calms me. He is nearby. We are together.

The knot in my chest loosens, and I realize that everything else will be okay as long as we are together.

"Finally awake?"

My eyes snap open at the unfamiliar voice, and I smash my body against the car door, putting as much distance between myself and my seatmate as possible. The car is dark, only the small lights from the car's console offering a small glow of light into the back seat, and I have to find the human shape in the blackness piece by piece.

"Sorry to startle you," she says. It is a 'she' I recognize now, but I'm still not sure who she is.

Definitely not Luka.

"Where am I?" My voice is raspy, and I clear my throat. "Who are you?"

The woman tilts her head to the side, her long blonde ponytail falling over her shoulder. "You don't remember?"

I shake my head slowly. My entire body is tense, on guard. I have no memory of how I got here, and a quick glance around the car tells me that, aside from the driver, we are alone. "Where is my family?"

The woman leans forward and looks into my face like she is studying me for signs of injury. "You don't remember me, Eve?"

It is still dark, but as she moves closer, I see her blonde hair and crisp business clothes. I remember what Luka told me.

"You are ... Cole's sister?" It is a guess, but now that I really look at her, I can see the similarities in their eyes.

"Rian," she nods.

I shake my head. This still doesn't make any sense. Even during the short time I was engaged to Cole Morrison, Rian was never around. I didn't even know she existed until Luka told me he'd met her earlier in the night.

When was that? Just a few hours ago? Talking to him after he came home from the FBI headquarters is one of the last things I remember, but clearly there is a large gap in my memory. How many hours have I lost?

And where is my husband?

Working for the FBI probably meant Rian couldn't socialize with a known gun trafficker, even if he was her brother. Cole didn't feel the need to mention she existed. Maybe I would have learned about her eventually if I'd stuck around and become his wife. But apparently they were closer than I realized if she was willing to use her authority as an FBI agent to hunt down the man responsible for her brother's death.

"I'm sure you are confused," she says, reaching out to lay a hand on my arm.

I pull away from her reach, and then feel bad for doing so. What if she really is trying to help me?

My head is still swimming. Nothing is making any sense.

She presses her lips together and folds her hands in her lap. "We came to your house to talk with your husband."

"We?" I ask, looking towards the driver.

She digs in her pocket and pulls out her FBI badge.

"Is he in trouble? You already talked to him tonight. What is going on?"

"Just business," she says sharply. Then, her eyes soften. "While we were there the second time, you went into a kind of … fit."

"What does that mean?" My heart is like a jackhammer in my chest, beating so hard I can feel the beats in my entire body. "You didn't come back a second time. It was just Luka."

"You were delusional," she says, waving a hand near her temple to silently suggest I went crazy. "I'm not sure if it was the stress or dehydration or what, but you were going mad. We had to get you out of the house."

I smack my lips together. They are so dry. My tongue feels like a piece of chalk in my mouth. Maybe I am dehydrated.

"But where is Luka?" I ask, looking into the third row of the SUV even though I know it is empty. "Where is Milaya?"

"She is with Luka at your house," Rian says in a soothing tone. "Don't worry. We are just taking you to get checked out. I offered to drive you so Milaya wouldn't have to get out so late."

I sit up and twist to the window. We are driving quickly—definitely on a highway—and the sides of the road are lined with thick trees. We aren't even in the city.

"Are you taking me to the FBI headquarters?"

"No, a hospital," she says. "You aren't being arrested. We are just taking you to be seen by a doctor."

In the middle of nowhere? Why wouldn't they have taken me somewhere in the city? And why wouldn't Luka have come with me?

Luka would have come with me. I know it.

Something is wrong here.

"Is Luka going to meet us there?" I pat my thighs, searching for my cell phone, but I'm wearing pajama shorts. No pockets. No purse. No phone.

"He is going to stay at the house with Milaya," Rian says, sounding slightly more annoyed this time. "Don't worry. We will just have you seen by someone, make sure everything is okay, and then we'll take you right back home."

Everything in my body is telling me something is very, very wrong.

My head feels heavy and my temples are pounding like I just woke up from the world's worst hangover. But I wasn't drinking the night before.

And as far as delusional fits go, I've never had one. No nervous breakdowns, even when I was kidnapped by my own father. If I could handle that, then certainly I can handle a raid by the FBI.

When I look over at Rian Morrison, she is smiling at me, but the expression doesn't reach her eyes. There, I find only cold assessment.

It is the agent in her, observing me, searching for any signs of what I'll do next, of what I'm thinking.

Why Rian?

She made it clear in her conversation with Luka that she blames him for her brother's death and wants revenge.

Is that was this is?

Because it certainly isn't official.

If the FBI was going to take me into custody, there would be more people here. I would be handcuffed. I would have some memory of being arrested.

No, this is off the books, and I know if I don't get out of here as soon as possible, something bad is going to happen.

Rian opens her mouth to say something else, but before she can, I haul my arm back and slam my fist into her mouth. Her top teeth cut into my knuckle and pain explodes through my wrist. I cry out but there is no time to slow down.

I have to fight.

I grab her ponytail and yank her head forward, trying to throw her off balance. The car jerks and skids on the road, and Rian is trying to yell things at the driver, but my blows are coming too fast.

Luka taught me to fight. At the time, I thought it was unnecessary. I had pepper spray in my purse and a rape whistle on my keychain. Plus, I had Luka and was under near-constant guard by a member of the Bratva. Why did I need to learn to defend myself?

Now, I'm glad he took the time to teach me.

I yank Rian forward and ram my knee upwards towards her face. She pulls back in time to avoid the full impact, but I still feel her nose crunch beneath my kneecap.

The back seat of the SUV is cramped and small, making it hard to move, but I throw my seat belt off and crawl onto the seat on my knees. I wrap an arm around Rian's neck, using my other hand to swat her clawing fingers away.

I know her nails are digging into my skin over and over again, but the adrenaline pumping through my veins has processed all of that as background information. Not important right now. The only thing that matters now is fighting and getting away.

Fight. Get away.

Back to my family.

"I'll send Milaya away," Rian screams. Her voice is shrill and panicked. "I'll send her to another country, and you'll never see her again."

Her words give me pause for only a second before I tighten my hold on her neck. If she kidnapped me and Milaya, then the likelihood that she was ever going to give Milaya back was slim anyway. Fighting doesn't lessen my chances of seeing her.

For a brief second, I allow myself to think about what she has done to Luka.

If she has taken me and Milaya, then where is he? Is he alive?

I push the thought from my mind as soon as it materializes. I can't live in that pain yet. Not until I know for sure. Until it is proven otherwise, I'll believe Luka is alive.

I just need to get the hell out of here and find out.

Rian is going limp in my arms, the fight falling out of her, and I think I am succeeding in suffocating her, but then I feel a sharp pain in my thigh.

I look down to see a syringe jammed into my leg, pumping a clear fluid into my body.

"No," I growl, throwing my body forward to pin Rian against the leather seats.

I pull the syringe from my leg, but it is too late. There is nothing left. Whatever it was, it is coursing through my veins now, which means I likely only have minutes left to fight.

My movements become hurried, panicked. Move by move, I lose the upper hand.

Rian kicks a leg up and around my back, leveraging her weight to roll over me and pin me on the floorboards.

I kick both feet up and into her stomach, knocking the air out of her, but before I can use the advantage, the rear passenger door opens and the hulking figure of the driver is standing over me.

His hands are warm and meaty, and they clamp onto my arms like I am nothing but a toothpick in the grip of a giant.

He hauls me out of the car and onto the crunchy grass of the ditch, throwing me back in the dirt.

I try to scramble to my feet, but my vision is blurred. My connection to my arms and legs is slipping, and even the simplest movements feel like a chore. Wet sand collects in my hands and my brain has liquefied and is sloshing against the sides of my skull.

I push myself away from the car, scooting further into the brush alongside the road, all the while Rian and her driver are moving towards me.

Rian looks wrecked. Her white shirt has blood around the collar and her lip is already swelling up. Even as I slip from consciousness, I can't help but be a little proud of my fight.

"She is gone," Rian says, though I can't see her anymore. "Put her back in the car."

Suddenly, I'm floating. My head lolls back, and I open my eyes to look up at the sky. At the stars.

Except, they aren't the stars.

Just above the tree line in the distance, I can see the lights of the city behind me. The lights of home.

I imagine being there with Luka and Milaya.

We are at the butterfly conservatory. A large building with floor-to-ceiling windows and skylights and a vast garden stretching in every direction.

Luka complains about the humidity and pulls at his shirt, but when he sees the smile on Milaya's tiny face, he can't help but smile, too.

We are both slaves to that smile. Anything we can do to make her happy, we will.

For a second after she was born, I was jealous of the way Luka looked at her. At the way he clearly worshipped her. But then, I realized how lucky I was to have a man like that in my life. A man who cared for his daughter more than he cared for himself. Who would do anything to protect her.

Then, he looked up at me, and I recognized the look. It was the same one he gave our daughter, and I knew.

He worshipped me, too.

Milaya bats her tiny hands at the butterflies that flutter close to her stroller, trying to grab them, but they move too quickly. She turns her head from side to side, eyes wide and full of wonder.

I cling to the moment, knowing one day I'll miss this.

A man appears at the corner of my vision. A dark shadow on the otherwise bright day. I turn to look at him, but Luka angles himself in front of me and Milaya, blocking my view.

I stretch to look around him, but I see the tension in his shoulders and follow the line up to his face. His eyes are narrowed. His gaze is on me, but his attention is somewhere else. Once again, I try to see around him, but he moves to block my view and then grabs my chin.

When I look into his eyes now, they are soft. My favorite shade of green. Like sunlight through spring leaves.

All thoughts of the man behind us disappear as Luka wraps an arm around my waist and pulls me against him. His lips flutter against mine, softer than butterfly wings, and I melt into him.

2

LUKA

As soon as my eyes drag open, I'm on my feet.

Holding onto furniture and walls for support, I stumble through my bedroom and into the hall.

"Hello?"

I know Eve isn't here and she and Milaya are gone, but we have security. Men from the Bratva who watch the house in shifts.

Ever since Eve was kidnapped by her father, I've made sure we have security on the property. Even if our system failed, the guards should have noticed something was going on.

"Hello?" I scream, voice hoarse and dry.

The house is eerily silent, and I stop at the top of the stairs, trying to listen for any movement. There is nothing, and I grip the handrail so hard on my way down the stairs that I'm surprised it doesn't break off in my hands.

Eve wanted me to quit smoking. If I hadn't been outside smoking a cigarette, this never would have happened.

The Irish wouldn't have gotten into my house and taken my wife and child.

All of this is my fault.

I reach the landing and move towards the back of the house where the guards should have been keeping watch from the security room.

As soon as I walk into the small hallway where the door to the security room is, I see the blood.

A thick red puddle leaks out from beneath the door. It is congealed and sticky, meaning it has been there for a while.

How long have I been unconscious?

I turn the handle and toe the door open. It opens a couple feet before it catches on something and won't open any further.

It is a body.

"Shit." I slam the door closed and lean back against the wall, hands tugging at my hair.

The Irish did this. I know that. The raid earlier in the evening was a distraction. Rian Morrison had a recording of me killing her brother, which gave her enough evidence to bring me in but not enough to hold me.

But that doesn't matter. It was a distraction.

While I was out of the house, they laid their trap.

They turned off the security alarms, killed my guards, and lay in wait.

They could have taken Eve and Milaya while I was gone, but that wouldn't have been good enough. That revenge wouldn't have been sweet enough.

I was supposed to come home and see my family safe and sound. They wanted me to relax, to take a deep breath and think everything was fine so that it would hurt all the more when they ripped the rug out from underneath me.

And oh man does it hurt. It hurts like hell.

I clench my fists, squeeze my eyes closed, and try to organize my still-cloudy thoughts into a plan.

I need to get my family back.

The Irish took them, but at the behest of Rian Morrison, no doubt. I could sneak into the New York City FBI field office and demand answers. Rian wouldn't have the gall to kill me on government property, especially government property where she works.

Except, I don't know that for sure.

If there is anything I've learned throughout my lifetime, it is that a guy like me can't trust the government. Especially the FBI.

They are supposed to protect and serve, but that doesn't extend to criminals like me.

They don't care about my missing family or my heartache. If I waltz back into that building of my own free will, I'll likely be detained and held indefinitely on a shit ton of charges. And that won't help me in the search for Eve and Milaya.

Plus, Rian may not even be there. She was at the headquarters when I left, but she could have followed me home to help run this covert attack.

I'm standing outside the security room wishing there was a way to know for sure who carried out the kidnapping, when I realize I'm standing two feet away from a wall of security cameras.

I jump up and, avoiding the puddle of blood, push the door open.

Once again, it catches on one of the bodies inside, but I turn sideways and squeeze into the room.

My guys have been shot in the back of the head. They probably never even saw it coming. One of them is on the floor, blocking the door from opening, and the other is slumped over in his chair, head resting on the table in front of him.

I nudge him sideways off the chair with a whispered apology and then drag the chair away from the majority of the blood.

The small room is thick with the tangy scent of iron and the smell is making me queasy, so I work quickly.

I pull up the cameras for the upstairs hallway and scrub back several hours. Whatever drug they used to knock me out did the job. I was passed out on the side of the bed for almost two hours.

Finally, I see Eve and I walking down the hallway to go downstairs. From there, we talked in the kitchen for several minutes, and then Eve went back upstairs. She walked into our bedroom and out of sight of the camera, and I know that downstairs, I was walking out to the front porch for a smoke.

Then, nothing.

No movement, no sound.

For a minute, I almost think the image is frozen.

And then, I see him.

A shadow in the corner of the frame, creeping down the hallway. He stops outside of Milaya's room, ear pressed to the door, and I want to throttle him. I want to run up the stairs and shoot him in the back of the head the way he had probably just finished killing my men.

But I know he isn't there.

This is a recording, so I grit my teeth and watch as he moves slowly towards the bedroom.

Following closely behind him is another man. This one much larger.

His shoulders are almost as wide as the hallway itself. Eve wouldn't have had a chance in a fight against someone that size, even with the training I gave her.

Though, when I see the men reemerge from the bedroom only a few seconds later, I realize there wasn't a need for a fight. Eve is already unconscious. Probably drugged in the same way I was.

The smaller man breaks away and goes into Milaya's room. A moment later, he emerges with my sleeping child on his shoulder, and a rage like nothing I've ever felt before rushes through me.

I slam my fists on the table and roar.

How was all of this happening while I was only feet away downstairs?

Knowing that I'm out of frame, standing on the porch, makes me feel sick. That I was so close, yet completely unaware. I've never felt more useless in all my life.

The small man carries Milaya down the hallway and out of shot, and the larger man carries Eve.

Now that he is walking towards the camera, I recognize him immediately. I should have known who he was as soon as I saw his large stature, but that doesn't matter. I know who he is now.

Sean O'Hearn.

He's known as "the Lumberjack" around the city. He's the main enforcer for the Irish mafia before they disbanded. Or, supposedly disbanded, anyway.

And his presence in my house means that Eve really is with the Irish.

Which means I know exactly where I need to go next.

It takes me an hour to get dressed and guzzle enough coffee to feel confident the drugs are out of my system and I am safe to drive, so by the time I get to the Irish pub it is just after three in the morning.

I haven't slept in well over twenty-four hours, and exhaustion burns the backs of my eyes, but in every other way that matters, I am wide awake. Adrenaline pumps through me as I approach the bar and pull the door open.

The pub was a favorite hangout of the Irish mafia when they were still in business, and I suspect it is still popular among a lot of them. I can only hope someone will be willing to talk.

Not including the bartender, there are only three people in the small space when I walk inside, and they all turn and stare at me. None of them are Sean O'Hearn. I tip my head and stroll inside, grabbing a seat at the bar.

Two of the men are at the bar chatting loudly with the bartender, laughing about some fight they saw at another bar earlier in the night. The other man is sitting at a table off to my left, drinking alone.

I don't want to draw much attention to myself, so I avoid looking at him directly, but I feel a tension radiating from him.

The bartender slides closer to me and raises an eyebrow in question. I order a beer and shift on the stool, glancing back over my shoulder.

When my eyes land on the thin man behind me, his grip tightens on his glass, and he sits up taller. He is clearly nervous.

The bartender slides my beer down to me, and I can feel him assessing me, trying to figure out where he may know me from.

I want to be out of here by the time he figures it out.

Whether the Irish mafia is really disbanded or not, there is a lot of animosity towards me, and I'm not in any mood to get in a four-versus-one fight tonight.

I sip the beer, not wanting to dull my senses any more than they already are, and look back at the table again. The man has turned away from me. He is hunched forward and hiding his face behind his glass.

But then, he peeks around the glass to see if I'm still looking at him. When he sees that I am, he darts back into hiding like a scared animal.

Whoever he is, he knows something.

I drop ten dollars on the bar and stand up, but as soon as I make a move towards the man's table, he runs—a full-out sprint towards the back door of the bar with no regard for being obvious or looking suspicious. The man is running for his life, which means he must have a good reason to be afraid of me.

The bartender yells after the man, "Hey! That back door is staff only!" But the runner doesn't care and neither do I.

I chase after him, jumping over an overturned chair and pushing aside a table that gets in my way.

The bar is narrow and the hallway in the back is a straight shot to the back door. I see it swing shut and lower my head, pushing as hard as I can to catch up.

The man might not know exactly what happened at my house tonight, but at the very least, he is an Irish mafia member and might be able to help me figure out where my wife and child are.

There are no lights in the alley, so I have to squint into the darkness to see the small man's shape hurtling through the dark alley towards the road beyond. I chase after him.

He is small but not fast, and my long strides have me right on his heels in a matter of seconds.

The end of the alley is coming up, but right before he can make it to the sidewalk, I lunge forward, tangle my hand in the back of his shirt, and yank him backwards.

A large huff of air bursts out of him when his spine hits the concrete. He collapses into a whimpering puddle.

I walk around him and press my foot into his chest.

"Why are you running?"

"Because you are chasing me," he says, trying to roll away.

I press into his chest harder until I'm sure another centimeter will crush his rib cage. The man strains for a second and then crumples back onto the pavement, gasping for breath.

"Let up, for fuck's sake," he says, weakly pushing at my shoe to no avail.

"I will let you up when you tell me where my family is."

He wrinkles his forehead, doing his best to look confused, but I can see the panic in his eyes. Like a wild animal searching for an escape route, I can tell I've cornered him. He knows he is fucked.

I flex, threatening to put more pressure on his chest. "Where are they?"

He winces and then lays his hands out on the pavement in surrender. "I don't know, man. I don't know who you are or what you are talking about. I was just in the bar having a drink and—"

I pull my knife and plunge it into his side before he even knows what happened.

His eyes widen and then his jaw goes unhinged. "You fucking stabbed me."

He clutches at his side and then lifts his hand up to see the blood on his fingers. A sob bursts out of his chest. "Shit. You stabbed me."

"Tell me what I need to know or I'll let you bleed out." I wipe my knife on the man's jeans and put it back in my pocket. "Where is my family?"

He blubbers, shaking his head. "Come on, man. I'm bleeding too much."

"Then talk fast!" I growl, driving my heel into his sternum. "The faster you tell me what you know, the faster you can find help."

The man is pathetic. He is almost crying on the ground, lower lip shaking like a small child's, and all of it makes me sick. Really, it makes me want to put the sad sack out of his misery.

"Did you just come to this bar from my house?" I ask.

His eyes snap to me, and I know I've hit the mark.

I grit my teeth and press my boot harder into his chest until I swear I can feel his heartbeat in the bottom of my foot. "Did you help kidnap my family?"

He shakes his head. "No. No. That wasn't my job."

"What was your job?" I tip my head down to the wound at his side. "Better talk quick. You're losing a lot of blood."

The man's face was going pale. Even in the dark, his skin seems to be glowing.

"Your wife was being kidnapped for an auction. It's a sale put on by the LeClerc Cartel. They deal with human trafficking. That is all I know."

My heart feels like it is lodged in my throat. The thought of sex-hungry men bidding on my wife. Touching her.

My hands are shaking.

"Bullshit," I bark. "Tell me more."

He sobs and shakes his head. "I don't know more. If I did, I'd tell you."

I know about the LeClerc Cartel. Rather than serving lowlifes with junkie girls and runaways, they cater to the immoral elite. Men with cash to spare who don't mind buying sex or slave labor. The Cartel has a large gathering every year where they show off their best merchandise. It is the biggest event they put on all year, and, if my memory serves, it is coming up on a year since the last event.

"When is the auction?"

"I don't know," the man says, slapping the pavement with his palms. His hand splashes in his own warm blood, and he groans. "Can I get up? Please?"

His voice is weak. Even if I do let him up, I'm not sure he'll make it to the end of the alley.

"Where is Milaya?"

He screws up his face and shakes his head. "Who?"

"My daughter!" I roar, furious that this piece of shit who helped kidnap my daughter doesn't even know her name.

She meant nothing to him. Just another job.

"I never saw her," he says. "My job was to take out the guards. That is it. Once the job was done, a separate car dropped me off here. I didn't see where they were taken."

I shift the weight on my foot, digging the toe of my boot into the soft flesh of his windpipe above his collarbone.

The man's eyes pop out and his lips go blue around the edges. He claws at my foot, panicked, but just as his eyes start to roll back in his head, I lift my foot and back away.

He gasps for air, but the breaths are shallow. His coughs sound wet and phlegmy.

He doesn't have long.

I want to stay and end him myself. I never had any intention of letting him live. Mess with my family, and you won't live to see another day.

But based on how much blood is in the alley, this man is dead anyway. And I don't have the time to spare. I need to find my family.

So, I walk down the alley and leave the man to bleed out.

3

EVE

Things come to me in flashes.

Brief moments of light so bright and quick that I don't know what is real and imagined.

My head hurts, but the sensation ebbs and flows, coming and going in waves until I can't pinpoint the source of the pain.

I open my eyes and see black leather right next to my face. I see my own arm draped over the edge of a car seat. I see the glowing knob for the radio on a car stereo.

Then, I see Luka.

He is in bed next to me, his strong arm wrapped around my waist. The woodsy smell of him curls around me like a blanket, and I take deep breaths.

Then, Milaya begins to cry.

I move to get up, but Luka kisses my shoulder and nuzzles his face against the back of my neck. His body is warm against me, and his hips circle against my backside. "Don't move. I'll get her."

I turn around and catch his lips with mine, sucking on his lower lip until he groans. "I'll be waiting."

Luka leaves, and I roll back on the bed and throw my arms over my head, sinking into the mattress.

There are few feelings as good as the after-sex glow. The warm, sated ease that seeps into every muscle, taking with it any worries I may have had prior. The best part of that glow, however, is snuggling into Luka's broad chest and wrapping myself in his warmth.

So, after he is gone a few minutes, I slip to the side of the bed, wrap the sheet around my body, and pad into the hallway to see if there was some kind of diaper explosion that is holding him up.

I stop outside the partially opened door to Milaya's room. The lights are off in her room except for a small cloud nightlight in the corner, and Luka is talking quietly.

"Everyone gets scared sometimes," he whispers. "When you get scared, you can just cry out for Mommy and Daddy, and we'll always come check on you."

I press my hand to my heart, afraid it might actually melt and drip down my rib cage.

"We love you so much, Milaya. More than we can say," Luka says. "Which is why I will do anything I can to ensure you are happy and safe."

Tears burn at the back of my eyes, and I swallow back a lump in my throat.

Luka isn't putting on a show for anyone. He isn't trying to impress anyone or prove that he is a good father.

He is simply being a good father.

Even when he thinks no one is looking, he loves our daughter so fiercely, and I have never felt so lucky in my entire life.

Still, flowing underneath the love and admiration, there is a touch of jealousy.

Not of Milaya or her close relationship with Luka, but a jealousy that stems from the fact that I never had that kind of relationship with my own father.

Before Luka, I never had a man look at me and swear to protect me. I never had a father figure who would have done anything to make sure I was safe.

Instead, I had a father who thought I was no good to anyone unless I was cooking and cleaning and popping out babies.

I had a father who tried to whore me out on multiple occasions and was willing to put my life at risk to reach his own ends.

I try to push the thought away, but I remember sitting in the chair at the warehouse where my father was holding me. I can see people standing around me, watching me like I'm a new exhibit at the zoo and they want to be entertained. I can practically feel their eyes on me, watching my every move, waiting for a sign of weakness.

Unlike the first time I woke up—dazed and unsure—I start awake this time.

I know where I am. Or, rather, where I'm not.

I'm not at home.

I'm not with Luka.

I'm not with my daughter.

My body jerks forward, and pain cuts into my wrists and ankles. I look down and see that my legs are zip-tied to the legs of a wooden kitchen chair. My hands, too, are secured to the armrests. I pull against the restraints, but the chair is sturdy, and I feel weak.

I look around the room and am surprised to see that I'm not in a dingy warehouse or a basement, but rather, an extravagant dining room.

A solid wood table runs the length of the room, plush carpet beneath it, and a large glass-fronted china cabinet runs the length of the right wall. Fine dinnerware and teacups line the shelves.

The left wall is all windows that look out over a rolling green lawn. I see a tree line and the sky beyond, but no sign of another house. No road with cars passing by. No visible connection to the outside world.

There is a swinging door to my right that looks like it could lead into a kitchen and a set of French double doors straight ahead. They are opened wide onto a sitting room. The furniture is modern—a blue, tufted velvet—with massive framed oil paintings covering the wall I can see.

And I recognize it.

The artwork, the décor, the grandeur.

I've seen all of it before, though it takes me a minute to remember where from.

Then, it hits me.

I've eaten in this kitchen before. Toured this very mansion before.

I look back at the table and can see myself sitting on the right side of the table, nervous and distant, passing a gravy boat around. Cole Morrison was sitting at my right. It was Thanksgiving almost three years ago.

Cole and I were engaged at the time, and before I called the entire thing off, I did my best to follow my father's orders. I went to Thanksgiving and met Cole's family after my father told me the Irish would retaliate against him if I didn't go. It was a guilt trip, but at the time, I thought it was my only option. I thought my father was asking me sincerely for help rather than manipulating me.

The meal was quiet and awkward. I tried to look more comfortable than I felt, but I was entirely alone.

Meeting the family of the person you are dating is always uncomfortable, but even more so when you aren't actually dating the man.

Cole's parents were nice, but cold. Even with Cole, there was a level of distance between all of them, like they were all being cautious not to offend one another or set anyone off.

That night, Cole walked me to my room, and I made a joke. I can't even remember what it was now—something about the awkwardness of the meal, I'm sure. I expected him to laugh with me. I expected the situation to be something we could bond over.

Instead, Cole exploded.

Until that moment, I'd never seen him be anything other than relaxed and calm. He wasn't a nice man, but he seemed at ease in most situations. He had a "roll with the punches" kind of vibe.

My joke, however, set him off.

His pale face flushed until I could see his scalp glowing red from under his blonde hair. He stepped forward, towering over me until I had no choice but to press my back against the door and cower.

"Who are you that you can come into my family's home and judge us?" he snapped. "You don't know my family. You don't understand anything about family. Even your own father pimps you out as his whore."

The rage in his voice took my breath away. I was too shocked to cry or argue. I just stood there, absorbing his fury, and trembling.

"That is what you are, isn't it?" he spat. "Just a fucking whore. A woman who thinks she is worth something because her father is an important man who stuck his dick in her slut mother."

I shook my head. Not because I was trying to argue with him, but because I couldn't understand the source of his anger.

It made Cole even angrier.

"Don't shake your head at me," he barked. "I'm not the one who allowed myself to be sold like a common prostitute. Remember that when you want to judge my life and my family. You are only good for spreading your legs, and a whore is all you'll ever be."

He was gone almost as soon as the tirade started, leaving me alone for the night to process what he'd said. And the more I thought about it, the more I realized I couldn't stay with him.

That rage—it came from somewhere deep inside of him. And I could tell immediately it was not an isolated incident. A life with Cole Morrison would be decades of navigating land mines that might make him explode at any time.

Plus, his words had hit home.

My father had used me as a bargaining chip to settle a dispute between himself and another family, and I couldn't allow it. I couldn't be forced into a marriage I didn't want.

That night was the night I decided to run away.

Cole apologized a few days later. He swore that he'd had too much to drink with dinner and was upset about something else, but I didn't buy it.

So, I left.

I left Cole and my father and New York City. And New York State.

For two years, I ran away from my problems.

And now, here I am. Right back in them. Drowning in them.

If memory serves, the Morrison mansion is in rural upstate New York. The view I have from the dining room of the desolate tree line is the same view I'd have from any window in the house. Screaming won't do me much good here. No one will hear me.

Still, I try.

I pull at the zip ties until my wrists and ankles burn, and I scream for help until my throat is dry and raw. Until the words feel like razor blades tearing from my chest.

Finally, after what feels like hours, I hear footsteps in the room next to me. Everything in my body wants to put distance between myself and the door. I want to ready myself for a fight or to run. But the ties don't allow me to do anything other than turn and look over my shoulder.

I see a built, blonde-haired man rush through the door.

For a fleeting moment, I think the man is Cole Morrison.

They have the same blonde hair and pale skin, the same square shoulders and loping, relaxed- looking walk.

As soon as he looks up, however, I realize he is much too old.

I don't remember his name, but I know it is Cole Morrison's father.

He stomps towards me and kicks the chair, rocking it over onto two legs. I have to quickly throw my weight to keep from tipping over.

"Stop your screaming," he yells. "Or I'll give you something to scream about."

"Why am I here?" My voice is raspy, and I have to work hard to make it loud enough to hear. "Where is my daughter?"

"Shut up," he says, pointing a fat finger at me, eyes wide.

"Please," I beg. "Just tell me why I'm here."

He plants his feet together and crosses his arms over his chest. He has on a suit, which seems like a very nice outfit to kidnap someone in.

"You killed my son," he says.

I shake my head. "No. I didn't."

He holds up a hand to quiet me, his top lip curled back in barely restrained rage. "You killed my son, so I don't owe you anything."

A desperate sob wracks out of me, and I sag forward, pulling against the restraints. "Please. Where is my daughter? That's all I want to know."

Cole's father is in my face in an instant, heat rolling off him in angry waves. Spit spatters on my face as he talks. "You can see your daughter again when I get to see my son."

Hopelessness opens up like a black hole in my chest, sucking in everything else. It absorbs my fear and anger and desperation. It eats and eats until there is nothing less. Until I'm a shell of a person sitting on the chair, Cole's father screaming in my face.

"You are going to be sold off like the trash you are," he says, standing back and crossing his arms again. "There are men congregating now who will bid on you like cattle."

I try to find the energy to be upset or scared, but I can't muster it. Not when I may never see my daughter again.

"You ran from my son like you could do better than him. You refused to marry him because you thought you were too good for him. Well," he says, his face splitting into a wicked smile. "You won't think so highly of yourself when you're standing on stage being sold."

Clearly, I'm being handed over to a sex trafficking organization. That is easy enough to surmise. But is this really all just revenge for Cole's death? A death I didn't even cause?

"I didn't kill Cole," I repeat again.

"Your husband did," Cole's father says quickly. "That's close enough. And now you will both suffer."

He walks around my chair in a circle, shaking his head. "You should have just married Cole. That would have saved you all of this heartache. Your father would probably still be alive." He shrugs. "Or maybe not. He was always an arrogant son of a bitch. Just like you."

"I'm nothing like my father," I say through gritted teeth.

Cole's father smiles even wider. "That's right. Your father kidnapped you, didn't he? In the end, even your own flesh and blood didn't think you were worth more than the price you could fetch."

Shame pierces my chest like a hot poker, and I turn towards the windows, trying to remind myself of my real worth.

I'm more than what the men in my life thought of me.

Luka has shown me that.

I'm treasured and valued. More than just a body to be used and disposed of.

No matter what this man says or anyone else, I'm worthy of more than this.

"Your own father thought you were common filth." He moves into my line of vision and lifts his chin, looking down his nose at me. "You could have married my son and become part of this family. You could have given us the grandchildren we've always wanted. You could have been happy."

Cole's angry explosion that night years ago proves this theory wrong. I would have never been happy with Cole Morrison because underneath the easygoing façade, he was a monster just like my father. Cole didn't value me, and he never would have treated me the way Luka does.

"But instead, you ran away," he says. "You ran away from my son only to be sold off to your husband—the man who killed my son."

Luka told me why he killed Cole Morrison. Because he betrayed our family and spoke ill of me, and Luka couldn't let him live.

In the end, Cole's own sense of self-importance got him killed, though I don't think his father would appreciate that interpretation of events.

"And now you are desperate to get back to your owner." Cole's father snorts in disgust. "You think your husband loves you? He doesn't. Just like everyone else, he knows you are only good for one thing."

He kicks out at my knee, spreading my legs apart, and I'm quick to pull them back together.

I know he is wrong. I know he is trying to get inside my head and break me, but I also can't ignore the painful wounds tearing open in my heart. Injuries that Luka has slowly and painstakingly sutured for me, now tearing open at the slightest bit of irritation.

No matter how far I try to run from my past, I will always be the girl who was broken by her father. Who was betrayed and abused and manipulated.

But just because that is part of my past, doesn't mean it has to be my future.

I lift my head and look Cole's father square in the eyes. "Luka loves me."

He laughs. "We'll see how useful that love is in the next few days."

"It doesn't matter," I say, actually believing my own words. "No matter what happens, my husband loves me, and I love him. You don't know anything about me."

His smile falters, and he takes a step towards me, eyebrow raised. "That may be true, but I know one thing about you, Eve Volkov. One thing that is all I need to know."

He leans forward until I can feel his hot breath on my skin. I want to look away, but I don't want to show any weakness, so I maintain eye contact. He gets close enough that my eyes have to cross to keep looking at him, and for a second, I think he is going to kiss me. But he stops just short of my lips.

"I know that you are never going to see your husband or daughter again."

With that, he turns on his heel and rushes out of the door.

I sit tall in my chair, watching him leave, but the minute his footsteps fade to silence, I sag down, chin on my chest, and cry.

4

LUKA

I pour more coffee into my mug, not bothering with cream or sugar. I just need the jolt of caffeine in my veins.

I haven't slept at all, and I can only run so long on adrenaline. Despite my best efforts, I feel my energy waning.

When I turn back to the men sitting around my table, however, I feel a slight surge of energy. My lieutenants are here, and we are going to get Eve and Milaya back. I know it.

"The Irish took them," I say flatly. The words roll off my tongue easily. They are facts, and I'm delivering them.

Underneath it, though, there is anger. Rage like I've never felt, and I know it could come exploding out at any second. "The Irish took my family."

"I thought they disbanded," Grigory says.

"They laid low long enough to make me feel comfortable." I hate admitting my own weakness, but if I want my family back, I have to be honest.

Grigory nods and looks down at his hands. Usually, he is more outspoken. He isn't afraid to challenge me, within reason, and ensure I am doing the best thing for the Bratva. Right now, though, he is quiet.

I know it is because I'm so on edge.

All of the men around me are avoiding eye contact, shuffling their feet, and twiddling their fingers. My frayed nerves are setting them on edge, so I take another long drink of my coffee, letting it scorch its way down my throat, and then stand tall.

"I'm exhausted," I admit. "I'm tired, and I need ideas on how to get my family back. Now."

The men offer up ideas at once. Eve and Milaya are mine, but in a way, all of these men think of them as family, too. That is what being in the Bratva means. We look out for one another. We defend one another. And the Irish broke into that family and robbed two of our own, and I know my men will do what they can to help.

"If they've been gathering in secret, then it shouldn't be hard with our underground contacts to figure out where. We can attack," one man says.

"Rian Morrison is the person behind this. Let's kill her. Chop the beast off at the head."

"Storm the FBI headquarters and take them back."

One by one the ideas are tossed up and then batted down.

We don't know where Eve and Milaya are. Until we do, we can't go into any building guns blazing or we risk killing them in the crossfire.

Or, even worse, they could be killed by the Irish in retaliation for any attack we wage. Whatever we do, we have to do it covertly. This isn't an instance when we can use brute force and get the results we want.

"We don't have the time to infiltrate their ranks," another lieutenant says. "We are good at fighting and killing. I say we stick to our strengths."

A few men nod in agreement, but even more shake their heads. "If you want Eve's death on your shoulders, then fine, bust into the local Irish hangouts and start announcing that we are hunting her down. But I, for one, think there has to be a more delicate way to go about this."

Slowly, the general enthusiasm for getting my family back starts to wane and tempers start to flare. The men are arguing about which course of action is best, raising their voices to be heard over one another until I can barely hear myself think.

"Enough!" I scream, slamming my coffee cup down on the table hard enough that it shatters. Ceramic shards spray into the air and coffee dribbles over the side of the table. The men look at me, wide-eyed.

"Truthfully, I didn't think any of you would offer up an idea better than mine, but I wanted to be sure."

They look at one another, clearly questioning my sanity, but I don't care. I know what I need to do.

"I may need your help later on, but right now, every step of this mission is up to me." I sit down in one of the kitchen chairs and rest my elbows on the edge, resisting the urge to lay my head down and go to sleep. "The Irish have clearly been planning this attack for a long time, so we need to be cautious. The last thing I want is for us to feel compelled to act and make a mess of things. That would only be playing into their hands."

"So, what do we do?" Grigory asks.

"You wait for my orders," I say. "You don't move or breathe or act without my permission, do you understand?"

Everyone nods, including Grigory. Then, he looks up at me. "So, what are you going to do?"

I sigh and press myself upright. My legs feel like cement blocks, but I know I can't rest yet. Not until I have a plan.

"I'm going to visit Rick Koban."

Grigory snorts and leans back in his chair, arms crossed over his chest, and a few of the other men join in, following his lead. But one sharp look from me is enough to smooth the annoyed expression from my right-hand man's face. He sits up taller, and the other lieutenants quiet.

I knock on the door just after lunch and step back, waiting for Rick to answer.

After the meeting with the lieutenants this morning, I laid down in bed and tried to sleep, but Eve's scent was everywhere. Every time I closed my eyes, my thoughts turned to her, alternating between dreams of her lying beside me and others of her being ripped away. I could hear Milaya crying, but when I'd slide to the end of the bed to go and comfort her, the noise would stop and the house would descend into complete silence.

Eventually, I gave up, swallowed down another mug of coffee, and headed for Rick's house.

His front porch is immaculate. No cobwebs or dust or lawn debris. Just smooth concrete and spotless bricks. He must have someone come out and clean it every morning.

The door opens slightly, and Rick peeks his head through a crack in the door. His hair is the same length and shade as mine, though his face is more weathered, grizzled. When he sees it is me, he opens the door a bit more, but it isn't a warm welcome by any means.

"Luka," he says with a nod. "To what do I owe the pleasure?"

"Do you mind if I talk to you?" I gesture around as though there are cameras floating above my head. "In private."

Rick twists his mouth to one side and looks hesitant, but in the next second, he opens the door and steps aside.

Before I even cross the threshold, I kick my shoes off and then carry them inside with me. Rick gestures to a rug next to the door where I can leave them and then pads down the hallway in socks.

"I wasn't expecting company, so excuse the mess."

I look in each room we pass, searching for any kind of mess, but I can't find it. The house is spotless. Which makes sense considering Rick's profession.

He is the leader of a "cleanup crew." The most popular cleaners in the entire city. They work with everyone and have been on the scene of every major Mafia hit for the last ten years. If anyone wants to ensure their murder scene is cleaned and free of DNA, Rick is the guy to call.

"The house looks beautiful," I assure him.

Rick smiles at me over his shoulder, and it is genuine.

A lot of the guys in our business do not appreciate Rick's particular talents. They respect that he keeps them out of prison, but they find him a bit too eccentric.

And to be fair, he is eccentric. Borderline obsessive. But I am willing to look past personality flaws if someone is loyal and a good worker. Rick is both, so he has earned my respect.

Rick leads me into a sitting room. The furniture is white and crisp. Every throw pillow is resting at the perfect angle as though he measured to ensure the coasters on the coffee table are each exactly one inch from every corner of the table. The room looks like it belongs in a museum.

"It has been a long time since I've heard from you," Rick says, gesturing for me to take the chair closest to the fireplace while he sits in the direct center of the couch. Rather than sink back into the cushions, he perches on the edge like a nervous bird. "You usually call."

"I'm usually not in the midst of an emergency," I say.

His brow furrows and his hollowed cheeks take on an even more sunken look. "Are you in need of a cleanup?"

"No, not today," I say. "Actually, I just need information."

Rick waves me away. "That isn't my specialty, Luka. You know I am a businessman, not a point of contact."

"And under normal circumstances, I would accept that response, but I'm afraid I can't today." I sit forward and rest my elbows on my knees. "I need to know everything you can tell me about the LeClerc Cartel."

He takes a deep breath in, and his eyes sag as he exhales. "I'm sorry, Luka. You understand. One of the many unfortunate dangers of being a powerful man such as yourself."

"You are a powerful man, too," I say. "You have a lot of information that could be very useful to me. Crucial, even."

He gives me a sad smile and shakes his head. "It is a key part of my business plan that I don't share any trade secrets with anyone."

"I know, Rick—" I start.

"I mean," he continues. "Imagine how it would look for someone like me, who is dependent upon every criminal in this city trusting him, to throw all of that away. And for what?"

"Justice," I say. "I know justice isn't always clear. It looks different to everyone, but you know me. We've worked well together in the past, and I'd like to think you trust my judgment. So, if I tell you I need to know where the Cartel is holding their auction, I hope you'll believe me when I say it is dire."

I haven't allowed myself to think about Milaya much. Not directly, anyway. I can think about the fact that she is gone, but dwelling too long on what she is going through is simply too much. It starts a fire in my chest that is impossible to douse. But right now, I fan the flames. I let my veneer crack, revealing the desperation beneath. I want Rick to see how much I need his help. Because I want him to help me willingly. I don't want to hurt him.

"I do trust you, Luka," Rick admits, twining his fingers together. "And you know I would love to be of help to you, but—"

"But nothing," I say, cutting him off. "All I need for you to do is tell me everything you know about the LeClerc Cartel."

"Can you tell me why?"

I shake my head. "No."

Rick's mouth closes, and his eyes meet mine, and I know he understands how bad things are. And for the first time, I think I understand it, too. Getting my family back won't be easy.

"Please," I say. I'm not begging, and Rick knows it too. His eyes follow my hand down to my waist, and he can see the bulk of my gun tucked away beneath my waistband. He knows what I am capable of. After all, he has cleaned up plenty of my crime scenes.

He sighs and stands up, folding his hands behind his back. "If we are going to get into this, I at least need some tea."

He turns and walks away, gesturing for me to follow. "Join me in the kitchen, and I'll tell you what you need to know."

If he had recently eaten lunch, there is no trace of the dishes now. The marble countertops are spotless and shining and the stovetop looks like it could be brand-new. Rick grabs his electric kettle, fills it, and then flips it on. He turns around when the kettle whirs to life.

"What do you want to know?"

"Everything," I say quickly. "Anything you can tell me. As much as you can tell me."

He hums. "What do you already know?"

"The LeClerc Cartel deal in human trafficking," I say. "They sell mostly to the elite, so it is a classy operation, at least as far as those things go. But honestly, that is about the extent of it. I'm in the dark here, Rick"

"Okay." The kettle clicks off, and Rick drops a tea bag into a mug, fills it with steaming water, and then turns back to me, his fingers curled around his tea. "Do you want any?"

I impatiently decline and bite my tongue as he takes a cautious sip of his tea. Then, he leans against the counter and takes a deep breath.

"The LeClerc Cartel auction is going to be a five-day event at the Crooked Tree Inn. It's a historic place. Very upscale."

"Five days? Why so long?"

He shrugs. "The men there are going to spend a lot of money, so the Cartel likes to make it worth their time. Plus, it gives them time to peruse the selection." He looks at me nervously and then brings the cup to his lips, taking a small sip. "And *sample* what they may want."

Heat floods my chest, and I clench my hands. *Breathe, motherfucker*, I tell myself. "How do I get in?"

Rick sets his mug down on the counter and crosses his arms over his narrow chest. "It is exclusive, obviously, but bidders can vouch for one another."

"Are you a bidder?" I ask.

Rick nods and then turns and walks out of the room without another word. For a moment, I think I'm supposed to follow him, but then he returns with something in his hands. When he holds it up, I realize it is a mask.

"They send these to the bidders a few weeks early," he says, turning the black mask over in his hands. Printed on the right temple is a small line drawing of the Cartel's symbol—cracked bull horns. "I wasn't originally on the list, but Levi Cornish gave it to me."

"The thief?" I ask. I've never met him, but I've heard his name around. Like Rick, he works with everyone, going wherever the money is and stealing whatever he is assigned.

He nods and then chuckles, holding the mask out to me. "He thought I needed to get laid, but clearly, you need this more than I do."

The mask is sturdier than I expected. It is a hard plastic covered in a durable, smooth fabric. I hold it up to my face for a moment, looking out from the eyeholes, and then pull it away.

"Is the mask just a ticket or do I need to wear it?"

"Both," Rick says. "It should be enough to get you through the door no questions asked, but you need to wear it once you are inside. This event is attended by a lot of other men on your side of the law. Many of them have worked together before, so as much as possible, the Cartel likes to avoid any bad blood or vendettas rising to the surface. So, everyone covers their faces. It isn't a perfect system, but it usually provides the right level of anonymity to keep the men inside calm."

"You sound like you've been before."

"Once," he admits. "Right when the event first started. But once was enough for my taste. And if we are being honest, I'm surprised you are interested in going at all."

"I wouldn't be going if it wasn't necessary."

He nods and then tilts his head to the side. "Is everything okay with Eve?"

The mention of her name sets me on edge, and I grit my teeth. I do my best to smile. "As far as I know."

He pulls his brows together. "Word has been going around that you've been domesticated. Everyone thought you were enamored with your partner. I'm only surprised you'd be interested in another woman so soon after the birth of your daughter."

Rick may be guessing at the truth, wondering if my urgency might hint that something is wrong with Eve, but I can't reveal anything to him. As he has made clear, his loyalty is not with me, but his career. If someone were to come along and offer him a sizable amount of money, I have to assume Rick would sell out my plans in a second.

And I can't blame him.

He owes me no loyalty, therefore, I do not owe him the truth.

Plus, the truth feels like a sucker punch to the gut.

I let my family be taken. I allowed myself to become complacent, and now my family is paying the price. It is a shame I've never felt before, and I'm not keen to share it with anyone else.

"It is never too early to spice things up," I joke, acid rising in the back of my throat with every word. Then, I reach into my pocket. "I assume this information isn't free. What is your going rate right now?"

He waves away my wallet, and I'm momentarily stunned, thinking he is refusing payment. Then, he wrinkles his nose. "I don't deal in cash. It is absolutely filthy. A one-dollar bill is covered in more germs than a public toilet seat."

I slide my wallet back into my pocket.

"A money transfer will suffice," he says. "Five hundred and we'll call it even. Only because you didn't actually pull your weapon." He raises a brow in mild amusement.

"I wouldn't have actually shot you, Rick," I say warmly.

Rick shakes his head. "Don't lie to me, Luka. Keep your secrets but be honest with me when you can. You'd shoot me in an instant. We both know it."

I tip my head towards the recognizable bulge at Rick's own waist. "You are not unarmed."

"I'm not," he admits, glancing down at his hip. "But I never lied about my intentions. If you had pulled your weapon on me, I would have fought for my life."

I laugh as he leads me towards the front door. "Then let's pray my draw will always be quicker than yours."

He opens the door and ushers me out. "And I'll pray the same."

I step outside but before I can turn around and say anything else in parting, Rick slams the door and slides the bolt into place.

Our conversation is over.

5

EVE

I've been in the Morrisons' mansion for hours, but I haven't seen anyone since Cole's father came to see me.

I watch the sun move across the sky through the wall of windows and try to focus on anything other than my gnawing hunger and thirst, but it becomes more difficult as time goes on.

Then, I hear a distant door open and close.

For a moment, there is a flood of relief.

Finally, another person to talk to. Someone to explain to me what is going on. Maybe someone coming to take me to the restroom or feed and water me. (I'm ashamed at how quickly I've acclimated to my environment—already describing my needs like an animal in a zoo.)

As the quick footsteps grow closer, however, fear opens up like a pit in my stomach.

What are they going to do with me? Cole's father told me I would be sold. Are they coming to take me now?

Even though I know what their plans are for me, part of me expected that Luka would arrive to save me before any of that happened. A small part of me clung to the idea that I would be rescued before anything truly egregious happened.

Now, however, I'm not as sure.

Especially because, if I know anything about Luka, he'll be looking for Milaya over me. I know he loves me, but I also know how much he loves our daughter. And he knows how much I love her, too. He knows that I would want him to find her over me, so that is surely what he is doing.

I sit tall in my chair, stretch my aching spine, and lift my chin.

I will just have to save myself.

Cole's father appears in the open doorway, and his face is twisted into a mask of rage and anger. His eyes are almost black with it.

"What is going on?" I ask, unable to help myself.

He pauses for a moment in the doorway and then stomps towards me, his footsteps shaking the table and the china in the cabinets.

I lean back in my chair until the back cuts into my spine, but there is nowhere to go. Nowhere to escape. My wrists and ankles are raw from trying to break the zip ties, so I know there is no use.

He pulls out a water bottle, wielding it like a weapon, and I shake my head. "What are you doing? What is going on?"

He charges towards me, barely stopping in time to avoid running me over, and then grabs my hair. I scream, my neck snapping backwards painfully, and then the bottle is at my lips. The water floods my mouth and throat, and I cough against it, trying to breathe.

"Drink it!" he yells, shaking my head by the hair. "Drink it."

Moments ago, I was desperate for water, for anything to quench my thirst, but now, I just want air.

"Stop fighting it," he says, tipping my head back farther.

I try to swallow the water in my mouth but the angle of my head makes it difficult to swallow. I force myself to quell the panic in my head, get my shit together, and make my throat do its job. It's either that or drown.

Once my mouth is clear, he releases his hold on me slightly—only to yank my head back again and start the process over.

I do my best not to resist, but Mr. Morrison jerks me around so forcefully that my instincts scream at me to fight. I tense up, trying to protect myself even though I do not have any way to do that.

More and more water is poured down my throat, and I swallow it until my stomach hurts. Until I miss the feeling of being thirsty.

When the bottle is empty, Cole's father crumples it in his hand and throws it under the dining room table. He turns to leave, and I call out to him.

"Wait, please," I cough. Droplets and drool run from my mouth. I feel utterly exhausted all of a sudden.

He turns slightly, looking at me out of the corner of his eye.

"I have to use the restroom," I say.

"Go ahead," he says, tipping his head towards my chair. He turns to leave again, and I'm desperate to keep him in the room. Right now, he is my only connection to the outside world, and I don't want to go back to being alone again.

"Where is Colleen?" I ask.

I can't believe I remember Cole's mother's name. Though, considering his name was inspired by hers, perhaps it isn't so surprising.

Cole's father turns to me, eyes narrowed. "My family is no longer any of your concern."

I would like to disagree with him, but my head feels fuzzy, and I can't find the words.

In the brief window of time when I was Cole's intended, and I hadn't decided I could never marry him, I hoped his parents would become family to me. His mother was a cold woman, but I could tell she loved her son, and I hoped that would include me someday. Though, now that her son is dead, and I am partially responsible, I have to assume she hates me as much as her husband does.

Before I can find the words to keep him in the room any longer, Cole's father turns and leaves. A few seconds later, I hear the front door open and close. And then I'm alone.

My bladder is full and uncomfortable and my body is stiff from being in such a strange position for so long, but I tip my head back and stare up at the ceiling. The tiles begin to bend and blur and spin, and I let my blurry vision distract me.

Until I realize what is happening.

My body is growing heavy and numb. My mouth is sagging open. My eyelids are drooping.

I've been drugged.

Clearly, I wasn't being force-fed water for my own hydration. They were drugging me. There was something in the water to knock me out. But why?

My heart stutters in my chest.

Was it poison? Is this how I die?

I shake my head, trying to calm myself down. They wouldn't kill me this way. Alone in a room, tied to a chair. After the way I've been treated, they clearly have bigger plans for me. Plus, Cole's father mentioned the auction. I am to be sold. They wouldn't kill me if they wanted to make money off me.

Strangely, the thought calms me for a moment. I'm only being sold into human slavery, not murdered.

Woo-freaking-hoo.

If nothing else, at least it means there is a chance I'll see my family again.

My eyes drop closed, too heavy to stay open another second, and in the blackness, Luka and Milaya appear.

He is cuddling her to his chest, rubbing his nose to hers, and he waves me over. I move towards them, hand outstretched.

But just before I reach them, the image swirls like smoke and is gone.

As soon as I wake up, I take in my surroundings and realize I'm alone.

Then, I throw my weight up and forward, scooting my chair forward.

Before this moment, I was too afraid of being heard to try anything so daring, but I'm not afraid anymore. Sometime in the night, my drugged mind came to the realization that the Morrisons can't hurt me. Not really, anyway. They can tie me up and leave me without food, but I'm supposed to be sold. No one will want to buy me if I'm bruised and broken. So, there is no reason not to try and escape.

The handles on the china cabinet are in the mid-century style. Long horizontal metal handles with sharpened points. Perfect for cutting through plastic zip ties. If I can just get to them, then I can break through the zip ties and escape.

I'm not sure exactly where I am, but it is my best chance.

I use my toes to counterbalance the chair when it starts to tip and then throw my weight again, scooting forward an inch.

It may take me an hour to get to the hutch, but I have to try.

Based on what I can see through the window, early morning fog is settled low over the ground and the trees, so hopefully no one will be in to check on me for a while.

I scoot forward again, the chair legs scraping and banging on the wood floors, and then again. It is noise, but the house has been empty so far, so I have no reason to believe anyone is inside.

Then, I hear a footstep overhead.

A single thump followed by the creak of the old wood as the weight settles.

I freeze.

"Did you hear that?" The voice is distant but right above me.

I know that voice.

It is Rian Morrison's.

I grit my teeth but keep going. Instead of throwing my weight, I use what little mobility I have in my toes to slide the chair across the floor. It is loud, but a low sound that is probably more difficult to hear upstairs.

"She is tied up," a deeper voice says. It is Cole's father. They are both right upstairs. "She can't go anywhere."

I nod, trying to telepathically encourage that line of thinking. *I can't go anywhere. I'm tied up. Stay upstairs. It is fine.*

I slide the chair closer to the stand. I am crawling at a snail's pace, and somewhere deep down, I realize it is futile, but I can't give up. Not now. Not before I've really tried.

"It is about time we check on her anyway," Rian says, footsteps moving across the upstairs. "I'm going down there."

Hope sinks in my chest like a stone in the ocean, and I lay my head back and stare up at the ceiling as she moves down the stairs and into the dining room.

The door opens. "You look like shit."

I sit up and see a put-together Rian standing in front of me. She has on a royal blue pencil skirt with a cream shirt tucked in, the buttons done up to her throat. She looks like a villain from a science fiction movie.

"Smell like it, too," she says, wrinkling her nose. "We did our best to clean you up after you had your little 'accident.'"

I don't know what she means until I look down at myself and realize I'm in different clothes. I'm no longer in my pajamas but in a cotton pair of sweatpants and an oversized T-shirt.

My bladder is empty. I peed myself.

"You force-fed me water and refused to let me use the restroom," I say. "I'm not sure what you expected?"

She is across the room in an instant, her face less than an inch from mine. "I expected you to be better than a dog from the pound. Though, I shouldn't be surprised. You are nothing more than a *bitch*."

I open my mouth to argue, but as soon as I do, Rian pulls a bottle from behind her back and shoves the top of it between my lips.

Water floods my mouth and I spurt and gag on it, wrenching my head away. Rian grabs the back of my neck, digging her nails into my skin, and yanks me forward. She tries to force my mouth over the bottle, but I keep my lips and teeth firmly closed now.

Her father appears behind her, his face red and angry, and stomps over to help.

He moves around behind me and presses his palms into either side of my face, squeezing down until it feels like my jaw will shatter.

"Open up," he growls, squeezing even harder.

"We can't mark her," Rian hisses at him. "Bruises on her face won't sell."

Instantly, his grip lightens, and I realize I was right. They can't touch me. Not really.

He moves around and kneels in front of me. He wriggles his finger into my mouth, and though I try to resist, he is able to wrench my mouth open and hold it there while Rian pours water down my throat.

I spit half of it back out, but the other half goes down, and within a few minutes, I start to feel drowsy again.

Then, for what feels like the millionth time since the FBI raid on our house, the blackness takes me away once more.

The next time I return to consciousness, I'm lying down. There is nothing around my hands and ankles, and for one blissful second, I think it was all a horrible nightmare.

"Grab her head."

Rian Morrison's voice is like a shot of adrenaline straight to my heart. My body goes rigid when I feel sweaty hands grabbing at me.

Instinctively, I kick out at the hands and begin thrashing.

Rian lets out a yelp, and I hear a deep growl behind me. Her hands clamp down hard on my calves, but I fight against them.

I still don't have my full strength yet because the drugs haven't totally left my system, but I can still fight.

I open my eyes and realize I'm in the back seat of an SUV. Maybe the same one they used to take me to the house. I'm not sure. But I see a different house in the distance. Or, really, a large manor. There is official signage above the door, letting me know it is a business of some kind, but I'm too keyed up to read it.

Rian tries to wrap her arms around my legs, but before she can, my bare foot connects with the underside of her jaw. I hear her teeth crack together, and she falls back into the dirt.

A deep voice I assume belongs to the driver tries to grab my arms, but I slip out of his grip and through the door where Rian was standing. I have a better chance of fighting her than a grown man.

My feet hit the dirt, and I throw myself forward into a run, but my legs are still wobbly. My knees feel like jelly, and I trip over Rian's leg and hit the ground.

I scramble quickly, but Rian recovers just as fast and throws herself over my body, smashing my face into the dirt.

"Enough!" she yells.

Hardly, I think.

I hurl my weight to the right and then bring my left hand around, my fist smashing into Rian's nose.

It is a weak punch, but it is enough to knock her back for a second, freeing me up to crawl out from under her body. I only get a few feet away before she is on me again.

Her FBI training is outdoing my self-defense classes, and I can hear the driver moving around the back of the car. I won't get away. There is no chance.

"You'll want to stop fighting now. We have Milaya," Rian growls in my ear.

My daughter's name stops me in my tracks. It sends a chill down my spine, dousing the fire inside of me.

"We have Milaya," she repeats. "And if you don't do as you are told, we will make sure she suffers."

I let my cheek fall against the dirt driveway. "Please don't kill her. Please. She is only a baby."

"Kill her?" Rian scoffs. "That isn't suffering. That would be a gift compared to what I could do to her."

My arms and legs are trembling from the unspent adrenaline in my body, but I hold still. I don't kick or fight or yell. I just contain the rage and let Rian pin me to the ground.

No matter what happens to me, I can't risk Milaya's safety. I'll do anything before I let them hurt her.

They've got me. There's nothing I can do. So I go limp.

Rian and the driver drag me to my feet and lead me through the front doors of the Crooked Tree Inn.

6

LUKA

I've only slept in thirty-minute dozes. And never lying down. Sleep only comes when I'm least expecting it. I've woken up with my head on my desk, cheeks pressed against my laptop keyboard. I jolted awake in the middle of eating dinner. Or, at least, what little dinner I can stomach.

Without knowing what is happening to Eve or where she is, any normal human activities feel impossible.

Instead of rest, I push my body to the limits. I spend an hour or more at a time in my home gym, running the adrenaline off on the treadmill and lifting weights, trying to find even a moment of reprieve.

But there is none.

When I'm not burning off energy, I'm doing what I can to find out anything about the Crooked Tree Inn and the LeClerc Cartel.

In this situation, knowledge is power. The more I can find out about the Cartel's practices and the location of the auction, the better off I'll be.

It isn't enough to just walk into the inn and buy Eve. They might be expecting me or I might be outbid. I have no idea what kind of men to expect at this thing. Will they be wealthier than I am? Will I have to watch men test out my wife the way Rick suggested they might?

The thought alone makes me turn the speed of the treadmill up faster.

Sweat is pouring into my eyes, but I can't stop yet. Not until my legs are shaking. Not until I collapse. That is the only way I can stay seated enough to do any valuable research. Otherwise, I pace, anxiously waiting for the time when I can leave and head to the inn, hoping Eve will be there.

When my legs feel like rubber, I take a quick shower and then move into my office.

My computer is still on, loaded to a page about the LeClerc Cartel. The only information I've been able to find is a few investigative journalism pieces from a few years prior and then a forum for at-home detectives who are trying to bring these men to justice.

One of the commenters laments that the Cartel went underground when a local magazine wrote the last article about them.

These journalists aren't doing us any favors. LeClerc needs to be an undercover operation. That is the only way to find out where they hold their auctions. As soon as something ends up in the paper, they go deeper underground.

The only thing I've found out is what I already know. The LeClerc Cartel sell labor and sex slaves. They are known for serving an elite clientele with the best "merchandise" around.

Thinking of Eve as goods for sale makes me sick.

Rick gave me the address of the auction location: a small inn upstate.

Based on satellite view, it is in a rural area, and based on the website of the Crooked Tree Inn, the rooms are luxurious.

Otherwise, nothing.

No blueprints or layouts—those are mysteriously absent from the file depository of the county's architectural commission. Not a surprise, really. Men who succeed in businesses like this rarely let such vulnerabilities linger unaddressed. As far as I can tell, I'll be going in blind, with nothing that could help me plan a good exit strategy should I find myself in a position where Eve and I can make a break for it.

I let my head fall forward on my arms and take a deep breath. I just finished in the gym an hour ago, but I can already feel my anxiety elbowing its way back to the forefront.

I check the time. I have another hour before I need to leave for the inn. I would spend the time packing, but Rick told me not to bother. They won't allow me to take any luggage inside, anyway. So, I'm about to stand up and head back to the gym for one last run when there is a knock on the door.

"Come in."

Grigory Kamarov steps inside.

He is my right-hand man, but since Eve disappeared, he has kept his distance. It is what I told him to do. I don't want to see anyone. Definitely not anyone from the Bratva. Admitting that I've lost my family is too shameful. Seeing the faces of men who trusted me makes it even worse. It makes me feel unworthy.

"I've been calling you," Grigory says, folding his hands in front of him. His head is bowed forward, shoulders shrugging inward. He is trying to make himself appear smaller, probably to avoid the rage that has been leaking out of me like water from a cracked glass.

"I haven't been taking any calls." I didn't turn my phone off because I didn't want to miss a call from Eve, but I avoided calls from known numbers. Even Grigory's. I knew if he had anything dire to tell me, he'd show up at the house. "Do you have something to tell me?"

"No good news, if that is what you mean," he says, looking down at the floor. "But the men wanted me to come check on you."

"Well, you did." I gesture towards the door. "Thanks."

On instinct, he moves towards the door to follow my order, but then he stops. "I'm sorry, but I can't go without asking what the plan is."

"The plan is my concern."

Like the commenter on the detective forum said, any attempt to infiltrate the LeClerc operation has to be undercover. The fewer people who know about it, the better my chances are. It's like the old saying: three men can keep a secret, if two of them are dead. I won't run the risk of a mole turning me in before I can rescue Eve.

Grigory nods. "I respect that, but we all just want to do what we can to help. We love them too. Eve and Milaya are our family."

"No, they aren't," I snap, standing up, pent-up energy bursting out of me like a bomb. "They are *my* family. *My* responsibility. Not yours."

Grigory keeps his eyes on the floor, accepting my rage even though he doesn't deserve it. "Respectfully, I have to tell you that your family is our family."

I take a deep breath, calming myself down, and collapse in the chair. I want to thank Grigory. The outburst saved me another trip to the gym. Suddenly, I feel drained. Physically and emotionally. Like my very soul is tired.

"We just need to know that you aren't going to get yourself killed," Grigory says. "The men are worried that we are in the dark. We will follow your orders. Whatever you want us to do, we will do. Is there anything you can tell us?"

I think through my plan—what little of it there is—and sigh.

Grigory needs to know.

So I tell him about the Cartel and the auction. I tell him what Rick told me and pull the mask he gave me out of the top drawer.

"I want to do this on my own. Not because I'm proud, but because it is the safest option. We can't attack the Cartel the way we would a rival family. They are too secretive and there are too many unknowns. So, I'm going in alone. This mask will act as a ticket, and I'll get inside and try to get Eve out."

"Are you going to bid on her?" Grigory asks.

"I'm not sure," I admit. "I will have to get inside and formulate a plan."

He looks unsure, but he nods. "So what do we do?"

"The auction starts tonight and ends in five days," I say. I grab a piece of paper and scribble down the address of the inn. "If you don't hear from me then, get as many men as you can and come to this address. Be ready for a fight."

Grigory studies the address for a moment like he is memorizing it and then looks up at me. "If we don't hear from you in five days, we'll come ready to save the three of you. Or die trying."

I nod slowly, silently thanking him for his loyalty. He tucks the address in his jacket pocket and leaves.

And, finally, it is time.

I am alone.

The drive to the inn takes almost an hour, but it feels like mere minutes.

I park in the back of the lot, shift the black mask over my face, and get out of the car.

I'm in a dark gray suit with a black button-down underneath. It is well-tailored and marks me as a man of taste without being too outlandish. I don't want to stand out.

There are other men in the parking lot, all of them wearing masks. From what I can tell, the inn has been rented out for the weekend. There are no ordinary guests milling around, which makes sense. The Cartel wouldn't want bystanders to their illicit activities.

I vaguely recognize a few of the men as prominent businessmen. They are wearing masks to hide their identities, but everything else about their appearance remains unchanged. They wear the same suits and carry the same weapons as they do in their day-to-day lives.

One man I can place instantly. His name is Peter Struthers and he is the president of a large bank. He is a hefty man with a round middle, which is difficult to hide, but he makes his identity even more obvious by wearing a pocket square with the bank's logo embroidered on it.

I seem to be the only attendee of the event attempting to fly under the radar. Rick said that the masks are there to keep men from recognizing one another and rehashing old feuds, but clearly the other guests are uncomfortable going unrecognized. They flaunt their wealth and their power in their clothes and the way they carry themselves. Which is fine with me. It will make it all the easier to ascertain who they are and how I can outsmart and outbid them.

If there is one thing my father taught me, it is how to read people.

As leader of the Bratva, I have to know who is a threat to me, and the easiest way to do that is to watch people. To study them, to be proficient in body language, verbal tics, all the little signs and tells that mark a person as himself. Knowing who a man is can help you predict what he will do next. And that could be the difference between life and death—not just for me, but for my wife and daughter, too.

Also, those skills make me even more aware of my own behavioral cues. If I want to go unnoticed, I can't let my own tics give me away.

I walk to the entrance with my head held high, but casually so. I let my arms swing at my sides, and I even smirk, something I usually reserve only for Eve.

As soon as I get to the door, it opens, and I realize the level of security this event has.

There are armed guards standing just inside the door. They wear headsets and their suits are bulky enough that I suspect they have on armor.

"Sir," the bald guard who opened the door says. His words are respectful, but his eyes narrow as he takes me in. "I'm afraid there will be no electronics or weapons beyond this point."

He tips his head to the other guard who is holding a basket.

"Really?" I ask, raising my eyebrow before remembering I have a mask on. "Feels a little juvenile, no?"

One of the guests behind me laughs at my joke, and the guard snaps his attention to him. The laughter cuts off mid chortle.

"It is for your protection as well as that of the merchandise," the guard says. "Tempers can flare and it is easier to control fists than guns."

I can't argue with his logic, and even though everything inside of me wars against it, I drop my gun and my cell phone into the basket. I know it isn't a big deal. I have plenty of experience fighting hand-to-hand should I need to, and even the guards, while muscled, look like they are more bark than bite. In a pinch, I could incapacitate one of them and steal a weapon.

The guard slaps a label on the side of the basket and shoves it into a safe before grabbing another empty box and holding it out to the man behind me.

Beyond the security checkpoint, no one asks me for a password or a ticket or any kind of identification to prove that I am supposed to be at the event. Apparently, Rick was right. The mask is all you need.

I walk further into the entryway and take note of the staircase that wraps around the edge of the circular room, leading to a large landing area on the second floor with a balcony. The room is all dark wood and crisp white walls, clearly updated recently to cater to modern sensibilities.

Under the balcony is a large doorway that opens into a general congregating area, though there is no one inside.

Then, suddenly, a man appears to my right.

"Sir," he says, bowing low, one arm pressed to his stomach, the other at his back. "Would you come with me?"

Before I can respond, he turns and moves through a door to the right. I follow. The door opens into a long hallway, and he walks halfway down it before stopping in front of a door, unlocking it, and holding it open for me to go inside.

The room is all shades of gray and black with a bright white bed and pillows. It is almost like I've had a stroke and can only see in black and white.

The door clicks shut, and I turn around, my back to the far wall. I don't want to give anyone the opportunity to sneak up on me.

"Welcome," the man says. "My name is Edgar, and I will be your guide this weekend. I am here to answer questions, assist you through the process, and fill any reasonable requests you have."

He emphasizes the word *reasonable*.

"This room will be yours for the next five days, and as soon as you remove your mask, I will leave you to get settled."

I freeze. "Aren't the masks meant to protect our anonymity?"

He nods. "Among the other guests, yes. But the hosts want every person present to be known by someone working. I'm sure we have nothing to worry about with you, sir, but knowing that someone knows their identity helps the other guests operate within the normal bounds of human interaction."

I'm not sure what normal interaction can occur at an event when human beings are being presented as cattle for purchase, but I suppose I understand.

Still, anonymity was the main pillar of my plan. Without it, I risk being kicked out.

Or worse, killed.

"That is not what I signed on for," I say.

Edgar frowned. "You are entitled to that opinion, though if you do not remove your mask—only briefly, of course—then you will be asked to leave. I am sorry."

I run my tongue over my teeth, glad Edgar can't see my deliberation. Then, slowly, I reach behind my head and undo the silk tie. I tip my head forward to catch the mask, and then run a hand through my hair as I stand tall again.

Edgar studies me blankly for a moment before his eyes widen.

My hands clench around the mask, and I'm prepared for whatever comes next.

If he recognizes me and has been instructed to alert someone, I'll kill him. He seems like a nice enough man—as nice as someone who works for the LeClerc Cartel can be, anyway—but I've killed nicer men for less. No one will stand in the way of me saving my family.

However, just as fast as recognition crosses his face, respect follows.

He lowers his eyes and tips his head forward. "I had no idea I was in the company of such a powerful man. It is an honor to assist you for the duration of the event, sir."

My brow furrows. "You recognize me?"

"You are the leader of the Volkov Bratva, are you not?"

He is not entirely sure, I can tell, which means he may not know my connection to Eve.

I nod once. "I am."

Edgar responds by dipping his head even lower. "It is my pleasure to be in your company. Do you have any other questions about the process for this weekend?"

"How will my identity be logged?" I asked. "Will it be recorded anywhere?"

"Only in my mind," Edgar answers quickly. "Given the nature of the event, the Cartel understands that our guests want the highest level of privacy, so your presence here will not be recorded anywhere except in my memory."

"And one person's memory can hardly stand up at a trial," I say with a nervous smile.

Edgar laughs, though I see his nerves in the tightness of his neck. His role here is just as precarious as mine. He could utter one word of my presence and end my entire plan right now, but he also has to be wary of me. If I were more superstitious, I could have him killed simply for being the only person here to see my face.

It is this mutually assured destruction that comforts me.

Edgar folds his hands behind his back and turns to a closet in the corner. He pulls open both doors to reveal a row of differently colored and patterned suits. "Since you are not allowed to bring any luggage with you, clothes have been provided. They are all new items tailored to the specifications given when the mask was registered, though other arrangements can be made if they do not fit."

Rick registered the mask, so it is a good thing he and I are close in size. He is thinner than me, which may prove to be an issue, but nothing much will be lost if I have to walk around with an unbuttoned suit jacket.

"Thank you."

"More casual items are in the drawers below," Edgar says, pulling out one of the wooden drawers to reveal neatly folded boxers, socks, and sweatpants. "If you need anything else, do not hesitate to alert me."

Edgar then bends low to open the lowest drawer. "And an array of personal items has been provided should you need them. Rest assured, everything is new."

I don't know what he means until he steps aside, and I see boxes of condoms in every size as well as an open-topped wooden box of various sex toys.

My heart feels like an anchor in my chest. "Maybe you should educate me on how this weekend will work, Edgar. This is my first time attending such an event."

"Of course," Edgar says, closing the drawers and then the closet doors and turning to face me. "Each night, various women will be available for bidding. Each guest can make bids on the woman of their choosing and, if they wish, take them for the evening. That is simply a 'test run,' as we like to say. The auction on the final day will be for permanent placement."

I nod and swallow hard. I will have to fight for Eve every single day.

Every night, there will be men fighting to spend the night with her. To fuck her as though she is nothing more than a common whore.

The idea sends rage burning through me, and it is all I can do to keep from lashing out at Edgar. From strangling him with my bare hands and tearing through the inn in search of Eve.

Somehow, though, I choke back my anger and put on a friendly face. "Understood."

Edgar nods, oblivious to how close he is to being collateral damage in my fight to find my wife. "I will give you time to settle in, sir."

My entire body is tense as Edgar bows once more and leaves, closing the door behind him. I contain my rage for another few seconds, giving him time to get far enough away, and then I haul back and slam my fist into the closet.

The wood dents under my fingers, sending a jolt of pain up my arm. I curse and shake my hand out, but the pain helps focus my muddled thoughts.

I can't relax or become complacent. I have to be vigilant every second.

Getting Eve out of here unscathed depends on it.

7

EVE

I move through the back doors of the inn in a despondent daze.

There are no ties on my hands of legs or anyone restraining me, but I might as well be a dog with a leash and muzzle.

Rian incapacitated me by mentioning Milaya. Now, I can't do anything that could put her in danger. All I can do is follow orders.

Which I do.

I'm led inside and herded into a group with other women. By my count, there are roughly thirteen of us, all different ages and ethnicities. The only commonality is that everyone around me is gorgeous.

We are shepherded single file by men with guns wearing body armor, and they roughly nudge women in the back if they walk too slow or fall out of line.

"Stop here," one of the men barks when we get to a cement-walled room. Based on the shelves of canned goods and boxes around us, it looks like a storeroom for the kitchen.

One of the guards stays behind while the other goes through a door ahead of us.

Someone in line a few women behind me is crying softly, sniffling incessantly. I understand her feeling, but the noise is grating in the echoey room.

"Enough," the guard barks, stepping towards the line and getting in the woman's face. "Crying isn't going to help."

The woman only cries harder, and the man presses his gun to the side of her head. His voice is low and full of acid when he speaks.

"I can kill you and claim you tried to run."

Immediately, everyone around me stands taller and the woman's cries end abruptly with one last sniffle.

The guards can't hurt us, but they can stop us from leaving. And right now, he is the only guard on duty. Which is as good as making him God.

I look over my shoulder to see which guard he is. I want to be sure and steer clear of him as much as possible in the days ahead.

As soon as I look back, however, the guard's attention snaps to me.

He has a thick black mustache and matching salt-and-pepper hair. If I had passed him on the street, I would have taken him for a small-town sheriff or a butcher. He looks like a friendly neighborhood man you'd share pleasantries with on your morning commute, not a guard for a criminal Cartel.

I turn to face forward again, but it is too late. His footsteps echo through the room, matching the pounding of my heart.

"Is there something you'd like to share with the class?" he yells into my ear.

His words vibrate against my eardrum painfully, but I don't flinch. I shake my head.

"I can't hear you!" he screams, making it so I'm afraid I won't be able to hear anything ever again.

"No," I say, adding a hasty "sir" at the end.

"Then I'd suggest you mind your own fucking business."

He is standing close to me. Close enough I can feel his hot breath on my face. And I know he is trying to intimidate me.

But I've faced worse than this mustachioed guard. My father, namely.

It is obvious by the way he wields his weapon that his gun is simply an extension of his cock. He craves control and his gun helps him get it. Even when it comes to terrified, defenseless women, he has to wave it around and throw his power in their face. He probably has to threaten to murder us so he can get it up later when he is alone.

In a lot of ways, he reminds me of Cole Morrison.

I want to tell him all of this, but I trust him to carry out his threat of shooting anyone who disobeys him, so I just stare forward, eyes boring into the blonde head of the woman in front of me.

Even while I'm pretending to be effectively cowed, the man hovers over me for a second, ensuring he gets his point across. Then, he continues pacing up and down the line.

Several minutes later, the other guard comes back and we are led through a dim hallway. One by one, we are assigned individual rooms. The guards come along the line and push each of us into a doorway.

We all learn as soon as the first woman falls that we should stay on our feet. She receives a swift kick in the stomach for her lack of balance.

When I'm shoved to the right, I stumble through an already open door and into a small gray room.

The walls are dingy and the ceiling is water-stained. Everything smells faintly musty, and I can tell from across the room that the mattress is lumpy. This must have once been servants' quarters for the inn. No guest in their right mind would have paid to sleep here.

I'm so disgusted by the room around me that it takes me a moment to notice the woman standing quietly in the corner. When I do see her, I jolt in surprise.

"I didn't know anyone else was in here."

The woman nods her head in silent apology. She looks to be about my age with pale blonde hair that is almost white. It hangs around her face in thin sheets, emphasizing the harsh lines of her cheekbones.

"I'm here to assist you in preparing for the auction," she says, voice barely above a whisper.

I raise an eyebrow. "Nothing I've experienced so far has led me to expect my own personal maid."

Her mouth pinches together, and I think I see it lift at the corners, but before I can really get a good look, she turns to a narrow door set into the back corner. She pushes open the door to reveal an equally dingy bathroom.

"I've run a bath for you to wash," she says. "There are razors for you to shave yourself. I'm supposed to tell you that any attempt to use the razor for any purpose other than shaving will result in punishment worse than death."

A shiver runs down my spine.

It does seem dangerous for the Cartel to offer women in this position a weapon. Not only could it be used on them, but it could be used on themselves, which would no doubt ruin the auction.

However, there is no risk of me hurting myself. As much as I don't want to be bid on and purchased, I can't give up hope that I'll see Milaya and Luka again.

Not yet.

"Noted," I say, brushing past the woman to go into the bathroom. I move to shut the door behind me but meet resistance.

The woman is standing behind me with her hand on the door. "Sorry, the door has to stay open."

"I see they want to strip us of all of our dignity," I say.

She shrugs and then lowers her head, her lips barely moving as she speaks. "Basically, yes."

The quick surge of annoyance fades as I realize this woman doesn't enjoy her job. She is simply doing what she has to do, just as I am doing what I have to. So, I move into the bathroom and slip out of the loose-fitting sweats and T-shirt Rian Morrison put on me.

I don't have underwear or a bra, but I assume there will be clothes provided for me. Surely, the Cartel wouldn't present me in sweatpants.

"I have clothes for you to change into," the woman says, reading my thoughts.

I look up and see that she is still in the doorway, but looking the other way. She is offering me as much privacy as she can.

The tub is old with dark grout around the edges and a rusted tap, but the porcelain itself is clean and, when I slip my leg in, the water is warm. After days of being in the same clothes and tied to a chair, my body is sticky and sore and the water feels like an embrace.

I sigh as I slide in.

Even a week ago, I never would have set foot in a tub like this. I would have taken one look at the bathroom and turned around. Now, however, my standards are lower. I will do almost anything to wash away the grease caked along my scalp and the oil on my face.

I cup my hands under the water and pour it over my eyes. Then, I tip my head back and submerge my hair. Even before shampoo or soap, I feel infinitely cleaner. I grab the shampoo on the edge of the tub and pour a generous dollop in my palm.

The shampoo is clearly top of the line. It is silky with a strong lavender scent. The Cartel may not be providing nice lodgings for the women they plan to sell, but apparently, they want to make sure we look and smell our best.

Part of me wants to leave this room smelling like manure and looking like I rolled around in an oil slick, but I can't resist the feeling of being clean. So, I use the conditioner and then the bodywash, lathering myself all over until the water is milky and suds float on the surface.

"Where is the razor?" I ask.

The woman opens a drawer beneath the sink and hands me a razor. As my hand wraps around the handle, she meets my eyes, and I can see her trying to assess whether I'm a danger to myself or her. I smile, not sure whether that is more or less comforting for her.

I shave quickly, not worrying about missing spots. Any man who ends up touching my legs will be doing so against my will, so I kind of hope he feels more stubble than he likes.

When I'm done, I pull the plug on the tub and then turn on the faucet and rinse the last remnants of soap from my skin. There is a towel hanging from a bar next to the tub, and I wrap it around myself quickly, folding back the top corner of the towel before tying it in a knot. Then, I slip past the woman and into the room.

She moves around in the bathroom for a minute before she comes into the room and stares at me.

"Where is it?" she asks.

I lift my brows in surprise. "What?"

"The razor," she says, tilting her head to the side. Her eyes are downturned and sad. "I can't find the razor blade."

I shake my head and hug the towel tighter to my body. "I left it on the side of the tub. Maybe it fell behind the toilet."

Her forehead wrinkles, and I recognize the expression as pity. "I already checked."

I clutch the corner of the towel, feeling the bulk of the razor beneath it. I planned to slip it into a fold of my outfit or inside my panties while I was getting dressed. Having anything—even a small razor—would be better than going out unarmed.

"I'm sorry," the woman says, taking a slow step towards me. "But I can't let you leave this room with it. It will be bad for both of us."

I cautiously let the razor fall from the fold of the towel and into my palm, and I contemplate attacking this woman. Maybe if I kill her, or incapacitate her, at least, I could run down the hallway and through the door I was brought in. There are a lot of trees around the inn. I could slip into the woods and run for the nearest road. It could work.

"Please," the woman says, her shoulders sagging forward.

The woman is terrified. Not of me, but of the Cartel.

Like me, she is a slave. Forced to work for them and prepare the women they sell. And what will happen to her if I escape? Even if I don't kill her, I feel certain the guards wouldn't let her live down her mistake. She would be beaten and killed.

And I can't do that to an innocent woman.

I sigh and hold out my hand.

Still cautious, the woman steps forward, palm out, and I drop the razor into her hand.

Quickly, she retreats into the bathroom and stows it beneath the sink. When she returns, she looks more at ease, though still pained.

"I understand the instinct," she says. "I know that you want to fight, but the rules here are different."

"Fuck their rules," I say calmly.

"I'm not talking about their rules," she says. "Out in the world, fighting is surviving. But here? You have to lie low. You have to do what you are told not because they told you to, but because if you don't, you'll be worse off than you are now."

"I don't see how that's possible," I say.

She steps closer to me, voice low, eyes nervous like she expects someone to be listening to us. I glance around the room as well, wondering if there are any cameras.

"You can't escape if you can't walk," she says, leveling her gaze at me. "And that is what will happen if you try to fight your way out of here. The inn is too heavily guarded for you to have any chance, especially with nothing more than a razor blade."

My face warms with embarrassment. It was a bad plan.

She walks past me and picks up a red dress that is laid out on the bed. It is tight and ruched on the sides with a deep V that is guaranteed to show off most of my chest. Next to it on the threadbare comforter is a black pair of lace panties.

I awkwardly get dressed, doing my best to keep the towel around me while I pull up the underwear. I'm not ashamed of my body, but I don't like the fact that I have no choice about who sees it.

I suspect that, soon enough, I will have to get over that feeling. I won't have any choice about a lot of things.

Once the underwear is on, the woman unzips the side of the dress and then holds it open like she wants me to step into it.

"I can do it myself," I say gently, taking the dress from her.

She gives it to me and then moves against the wall.

The dress is skintight, but it fits. It isn't uncomfortable or too tight in any area. It feels eerily like it was tailored with me in mind.

"How is this going to work?" I ask, pulling the zipper up my side.

"What?"

"The auction," I say. "What is going to happen first?"

She shakes her head. "I'm not supposed to say. They will explain everything to you."

"I'd rather you explain it," I say earnestly. "I don't trust them."

She bites her lip and then tips her head to a pair of black stilettos on the floor. "Those are for you, too."

I put the stilettos on and then sit back on the edge of the bed. Like I guessed when I walked into the room, it is lumpy. Though, if my guess is correct, I won't be spending much time in here, anyway.

"Is there anything you can tell me?" I ask, fastening the buckle on my heel. "As much as possible, I want to know what to expect. I don't want to be taken by surprise."

She blinks, her eyes wide and nervous, and rubs her fingers anxiously across the hem of her shirt. "The red dress means you are more expensive."

"More expensive than the other women?" I ask.

She nods. "Red indicates that you come from better stock."

Better stock.

The words make me feel sick to my stomach. Feeling like an animal is different than being described as one.

For the first time, it really hits me how little anyone here cares about me. To them, I am nothing more than merchandise. I am only as good as the price I can fetch.

Also for the first time, I'm terrified.

"What a compliment," I bite out sarcastically, pushing through the sudden thickness in my throat. I don't want anyone to see me cry. Even this woman.

I realize that I don't even know her name.

She steps forward and extends a hand to help me to my feet. I place my hand in hers, feeling her cold fingers on my skin, and stand on shaky legs. Getting accustomed to the heels will be a process, given what my body has been through in the last few days.

"Who are you?" I ask.

"Just a servant," she says quickly. "Here to assist you."

"No." I shake my head. "I mean, what is your name?"

Her eyes widen in surprise, and then the fear returns. "Names aren't important here."

She spins away from me quickly and pulls open a drawer in the rickety dresser behind her. When she turns around, she has a shimmery red leather collar in her hand. It looks like a high-class dog collar. Dangling from it is a gold charm.

"This is for you," she says, unhooking the clasp and holding the collar out towards my neck.

I jerk away from her so quickly I almost lose my balance. "What is that?"

"It is how you will be recognized during the auction." She tips the charm towards me so I can see the number '7' engraved on the face of it. "You are Number Seven."

I shake my head. "No way. I'm not a fucking dog."

"It is easier to go along," the woman reminds me in a trembling voice. "It is just one of their rules."

"My name is Eve." I lay a hand over my heart, feeling the beating against my palm. It is a good reminder that despite the way I may feel in this situation, I am still a human being.

"I know," the woman says softly. Then, her eyes dart around the room again and she leans forward. "And my name is Kari."

"Kari," I say, testing the name out.

She shushes me quickly. "Don't use it. And don't use your own name unless specifically asked. It will be easier that way."

I want to fight, but I have no idea what is next for me, and I have a feeling I will need all of my energy. So, I concede this battle.

Kari lifts the collar to my neck, and I lift the still-damp waves of my hair to let her fasten it.

The material is smooth against my skin, but I can feel it tighten around me with each swallow. This thing could be made of pure gold and rubies. It doesn't change the fact that it is a fucking collar.

8

LUKA

I search every nook and cranny in the room in hopes of finding something I can fashion into a weapon. But the room is clean.

Even the glass from the picture frames has been removed in an abundance of caution. I tap on the mirror in the bathroom, but it is apparent that it is some kind of reflective plastic rather than actual glass. So, unless I want to braid the clothes in the closet together to use as a noose, I have no choice but to leave the room with nothing more than the clothes on my back and my mask.

I half expect to find Edgar lurking outside my doorway when I open it, but the hallway is empty. As I walk back towards the lobby, though, I hear soft voices. I follow them.

The armed guards who were standing by the door before are gone now, though I am certain there is still heavy security all around me. The whole building is tingling with pent-up aggression, like a vibration in the walls themselves.

I walk through the entryway and through the door underneath the balcony into a sitting room. There are plush white couches and chairs around a central fireplace that stretches all the way up the wall and through the peak in the ceiling.

Several masked men and women sit around on the furniture, clutching drinks in their hands.

I spot a bar cart against the far wall and make my way over to it, pouring myself two fingers of bourbon.

"Were you here last year?" a man with a white mask in the shape of a fox asks.

The woman sitting next to him shifts in her seat. "I don't think questions like those are common courtesy around here."

"Oh right, of course," the man says. "I forget all the secrecy. I have never been too fond of it, so I wouldn't mind ditching my mask now, though I know it would ruin the integrity of the evening."

I almost laugh at the idea that this event could ever have any integrity at all, but I don't. I quietly take a seat in a chair far away from the rest of the guests and sip on my drink. Luckily, the masks cut off just above the lip, allowing for unencumbered eating and drinking. But I can't imagine feeling something as trivial as hunger while I'm trying to track down my family.

I want to observe everyone. I want to have a good idea of who the people around me are because I have no way of knowing when that information could be useful. Foe or ally—it's impossible to say. And people like these have a way of changing sides when you least expect it.

For instance, I already know the man in the white mask is confident and thinks himself untouchable. One short conversation with him could probably provide me with his name and job title.

The woman is more reserved. She is wearing a fitted black skirt and jacket with a white button- down underneath, the buttons done up to her neck. She is either here to purchase a labor slave or she runs some kind of upscale brothel and is looking for a high-class worker.

Whatever the reason, she is here for business, not pleasure.

As I'm watching the rest of the room, I notice more and more eyes glancing in my direction. I do my best to look unimposing, but the tension in the room continues to rise.

I slouch my shoulders forward and lower my head, hoping to look smaller. It is difficult, though. I have been raised my entire life to be tall and proud and powerful. Even though I'm aware that everyone around me has tells that give away their station in life, I can't seem to control my own. They are innate.

"What about you?" Fox-Face asks, finally gathering his courage and throwing his voice over to me. "Were you here last year?"

The woman next to him on the couch sighs and adjusts her position. It is clear she finds the man annoying.

I take a slow sip from my glass and swirl it, while an awkward silence lingers in the air.

"I'll tell you if it ever becomes your business," I say, my voice striking a delicate balance between a joke and a threat.

The man gives a nervous chortle and then turns back towards the fireplace. If he didn't have a mask on, I'm certain his face would be glowing red.

A few more men wander into the room one at a time, taking stock of the other guests before taking a drink and claiming their own seat. When people aren't looking around at one another, they are checking the clock mounted above the fireplace.

The event should be starting soon.

Nerves twist my stomach, though I don't let it show. I do a head count and, in addition to a few people I saw earlier who are not in the room now, I guess there are ten bidders. To the right of the fireplace, there is a thin electric screen mounted to the wall, split into two columns. The first is a thin column numbered from one to fourteen and the other column is blank.

It is an intimate affair, which only serves to raise the stakes.

On one hand, it is good to know I'll only have to compete with nine other people for Eve, but then again, there will be even more focus on us now. If I do find her, people will surely notice if we spend too much time together or if I show her special attention.

They will either become suspicious or, due to the competitive nature of the week, more determined to make Eve theirs. People like this are here because they crave one thing above all else:

Control.

A rail-thin man in a dark suit and blood-red mask gets a drink behind me and then lingers near my chair. He doesn't say anything, but it is clear he has strategically chosen his location near me, and I intend to use that to my advantage.

"More people here than I thought there would be," I say.

The man turns to me, assessing my relaxed posture, and then lowers his own shoulders. "About the same as last year. Less than the year before that."

He must be a regular at this event.

"I suppose I've revealed how infrequently I attend the auction," I say.

"I already knew," the man says, glancing over at me. "The masks keep me from knowing exactly who you are, but I know who I've met in this room before. And I don't recognize you."

"Seems like there is more security this year, too," I say, moving on without responding to his previous statement. "Or maybe I was simply less observant back then."

The man takes a drink, his pointed chin dimpling as he thinks. "You may be right. Our hosts seem to want to show their muscle—indoors, at least. There are always armed guards around the perimeter of the property, of course, but they did try to keep the guns out of sight of the guests last year. One can only guess at their motivations. It tends to be a rather tight-lipped organization, no?"

I lean back in my chair and look into the entryway. The guards who were there before still haven't returned, but I see a shifting shadow standing on the other side of the fogged glass. They probably just moved outside to man the doors from the exterior.

"I wonder what happened to inspire the change."

The man hums in mild interest. "One of the women for auction always makes an attempt to escape. It happens every year. Perhaps they want to be more prepared this time. Though, the biggest threat is from the outside, not inside."

"You mean the police?" I ask.

The man nods. "And people interested in the event who don't have the funds. There have been threats before. Other cartels who want to come in and take the merchandise for free."

The man takes a sip of his drink and wanders closer to the center of the room, leaving me alone with my thoughts which are growing more and more frazzled with every second.

If this was any other mission, I'd call it off.

There are too many unknowns, too many different threats. I have to be on guard against the men inside, the guards outside, and the possibility of a third-party raid. Plus, I have no idea where Rian Morrison is or what the FBI has to do with any of this. The likelihood of success with the odds so stacked against me is slim.

I should get out.

But I can't.

Not when Eve and Milaya are on the line. If it meant keeping them safe, I'd strip my mask off in the middle of this room and allow the guards to gun me down.

I'll do anything to protect them.

So, I finish off the last of my drink and take a deep breath. It is going to be a long five days.

Edgar walks into the lounge a few minutes later, a pleasant smile on his face. He strolls to the front of the fireplace and opens his arms in welcome.

"Welcome," he says, nodding to every corner of the room. "I will keep my remarks brief. Now that everyone is here, I know you are all eager to begin, so let's do just that."

He takes a few steps towards the screen on the wall and gestures to the screen. "The bidding board should look familiar to those of you who have been with us before. To those of you who haven't, the board is where all official bids will be logged for each of the fourteen items on show this week. Feel free to bid whenever you would like, but bidding early does not guarantee anything. It is simply a way to express your interest. And in return for doing so, we will make sure you are rewarded each night."

The man in the fox mask laughs, causing the woman to his right to slide even further away from him on the couch.

From a business perspective, I understand how this works. The Cartel wants people to put in early bids to help increase the overall price by the fifth day. And to encourage early bids, whoever has the highest bid on any woman by the end of the day gets to take her to their room.

It's a cruel and efficient way to extract wealth from the extraordinarily wealthy moguls in attendance.

As a don, I am impressed.

As a husband, I am enraged.

I want to rip the bidding board from the wall and crack it over Edgar's head. Then, I'll use the broken shards to ram Fox-Face through the chest.

Instead, I swallow back the bile that has risen in my throat and try not to crush the glass tumbler in my hand.

"Bidding will end at 4:59 p.m. on Wednesday," Edgar says. "But until then, enjoy your stay and enjoy the show."

Like a ringmaster opening a circus, Edgar waves an arm towards a door on his right and strides backwards to the far corner of the room.

There is a beat of awkward silence when nothing happens and everyone is just waiting in breathless anticipation.

Then, slowly, a woman appears in the doorway.

She is wearing a purple dress that is tight, but still fails to hug her frail body. She looks like she hasn't had a proper meal in months. Her cheeks are hollowed and dark circles that makeup could never hide hang heavily under her eyes.

With slow, shaky steps, she walks through the door and across the fireplace to stand a few feet from Edgar. I can see her hands are trembling, and her eyes dart around the room like a nervous mouse.

The room draws in a low hiss of distaste. The woman is not quite repulsive, but she's far from the desirable jewel we've been primed to expect. Our eyes slide back to the door from which she entered, waiting for the next with bated breath.

A moment later, another woman appears.

This one is better. Healthier, fitter, though still not worth parting with any significant sums. She steps forward cautiously and takes her place next to the first.

Following the first two, the rest of the women file through the door one by one. Each time a woman steps from the shadows into the lounge, my heart clenches.

Is this one Eve?

Is she even here?

Have I wasted my time?

As one turns to five and then ten, the women become more attractive. Starting with Number Eleven, the women are all dressed in red. Their hair is shiny and healthy, their skin is smooth and radiant. They look like models more than slaves. Terrified models, of course, but beautiful. It is clear the Cartel are saving the best for last.

Number Thirteen walks out—a tall, strong woman with dark brown skin and curly black hair—and she isn't as afraid as the other women. She smiles at the group of men and women waiting for her, even winking towards Fox-Face. I consider myself adept at reading people, but whether her act is a façade or not, I can't tell.

I look at the bidding board and realize there is only one woman left. One more chance for it to be Eve. For me to be in the right place.

I bounce back and forth between wanting it to be her and hoping she is far away from this depravity.

On the one hand, it would be good to see her. To see that she is alive, at least.

On the other, I don't want to see her treated as cattle. I don't want to spend the next five days bidding on the woman I love, playing a dangerous game that might get us both killed.

I hold my breath as a shadow separates from the dark room and steps towards the middle.

When the fire's light hits her face, my heart breaks.

It is my wife.

At once, I'm consumed with relief and guilt and the desire to grab her and run and the knowledge that I can't do that without getting us both killed.

I stifle a moan, but luckily it is lost in the stir as Eve walks out.

She is easily the most beautiful woman in the room. And I know it is not only I who think so. Several men in the room sit forward and crane their necks to see. I want to snap each one of them in half.

She doesn't look scared, but she doesn't openly flirt with anyone in the room the way the woman before her did. Eve walks out with her chin held high, her chestnut hair falling in thick waves down her back, and plants her feet firmly on the floor. She doesn't shy away from facing the crowd in front of her.

And her gaze is devastating.

There is fire in her eyes. Anger and a promise. A promise that she won't let anyone here forget what they did to her.

She meets every set of eyes, and when our eyes meet, it is all I can do to not rip off my mask and run to her.

For a moment, I wonder whether she'll recognize me. Whether she'll be able to tell it is me based on my eyes and mouth alone, but I am farther away than the other guests, and her eyes fall on me only for a minute before flitting away.

"Okay," Edgar says, stepping forward and clapping his hands. "Everyone is free to mingle. Have a drink, talk to one another and the women. And don't forget, if anyone catches your eye, be sure to put in a bid."

For a moment, it is like a middle school dance. The women on display and the guests not moving. We just stare at one another uncomfortably, waiting for someone else to make the first move.

I would, but I don't want to draw attention to myself or my obvious preference for Eve.

Fox-Face, however, has no such qualms. He groans merrily as he pushes himself to standing, adjusts his pants around his chubby middle, and makes his way directly to Number Thirteen, the woman who winked at him.

Eve grimaces as the man passes by her, then marches towards a distant wall, pressing her back against it.

As soon as both sides make a move, the rest of the room stirs.

The auction week has officially begun.

I make myself another drink but don't taste it. I don't want to drink too much and dull any of my senses. I can't afford it.

So, I fidget with the glass, swirling it in my hands, and watch Eve move around the room.

She tries to stand against a wall, but Edgar walks over and quietly encourages her to join the party. They are too far away from me to hear what he says, but I guess his words are not as kind as the fake smile on his face.

A woman in a purple dress approaches me, but I don't even glance in her direction. Even when she is standing a foot to my right, I just stare straight ahead.

I don't want to talk to her or any woman in the room. Only Eve.

The woman tries to catch my eye for a few desperate seconds before she slips away to find another man.

I feel bad for dismissing her, but I don't want to give her any sense of false hope. I won't be making a bid on anyone but Eve. Ever. And the woman's time will be better spent cozying up to another guest at the auction.

Peter Struthers bumbles over to Eve and brings her a drink. She tries to demur, but he pushes it into her hand. I have to bite my tongue to keep from ripping his hand off.

I keep my eye on them as I circulate, doing my best not to tip my hand so obviously as to draw unwanted attention. Eve looks miserable talking to Peter. He is laughing and smiling and moving increasingly close to her, but she just stares at him with blank eyes. Though, her lack of enthusiasm doesn't seem to discourage him.

During the conversation, I notice Eve reach up and adjust something around her neck. That is when I notice the collar.

I was so distracted when she first walked in that I didn't see the red strip of leather fastened around her neck.

When she turns to avoid another of Peter's advances, I see the gold charm hanging from the front, and I curse under my breath.

They have a collar on her like she is a fucking animal.

Heat builds in my core, and my breathing grows heavier. My heart feels like a bass drum in my chest, and my vision tunnels until Eve is all I can see.

I have to get her out of here. I have to save her.

"Hey there."

I turn and see a hippy blonde woman standing next to me. She has dark makeup around her eyes and bright red lipstick on, which only serves to highlight how pale she is. I wonder when she last saw sunlight.

I want to dismiss her the way I did the first woman who approached me, but I realize that I have to show interest in the other women. If I want this plan to work, people have to believe that I am here to shop.

So, I turn towards her and raise an eyebrow. "I thought I was supposed to be the one doing the approaching."

She blinks, trying to decide whether I've just insulted her or not, and then smiles, her lips twitching from the effort. "I was always taught to go after what I want."

I reach out and pinch a strand of her hair between my fingers. She flinches from the brief contact, but then smiles. "And you are the most handsome man in the room."

"I have a mask on," I remind her.

"A mask can only hide so much," she says.

I glance towards Eve. She is now talking to Fox-Face. Her cheeks are the same shade of red as her dress, and I desperately want to know what he is saying to her.

"What do you do?" she asks.

I shake my head. "No. Nothing personal."

After several seconds of silence, the woman asks me about the weather. It is so cliché I almost laugh, but I can't muster it. Not when Eve is being hit on by every man in the room.

I talk to the woman for several minutes, letting her do most of the talking while I watch Eve move around the room.

Finally, she is standing back near the bar, and I can't resist her for another moment.

"You must excuse me," I say to the blonde woman, interrupting her in the middle of a sentence.

I weave through people, raising my glass in the air as I squeeze around the bodies, and then Eve is right in front of me. Mere feet away.

Her hair shines gold in the overhead lights, and she turns her head to register me in the corner of her vision, but quickly goes back to making her drink.

My heart is pounding as I approach her.

I don't know how to do this. I don't want to surprise her and blow the mission before it has even begun, so I can't just walk up and tell her who I am. I have to let her figure it out slowly.

So, as I pass her from behind, I curl my fingers around her waist and then drag them across her lower back.

She starts at the touch, but when I tug softly at the ends of her hair, she turns to look at me.

I look into her caramel eyes for only a second, but it is long enough to see the question she is asking.

Is that ...

I nod slowly, answering it for her, and immediately her eyes fill with tears.

Then, she bites her pouty lower lip and turns to keep making her drink, but her fingers are trembling.

She knows it is me.

9
EVE

I think I'm imagining it when I smell Luka.

The spicy scent of his cologne mingles with the woodsy smell of his skin.

I've been seeing him everywhere. Every time I close my eyes, he is there.

Surrounded by these horrible men and women who are studying me like a dog at a kennel show, I want nothing more than the familiar comfort of my husband.

Then, I feel a hand on my waist.

My instinct is to pull away and slap whichever disgusting man has put his hands on me, but then I feel the pressure of the fingertips along my back.

The touch is tender and intimate.

And so, so familiar.

Before this moment, I would have said there is no way I'd recognize

Luka by nothing more than the brush of his fingers, but in the instant his body touches mine, I feel relief.

It feels like arriving home after a long time away.

I turn to my left and see a tall, broad man wrapped in a deliciously tailored suit. A black mask covers his face, but I can see the tense line of his upper lip and his clenched jaw. Usually, there is a dark beard there, but I've seen my husband with a clean-shaven face often enough to recognize the square line of his jaw.

It is Luka. It has to be.

Still, I'm hesitant to believe it.

Have my delusions grown worse? Am I having full-blown hallucinations now? Could it really be him?

As though I've voiced the question aloud, the man in the black mask nods his head slowly, and tears well up in my eyes.

I bite my lip to hold in a sob and turn back to the bar.

Luka is here. He is here.

And the fact that he hasn't grabbed me and made a run for it means that he can't just take me and bolt. It means that I have to play along.

Even though I want to chase after him as he begins to mill around the room, I grab my drink with shaky fingers and turn in the opposite direction.

"In your case, I guess they really did save the best for last."

A man in a navy-blue suit with silver embroidery on it is standing next to me. He has on a white button-down underneath, open to reveal a swirl of brown chest hair.

Not waiting for any response from me, he reaches out to grab a lock of my hair. He twirls it around his finger like he already owns me.

"You are the sexiest woman in the room," he says.

His mask is the same shade of blue as his suit. It has a beaked nose like a bird that sticks out so far it almost hits me in the face when he leans in to whisper in my ear.

"I put a bid on you the moment cocktail hour started."

I spin to the board and see five hundred dollars typed in green next to my number. It is the only bid.

"Is that all I'm worth to you?" I ask, eyebrow raised.

I can't see the man's face, but by the way his head pulls back, I think he might be insulted. Then, he laughs. "Of course not. Believe me, baby, I have more money than any man in this room."

His suit is nice, but I don't imagine many people here have the kind of connections Luka has. He is independently wealthy and he is owed many favors from a lot of wealthy men. There are few money matters that he can't handle. And since I am apparently the prize, I know Luka will do whatever he can to walk out of here with me.

The man keeps his eyes on my chest, tracing the deep neckline of the dress over and over again like he is trying to remove the fabric with his mind.

"Men who have to say they're rich usually aren't telling the truth," I say with the smallest of smiles. I mean every word, but I want the man to think I'm flirting with him.

He does.

His mouth splits into a grin, and he steps closer to me until I can practically taste his overpowering cologne. It takes everything I have not to retch as he drawls, "Stick with me, and I'll back it up."

I lift an eyebrow and bring my glass to my lips, taking a slow sip.

The man watches eagerly. When I drag my tongue across my upper lip, his eyes widen.

"Keep that up, and I might have to go raise my bid," he says, his voice husky.

I smile and turn away from him, ready to move along to another man.

I want to make it clear I have no particular preference for Luka, but I also don't want to get myself in too deep with any other man in the room.

As I turn away, however, the man reaches out and grabs my hip.

Unlike Luka's soft touch, the man's fingers are hard and possessive. They wrap around me like a shackle and spin me towards him.

He moves closer to me until my drink is wedged between our bodies, the only thing keeping him from being flush with me.

"Running away so soon?" he whispers.

I see him glance over my shoulder, and then suddenly, he backs away. His lips are pressed together in a tight line, and he swallows nervously.

I'm confused until I feel the warmth of Luka's hand on the small of my back.

"Now, now," Luka says in a playfully deep voice. "We all have to share."

The man in the bird mask smiles and bows, either to me or Luka or both, I'm not sure. "Of course. Clearly, I am not the only man here with exquisite taste." He winks at me before throwing another cautious glance at Luka and then turning to survey the room. "You two have your fun, and I'll try to occupy myself with something else."

Luka presses his hand into my lower back, leading me towards a chair against a set of tall windows. He sits down and then gestures for me to sit on his lap.

I do my best to look the part of the nervous slave, but I practically leap onto him, grateful to feel his familiar bulk and warmth against me.

Luka wraps his arm around my waist and pulls me closer to him until his lips are right by my ear.

"Hello."

A shiver works its way down my spine, and I try not to melt into him. I want to press my lips to his neck and bury my face against his chest and let out every emotion I've been holding in since I was taken.

"How did you find me?" I whisper.

He draws a circle with his finger against my rib cage. "I'll always find you, Eve. Always."

For the first time in several days, I feel like I can breathe. The vise-like pressure that was wrapped around my chest is gone, and I take deep, greedy inhales in an effort not to hyperventilate with happiness.

"What is the plan?" I ask.

Luka shakes his head imperceptibly, and I follow his eyes towards the rest of the guests. No one is really looking at us.

Around the rest of the Bratva, Luka has enough power that no one wants to be caught staring. And even people who don't know Luka is the leader of a crime family avoid direct eye contact.

Luka is large and intimidating, and it works in his favor.

Now, though, he is wearing a mask and this event is rooted in competition.

People are watching us more closely than normal, but I notice they have the good sense to look away when Luka notices them. Still, this isn't exactly a safe place. There is no way to know who may overhear anything we say.

Luka readjusts me on his lap so I'm balanced between his muscular thighs, and his hand wraps around my back and smooths down the leg.

My dress is riding up dangerously high, and Luka takes full advantage, dipping his fingers below the hem until I can feel him caressing the black panties I am wearing.

A small sigh escapes my lips, and Luka presses his mouth to my ear. "Look like you are having a worse time."

I try to pull my face into a frown, but every brush of his finger against my inner thigh leaves me a little looser and brings more color to my cheeks.

I know I need to look miserable, like Luka is taking more than I'm willing to give, but I can't. I want to give him everything.

Before I can stop myself, I reach up and curl my finger down his face.

I can feel the beginnings of stubble on his jawline, and I want to drag my tongue across his face like a cat. I want to twine myself around his legs and claim him as mine.

I don't want to talk to any other men or be with anyone else. I just want Luka, and part of me hopes that if everyone can see us together, they'll realize they don't have a shot in hell of ever making me happy. Not the way he could.

Though, my happiness isn't their main concern. Not by a long shot.

"I'm going to take you home with me," Luka growls.

To anyone else in the room, he is just an auction guest making known his intent to purchase. But to me, it is a promise.

Luka is going to get me out of here.

All at once, the panic inside of me eases, making way for the other emotions I have pushed aside. Namely, guilt.

This is all my fault.

The reason Rian Morrison is after us is because of me. Because of my failed relationship with her brother.

"I'm sorry," I whisper, voice breaking around the words.

Luka frowns. "For what? You have nothing to apologize for."

"But I do," I say. "This is all my fault. If I'd been brave and told Cole Morrison how I felt from the start, none of this would have happened."

"Eve," Luka says so low I can only feel the vibration of the word in his chest.

I shake my head. "But I let myself be promised to him. I was too scared to run away and now you have to risk your life to save me, and—"

Luka's finger against my center silences my tirade.

I hold my breath, surprised by my own desperation for his touch.

But Luka doesn't move. He looks around the room to ensure no one is watching us too closely, and then he leans in, finger still poised against me like he has all the time in the world.

"You have nothing to be sorry for," he says, his breath warm against my neck. "This isn't your fault, and I'm going to fix it."

Unable to help myself, I shift my hips, pushing myself against his finger.

Luka slides his hand further under my dress, but before anything more can happen, the man who announced the start of the auction reappears and waves his arms to draw everyone's attention.

"I'm glad to see you are all having a good time," he says, looking over towards where Luka and I are sitting together in a chair. "But dinner is about to be served. So, if you all could follow me into the dining room, we will begin the next portion of the evening."

The quiet conversation grows louder as everyone migrates towards the dining room, and in the brief moment of chaos, I lean in to Luka. "Where is Milaya?"

Because of the mask I can't see his face, but I feel his body tense underneath me. "I thought Milaya might be with you."

My heart shrivels in my chest.

It is a wonder I am still alive at all.

The heat that was flooding through me only a moment ago because of Luka's finger turns to ice.

When I saw Luka, I assumed he'd saved Milaya first.

It hadn't even crossed my mind to be worried about her anymore because I was sure that Luka had her. Surely. Like a spy from a thriller novel, I knew beyond doubt that he'd come to save me dressed in a designer suit, wearing a masquerade mask. But I was sure that he knew I could handle myself long enough for him to find our daughter first.

I am the daughter of a Mafia don, after all. This world, while cruel, is what I know. Milaya is the innocent one. Milaya is helpless.

Realizing neither of us has any idea where our daughter is feels like a kick to the chest when I'm already down as low as I've ever been.

But I don't have time to linger on the thoughts threatening to choke the air from my lungs. At the urging of the master of ceremonies, Luka escorts me into the dining room behind the rest of the women and guests.

I expected a large room with one long table, however the dining room is set up almost like a restaurant. Scattered around the space are small tables with two chairs each and small candles flickering in the middle. Naturally, everyone walks in and begins to pair off.

This pairing becomes part of the festivities. Men jostle to sit with the woman they have their eye on, hoping to get more time with them. More than one man looks in my direction, but Luka doesn't leave my side.

I wonder whether I shouldn't go with someone else. Not only to help with our deception but because I'm not sure what to say to Luka right now. As happy as I am to see him here, I'd rather know Milaya is safe. I only blame myself for this entire situation happening in the first place, but I blame Luka for Milaya still being missing, and I'm not exactly sure how to navigate that emotional minefield.

There isn't much room for debate, however, when Luka leads me to a table near the corner of the room and pulls out my chair for me.

As I sit, he glares over at the man with the bird mask, making sure to mark his territory.

Luka orders for both of us, which is fine with me. Even if I looked at a menu, I wouldn't be able to focus on it. There is only one thought in my head:

Where is my daughter?

At the Morrison house, I only saw Rian, her father, and a driver. How many people could be working for them? Could Milaya be with one of them? I never saw Rian's mother, so maybe Milaya is staying with her, though that thought isn't exactly comforting. Everyone in the Morrison family hates me, so it is unlikely they will be kind to my daughter.

Before the food arrives, Luka reaches across the table and lays his hand down, palm facing up.

I look around the room to be certain no one is watching before I lay my hand over his.

His hand is warm, and he curls his fingers around mine, and though I'm angry and upset, I love him. So much. And having him here with me during one of the scariest times of my life is reassuring in more ways than I can express.

When waiters begin bringing the food out, Luka takes his hand back and puts on an air of indifference. I match his tone.

We eat mostly in silence. The tables in the room are close together and I am afraid to say something that could be overheard by someone else. It is more than just my life at stake now. If the Cartel discovers why Luka is here, they could be upset. And they don't seem to be the kind of people who will simply kick him out.

They'll probably just kill him.

And if he dies, and I'm sold into slavery, who will search for Milaya?

The Bratva, maybe, but I don't know how long they'll keep up the search. They are loyal to Luka now, but once they have a new leader, there is no way to know how long that loyalty will last.

"You seem to be a man with a lot of power," I say softly, pushing the cheesy pasta around my plate.

Luka narrows his eyes at me and nods.

"A man in charge of a lot of men?" I ask. "How are they surviving while you are away for five days?"

Luka sees my question for what it is. "They are waiting anxiously for the fifth day. They are lost without me."

They are waiting.

I stare at Luka, trying to see if there is anything he is holding back, but he is waiting for me to speak.

The men are just waiting for Luka. They aren't looking for Milaya or pursuing any leads.

My heart falls, and I stab a noodle with my fork. "It would be horrible to be that helpless. Me? I know how to take care of myself."

I glare at Luka over my water glass, and I can see in the flicker of pain across his face that he understands me. He leans forward, his green eyes shining and serious.

"You can take care of yourself?" he hisses, sitting back in his seat and looking around the room. "How is that going for you?"

My jaw drops.

The rest of dinner is uncomfortably silent, broken only by the sound of silverware clinking against our dinner plates.

The man hosting the event, Edgar, ushers everyone from the dining room to a large ballroom at the back of the inn.

The walls are high and painted a pale gold color. Large chandeliers hang from three points along the room, and there are stained glass windows along the back wall. If I wasn't being held prisoner, I'd think it was a beautiful place for a party.

Music plays softly through speakers located in every corner of the room, and once everyone is inside, the lights are dimmed and another bar is set up.

It is clear the intention is for everyone to get loose, though for all of the other women I can see, that seems impossible.

Only the woman before me in line, Thirteen, seems to be having even a remotely good time.

As soon as the lights dim, she moves to the center of the dance floor, dragging a guest by his tie, and begins to dance. Her enthusiasm encourages the other guests to find women of their own and make their way to the middle of the room.

The female bidders are less interested in the festivities and stand against the wall, content with studying the proceedings.

Out of all of the people present, I'm most scared at the prospect of being purchased by one of the women. With the men, it is clear what my purpose would be. But with the women, I'm not sure.

And, like the saying goes, the devil you know is better than the devil you don't.

Luka takes a half-hearted lap around the room before making his way back to me and dragging me out to the dance floor.

I'm still angry with him. For not trusting me. For coming to save me before he looked for Milaya. For telling me to my face that he doesn't think I can take care of myself.

However, as soon as we are together on the dance floor, hidden in a crowd of other people, with music pulsing all around us, I can't begrudge my body what it wants: to be near him.

Luka wraps an arm around my lower back and jerks my body against his. Our hips crash and grind together in time with the music, and I tip my head back, letting my hair shake loose.

Luka groans, and I lift my head to see him staring at my chest. His eyes inch up slowly until our gazes meet, and he shakes his head.

"I'd appreciate it if you could be less sexy," he says as quietly as possible while still being heard over the music. "You are making my job more difficult with every man you make interested in you."

"No one is paying any attention to me," I say.

Luka raises an eyebrow and tips his head to his right. I follow his gaze and see the man in the bird mask staring at me. He has a woman held in the circle of his arms, her back against his chest while she grinds into him.

But his eyes are locked on me.

I turn into Luka quickly, feeling sick. The momentary high I got from being close to him is fading, being washed away by dread.

"Even if we get out of here, they can hold Milaya over our heads," I say finally.

Luka looks around to be sure no one is listening, and then slowly dances me further from the crowd. "I'm not sure what you want from me, Eve. I'm here for you—"

"Exactly," I interrupt. "You should have gone after Milaya. I could fend for myself."

"How?" he barks a bit too loudly, drawing the attention of one of the women in purple. "I can barely fend for myself here. How would you have gotten out?"

I don't want to tell him that maybe I wouldn't have. Luka won't accept that answer, but it is the truth. I accepted that I might spend the rest of my life as someone else's slave. I came to terms with that, and while I would have done everything in my power to get out, I also would gladly follow that path if it meant Milaya would be safe with Luka.

"I did my best," Luka says. And for the first time, I see his uncertainty. His doubt.

Luka isn't sure he made the right decision, and now I'm making it worse. If I know anything about him, he has been beating himself up for the fact that we were taken in the first place, and now I'm making him feel guilty about the way he is trying to save us.

I want to wrap my hand around his neck and pull his lips to mine. I want to apologize and promise him that we'll find some way to make this all better.

But before I can, a heavy hand lands on my shoulder.

I spin and nearly get hit with the birdman's beak again. He smiles at me and then at Luka. "I believe I've shared her enough now, don't you?"

Luka's jaw clenches, and for a second I worry he is going to haul back and punch the birdman right in his hooked nose, but then he lets his hands fall from my waist and gestures for the bastard to step in.

I watch Luka disappear into the crowd, wanting nothing more than to follow him. But my attention is quickly drawn to the birdman's hands on my waist.

He grips my body like I'm a freshly caught fish that might jump from his grip. He is holding me so tight that I can barely breathe, and my chest heaves with the effort, which seems to only make him squeeze me tighter.

He talks to me, though I don't listen. Whatever he is saying, it doesn't require my response, and I'm glad because I would have nothing to say.

My thoughts are with Luka and Milaya and the bidding board in the lounge area. Has anyone else made a bid on me yet? Has Luka?

Who will I be going to bed with tonight?

The thought sends a chill down my spine, and then the entire room goes cold.

A woman is screaming. The sound echoes off the walls, drowning out the pulse of the music, and everyone freezes.

Except for me.

I immediately pull away from the birdman's greedy grasp and push my way through the crowd.

10

EVE

The guests are backing away from the center of the room, and when I push my way past another woman in a red dress, I see a shaking figure in the center of the room.

She is dressed in purple—according to Kari, that means she is a virgin—and she is curled in the fetal position on the floor, rocking back and forth and screaming.

"I don't want to be here! I don't want to do this. Don't make me do this."

The man who was dancing with her, Fox-Face, steps back and shrugs his shoulders like he can't imagine what led to her breakdown.

But I see a smile pull at the corners of his mouth. He is enjoying this.

Luka is frowning towards the woman, and when he sees me moving towards her, he shakes his head once quickly.

I want to listen to him and not get involved. I know it is better not to draw unnecessary attention to ourselves. However, when I see armed guards rushing from the corners of the room towards the shaking girl, I can't stop myself from running towards her.

I kneel down beside her and drape an arm over her back.

"Hi," I whisper in her ear. "My name is Eve."

The woman doesn't look up, but she stops screaming.

Sobs wrack her thin body. I can feel the bones of her back through her dress, and I wonder how long she has been held prisoner. For me, it was only a few days. But any longer in the Morrison house, and I would have been all skin and bones, too.

I run my hand down her spine and shush her the way I do Milaya when she wakes up in the middle of the night. "It's okay. It's okay, dear."

The guards break into the inner circle, but they stop when they see me next to the woman on the floor. I look up into their grim faces, hoping to find some level of humanity there, but there is only annoyance.

They look at one another, trying to decide what to do, and one of them nods his head towards the bar. They need to distract the guests because right now, they are all watching me and the woman intently, and this is not the kind of thing the Cartel wants to advertise.

Right on cue, Edgar steps forward and claps his hands to draw everyone's attention.

"Technical error," he laughs, ushering the crowd towards the bar. "These things can happen. Why don't I show you all to the house bar? It has a larger selection than the minibar, and our bartender can make anything you want while we deal with this."

Deal with this. As though the sobbing woman on the floor is nothing more than a computer bug.

"You have to pull it together," I say as gently as I can in the woman's ear.

Luka lingers as everyone begins to follow Edgar towards the exit, listening to him explain that there is a pool table and a secret vault full of "adult toys" they can peruse.

The woman shivers at the idea and presses her forehead against the tile floor.

"Things will be worse for you if you make a scene," I say, hating that I sound like Kari.

I want to tell the girl to fight. To scream and run and do whatever she can to get out of here, but I know that won't help.

She is shivering and weak and scared, and the guards would dispose of her in an instant.

"I know this is horrible, but if you want to live, you have to play their game."

The girl looks up at me, and I'm struck by her beauty.

Her face is gaunt with shadows under her eyes and cheekbones, but she has clear blue eyes the color of the ocean and full lips. Her red hair is wavy and thick and a delicate smattering of freckles cover her nose and cheeks. The purple collar around her neck says she is slave Number Eleven.

"What is your name?" I ask quietly.

She sniffles, her shoulders shaking with shuddering breaths from all of the crying. "Maddie."

The guard nearest to us clears his throat and narrows his eyes at me.

We aren't supposed to give our names, though I suspect he is only giving me a warning because they would rather I diffuse the situation than lose out on a woman who will clearly go for a hefty price.

"Okay," I say, grabbing her around the waist. "We're going to stand up, all right?"

She nods and stands on shaky legs like a newborn giraffe. I have to wrap an arm around her back to keep her standing.

The guards step back as we stand, and I look to them for permission, hoping I can lead her out of the room. They look at one another, and then slowly slip back to their posts, clearly grateful they don't have to deal with it.

"Let's just walk it off," I say.

We make it to the doors before Maddie starts to cry again. She sags against my side and shakes her head. "He is so horrible."

"Who?"

"The man," she says, gesturing over her shoulder. "The man in the fox mask. He is horrible."

"What did he say?" I already know the man is disgusting. I gathered that from his obvious enjoyment at Maddie's breakdown. But having further proof he is a pig would be nice.

"He just told me—" she hesitates, a shiver running through her. "He told me what he wanted to do with me. Later."

This girl isn't going to make it.

That is the first thought that enters my mind. If I get out of here and she is sold, she won't make it. She'll be dead within a month.

I walk Maddie into the hallway, which stretches in both directions and is entirely empty now. I have no idea where the other guests are.

"There is no way to make any of this easier," I say, choosing to turn right in hopes it will lead us back to the group. The last thing I want to do is be caught by a guard wandering in a prohibited part of the inn. "It is a horrible situation for us all, but if you freak out like that again, they'll kill you."

Maddie flinches, and I squeeze her shoulders tighter.

"I don't want to scare you, but that is the reality. The best thing you can do right now is try to find someone here who isn't horrible. Keep as much distance from the man in the fox mask as you can. My gut tells me that he gets off on your fear. Be confident and try to catch the eye of someone else. Someone who isn't as horrible."

"How?" she breathes. "Everyone here is horrible."

"That's true," I admit with a humorless chuckle. "But cling to the least horrible man you can find. You are beautiful, and if you play your cards right, you might end up with someone who isn't so bad."

The words feel like acid in my mouth, and I nearly choke on them.

Every person here is horrible except for Luka. But I have to give Maddie some hope. Without it, she'll be killed like the runt of the litter. She won't survive the week.

Maddie begins to cry again, and I run my hand down her back as I peek in every door we pass, hoping to find the group.

Luka is probably livid at me for separating myself from him and drawing the attention of the guards and the other guests, but I can't think about that now. Not when I don't even know where I am.

From the outside, the inn looks averaged-sized, but inside, the hallways are like a maze of identical doorways. I stop and try to listen for the other guests, but I can't hear anything.

Then, we turn a corner and run headfirst into Luka.

I bounce off his chest and stumble back with Maddie, but Luka doesn't move. He is like a brick wall, and he leers down at both of us, his eyes narrowed.

"The rest of the party is that way," he says to Maddie, pointing over his shoulder. "Third door on the right."

Maddie gazes up at him, her fear shifting to awe. She nods once, hesitantly, and then separates from me and walks away. She looks back at us as she moves down the hall towards the rest of the guests.

"What in the hell were you thinking?" Luka asks, grabbing me by the waist and pinning me back against the wall.

His words are gruff, but his hands are gentle and warm. He caresses my waist and hip in slow, sensuous circles, breathing heavily.

"I thought the guards might grab you, too," he whispers, leaning down until his forehead is pressed against mine. "I thought they might get rid of you for being too much trouble."

"I had to help her," I say sharply. "They were going to kill her."

"They could have killed you," Luka bites back. "That silly girl isn't worth a hair on your head; do you hear me?"

"We have to save them."

Luka's eyes go wide and then he drags a hand down his face. "Clearly, you didn't hear me."

"I did hear you, but I disagree."

Suddenly, Luka's hand is wrapped around my neck and he is tipping me back, back into a kiss.

His lips are soft but demanding, opening my mouth so he can flick his tongue against mine. I go fluid in his arms, unaware of how desperate I was for this connection until now. He steps forward, his hips grinding into mine, hitting me in all the right spots until I moan against his mouth.

When he pulls away, I gasp like a deep-sea diver who just lost her oxygen.

"My priority is you," he says, firmly, brushing his nose against mine. "And only you. I don't care about anyone else."

I'm still dizzy from our kiss, but I push him away and shake my head. "We can't just walk away and let them be sold."

"You are my wife," Luka growls in a low voice. "You are my priority."

"They could all be somebody's wife, too," I argue. "They probably have people who love them wondering where they are. Doesn't that matter to you?"

Luka tips his head back and stares at the ceiling, blowing out a frustrated breath, and then turns his green eyes on me in a glare. "First, you were mad at me for coming here to save you in the first place, and now you want me to save everyone?"

"I wasn't mad you came to save me, so don't twist my words." I jab a finger into his muscled chest, and Luka looks down at it, a warning in his narrowed eyes. "But now that you are here, why can't we shut this entire operation down?"

"Because I'm alone and without weapons," he says between gritted teeth. "Our only chance of getting out of here alive is for me to bid on you and hope no one realizes we are already married."

I cross my arms over my chest. "We have to at least try."

Luka huffs and opens his mouth to argue, but there is a small cough from the far end of the hallway.

Edgar has turned the corner, his hands folded behind his back calmly, but there is a question in his eyes.

"Sir?" he asks, turning to Luka. "Is everything okay?"

He must have heard our whispered argument, and I can only hope he was too far away to hear any vital details.

"Fine," Luka says dismissively, scowling.

I slide away from him, looking horrified. "We were just having a discussion."

"About what he plans to do to me later," I say, stealing a line from Maddie.

Edgar lifts his eyebrows in amusement. "Well, until then, why don't we have you both rejoin the party?" he says, nodding for us to follow him back towards the bar.

"I was going to have a smoke," Luka says, pulling a cigarette from his pocket. "Or is that not allowed?"

"Of course it is allowed," Edgar says. "I will fetch a woman to accompany you."

"This one will do nicely," Luka says, grabbing my arm.

Edgar clears his throat nervously and smiles. "I see you have a preference for this woman, but it would be unfair to keep her to yourself all night. We would prefer if she mingled with some of the other guests as well."

Luka looks like he is going to deck Edgar for the mere suggestion that I talk to anyone else, but then he takes a deep breath and nods. "Fine then. But I will smoke alone, thank you."

He stalks down the hallway towards the main lobby, and Edgar smiles after him.

As soon as he is gone, however, Edgar roughly grabs my arm and leads me to the bar.

"You are here for the satisfaction of our guests," he snaps, dragging me along faster than I can walk in my heels. "Keep your feelings to yourself, do you hear me?"

I don't answer, and Edgar pauses outside the bar.

"Do you hear me?"

"Yes," I say, glaring up at him.

When we walk into the bar, Edgar is smiling again and politely leads me towards the group, bowing as he walks away.

I feel alone without Luka in the room. Being able to look up and see him watching me helped me feel safe. Without him here, however, I realize how precarious my situation here is. At any moment, I could be sold to someone else.

If someone outbids Luka, it is all over. And there is no telling what Luka will do if that happens.

Several of the men who didn't show much interest in me before Maddie's outburst now move towards me as I enter the room. Just as Luka feared, drawing attention to myself only means more competition for him when it comes to bidding.

I take a deep breath and try to ground myself.

Luka is here to save me, but I can't depend on him. We are in this together, but I have to be strong on my own. Just like I told Maddie, I have to play their game and be cunning or I won't survive.

None of us will.

11

LUKA

After the woman's outburst during the dance, the night's event is transferred to the bar and never makes it back to the ballroom.

The guests seem content to drink and mingle with women, most of them acting as though the disturbance never happened, but I can't forget it. Not when Eve spends all of her energy catering to the poor woman.

Between every man she talks to, Eve cuts across the room to check on Maddie.

I love Eve for her kindness and determination, but right now, it is putting our entire plan in jeopardy. As much as I want to trust my wife and allow her to do what she thinks is best, her heart is overriding her brain. We can't save everyone. It simply isn't possible.

I would love to end the LeClerc Cartel for good, but I can't do it in the next four days. The only thing I might be able to do is get my wife out of here so we can find our daughter.

That's the only fucking option. So, that is my priority.

To keep Edgar and the other guests from getting suspicious, I briefly talk with a few of the other women, but it is hard to pay attention to them when my focus is locked onto Eve.

Since she ran forward to help the woman in the ballroom, more bidders seem to be paying attention to Eve. I can't see the bidding board, but I can only assume she has several more bids under her name.

Eve cuts into a conversation between Fox-Face and the weeping woman, sending the girl away, no doubt to keep her from breaking down again.

I can't stand watching this for another moment.

She is talking to the most odious man in the room, and—Edgar be damned—I want to talk to my wife.

I sit my drink down on the bar and begin making my way towards her to interrupt, but before I can, Edgar claps his hands again to draw everyone's attention.

Once he has it, he smiles.

"Well, this will conclude day one of your stay. I hope you all had a delightful time," he says, winking at Thirteen and Peter Struthers who are dancing closely in the corner to the soft music. "Now is the time for final bidding for the day. Only the non-virgins will be up for auction right now, so please keep that in mind."

Two guards wheel in the bidding board from the lounge, and as I suspect, the price on Eve has risen to over three thousand dollars. There are bids on a few other women, including Thirteen who has made her rounds flirting with every man in the room, but otherwise, not many people have taken a large enough interest in the other women to spend their money.

"Anything you spend tonight will be donated to our charity, Glory Tree, to help support impoverished individuals." Edgar throws out a wink as he says this.

I highly doubt that there is such a charity. It is simply the cover for their money-laundering operation. The money is going straight in the Cartel's pockets.

One by one, Edgar brings up the women, having them stand in front of the crowd while bids are thrown out.

A few of the women are given to the first bidder for an embarrassingly low price, but as he gets towards the last few women, competition increases. Thirteen ends up being sold to Peter Struthers for the night for two thousand dollars with some heavy pushback from the man in the fox mask, who already purchased another young women earlier in the lineup.

Then, Eve is called up.

Just like when she entered before, she keeps her head high and her face emotionless. She doesn't flirt or look scared. She simply looks strong, and as terrified as I am, I'm proud of her.

I raise my hand to increase the bid before Edgar can even make the call.

"Ooh," he says, whistling low. "This is going to be interesting."

The man in the fox mask increases every bid I make by one hundred dollars with no sign of slowing down.

Eve keeps glancing over at me, looking nervous, but I try to push all distractions from my mind. I have to stay focused. If I don't win, Eve will go to another man.

The thought alone burns me up inside and makes my hands shake.

I raise my hand again to increase the bid, and when Edgar calls out a higher price, the man in the blood-red mask I spoke to earlier in the evening steps forward and nods for his name to be added to the bidding.

I haven't seen him much all evening as he kept a rather low profile, but I can see the way he looks over at Eve. His eager interest seeps out, even from behind the mask.

"It looks like I better save my money for another evening," Fox-Face says with a laugh. "You two gents have it out."

Edgar is excited at the prospect of bringing in so much money, and though he isn't talking quite as quickly as an actual auctioneer, he is getting close.

Ever couple seconds I'm raising my hand, raising the bid higher and higher and trying not to reach over and strangle the thin man bidding for my wife. Finally, when the price hits four thousand, I've had enough.

"Five thousand dollars," I bark, turning to face my competition. "Will you match that?"

Edgar clears his throat. "That is my job," he teases. Then, he turns to the man in the dark red mask. "Will you?"

The man looks at me, drags his eyes down Eve's body, and then bows out with a courteous dip of his head.

Edgar grins as he directs Eve over to me. "That concludes the bidding for the night. If you won an auction, be sure to pay in the lobby before you head to your rooms. If you didn't, do not worry. There are three more nights ahead of us."

The thought makes me feel weary, but the dread is pushed aside when Eve walks over to me, a small, grateful smile pulling on her full lips. I wrap my arm around her shoulders and lead her out of the room.

For tonight, at least, she is mine.

As soon as I close the door to my room, I lock the door and rip my mask off.

"That was close," Eve sighs, sagging back against the wall. "So now what? What are we going to do about—"

I shush her quietly with a finger held to my lips as I study the room. I checked it earlier when I arrived, but I've been out of the room for many hours now, and I want to ensure no one came in and planted any cameras or listening devices.

I check under lampshades, under the bed, and along all of the window ledges and molding. Finally, after several minutes, I'm content that we are actually alone.

I turn to Eve who is still standing in the doorway, and I walk towards her, arms open.

She hesitates for a brief second before lunging forward and crushing her body against my chest.

I wrap my arms around her and breathe in the scent of her. She has been away for many days, and she smells slightly different than normal, but underneath it is the same floral scent of her body, and I inhale it greedily.

I want to soak her in, to stay her with her in my arms for as long as humanly possible.

But she peels her head off my chest and looks up at me with curious eyes.

"What are we going to do about the other women, Luka?" she asks.

I sigh, and she pulls further away from me. "We are going to do something about them, right? We aren't going to leave them."

"I'm not sure what we can do," I repeat. "We can try to take down the Cartel once we are out, but right now, I don't have the resources to do anything. Even winning you just for tonight was harder than I anticipated. And I have to assume the price is only going to go higher."

She bites her lip and shivers.

I pull her against me again. "Don't worry, I'll win you. Every night. You won't go with anyone else."

"I don't believe you," she whispers.

I jerk back from her. "What does that mean? You don't trust me?"

She looks up at me, her caramel-brown eyes glassy and wide. "I trust that you'll save me, but I don't believe you'll take down the Cartel. You are just saying it to make me shut up. You just want me to stop talking about it."

"Eve ..." I reach for her, but she steps back out of my range. The fire in her eyes is raging.

"No," she shakes her head and flips her hair over to one side, her fingers fidgety and nervous. "The least you can do is tell me the truth."

"The least?" I ask, anger creeping into my voice. "As if I haven't done enough already?"

"You should have gone after Milaya!" Eve yells. The force of her words seems to surprise her, and she pinches her lips together. "I could have taken care of myself."

"I only had a lead on where you would be," I argue. "My option was to miss my only opportunity at getting into this auction to save you or search in vain for a clue about Milaya's whereabouts that may not have ever come. Regardless of what you think about my decision, I did the best I could with the time and information I had. I'm so sorry that isn't enough for you."

She stares down at the floor, looking guilty, and then looks up at me.

"No, it's not enough, Luka. There are more women here. They need you. They need us."

Frustration bubbles up inside of me until I can't see straight. My vision goes blurry around the edges, focusing in on Eve's face, and I stalk towards her quickly.

She backs up against the wall, and I pin her there, her wrists in each of my hands.

"I don't want to save everyone," I growl. "I don't care about everyone. I only care about you."

"Luka, that isn't—"

I press my knee between her legs, making her gasp, and shake my head. "No argument. Those are the facts and they aren't up for debate. I only care about getting you out of here unharmed, and I won't hear any talk about anything that could interfere with that plan."

Her eyes narrow. "You may have bought me tonight, but I'm not actually your slave, you know?"

I step away from her all at once, putting a foot of space between our bodies. "Then leave."

She moves forward like she is going to. Her eyes are golden with anger, and she is breathing heavily, her chest heaving, drawing even more attention to the low cut of her dress.

"I'm not your captor," I whisper, reaching out to touch a strand of her hair. "You are free to do whatever you want when you are with me, you know that. So, if you want to leave and go back to your room, go. I won't stop you."

Just as the words are out of my mouth, Eve throws herself forward and crushes her lips against mine.

It takes me less than a second to curl her into my body and push her back against the wall.

Her hands are on my neck and curling in the hair at the base of my head, and I can't get close enough to her. I press my body into hers, grinding my hips hard. She moans and scratches her nails down my back.

There are too many layers between us. As soon as I start to shrug out of my jacket, Eve slides her hands under the collar and pushes it down my arms. Then she undoes the buttons of my shirt as fast as her fingers can manage.

Her hands on my bare skin are ice-cold, and I hiss in surprise, but she drags them lower, lower, curling her finger just above my pants and then dipping her fingers even lower.

Before she can do anything else to send me over the edge, I grab her wrists and pin them against the wall. Eve arches her back and looks up at me. Her eyelids are low, but there is fire in her gaze. Need. Overwhelming desire.

I press a kiss to her chest, moving lower until I'm between her breasts.

The dress is cut low enough that I can see the gentle curve of the underside of her breasts, as well, and I lick the sensual slope before pulling back the material with my teeth.

Her breasts bounce free of the material, and I circle my tongue around her pointed nipple before sucking it into my mouth.

"Luka," she moans, closing her eyes and resting her head back on the wall.

I play with her nipple until she is so hard it must be painful, and then I switch to the other breast and do the same thing.

She is so beautiful. It is no wonder there was a bidding war over her. Anyone in their right mind can see she is the most beautiful woman in the room.

Before I can stop myself, I'm imagining what the night would have looked like if I hadn't won her. If she had gone to another man's room.

The thought fills me with an indescribable darkness. I stand tall, back rigid, and growl against her warm cheek.

"You are mine," I growl. "Only mine."

She nods—desperately, painfully, like every fiber of her wants to let me know that what I'm saying is true.

Eve tugs her hand free of my grip, and I let go, allowing her to dance her way across my abdomen and lower to undo my pants. When she slips her hand inside, I catch my breath.

She wraps her hand around me and strokes me gently, taking her time.

Desire overwhelms me, and I try to grab her and haul her back to the bed, but she avoids my grip and drops to her knees in front of me. I stay perfectly still, breath caught in my chest.

Slowly, she pulls the suit pants down followed by the black boxers, and when I spring free of the soft material, she licks her lips and looks up at me. "And you are mine. Only mine."

I press one palm against the wall as she takes me in her mouth.

From this angle, I can see her working on me and her breasts bouncing free of the dress, and it is too much.

This night is supposed to last much longer than it is going to if she keeps this up, so I close my eyes and tip my head back.

Her cold fingers are wrapped around each of my thighs for grip as she plunges down on me as far as she can and then draws back slowly, utilizing the perfect level of suction. Then, she licks me from base to tip, and I can't stand it.

I grab her under the arms, throw her giggling over my shoulder, and walk over to the bed. When I throw her down on the mattress, she is smiling, and I take a minute to enjoy the sight of it.

I wasn't sure I'd ever see that smile again.

I spread her legs wide and kiss my way under her dress. The black panties she's wearing are delicate, and I rip them away with one tug. Then, I lick her opening.

Eve sighs and her legs open wider, giving me more access. I dive in greedily.

I lick and suck and flick until she is writhing, and I have to pin her hips to the mattress with my arm. When I add a finger, she nearly bucks us both right off the bed. Then I add another, pulsing into her, but it isn't until my lips wrap around the tiny bud at the apex of her thighs that she falls apart.

All at once, her body goes fluid and then rigid, and her breathing becomes erratic. There are long pauses punctuated with a gasp and the writhing of her hips.

Eve fists the comforter and bites down on her own cries as her body releases harder than I've ever seen. When she is done, she goes limp on the bed.

I wait a moment before I kiss my way up her body, and when I reach her arms, I pull her upright and unzip the dress.

She's putty in my hands. Undressing her is like taking care of a doll. I have to lift her hips as I drag the dress down her legs, but as soon as it is off, I forget about the effort it took.

She is gorgeous.

Every line, every curve of her body speaks to me in ways I didn't know a human body ever could.

Before Eve, I didn't think myself capable of love. I knew how to fuck and find my own release, but that was all sex was to me.

But now?

My climax is nothing without hers.

My pleasure is nothing if Eve isn't enjoying it with me.

Getting her off feels just as good as my own orgasm, and seeing her sated and lazy on the bed makes me harder than steel.

I crawl over her, kissing each of her breasts before she cups my face in her hands and drags me up to her mouth. We kiss, slow and passionate, her tongue curling around mine. Then she pushes me away and smiles a wicked smile, eyebrow arched.

"Your turn."

I let her push me back on the bed and straddle me, her knees on either side of my hips.

She is sublime mounted on top of me, and for just a minute, I try to forget where we are. I try to imagine we are home with our daughter in the next room and this is just a normal night and not potentially one of the last times we'll be able to do this.

I can't let that happen.

So I grip her hips and pull her onto me.

Her pouty lips part as I spread her wide, and when I'm in as deep as I can go, she rocks her body to settle onto me and sighs with contentment.

"God, we fit together perfectly," she hums.

I don't get a chance to answer because the next second she lifts her hips up and then works them back down.

She rolls her body over me again and again, moving to a rhythm I can't hear but can feel in the deepest corners of myself.

"Say it again," she whispers hoarsely, planting her hands on my chest.

"What?" I ask, thrusting up in time with her movements.

She looks down at me with lust in her eyes. "Tell me I'm yours."

I wrap my arm around her waist, tip her backward, and switch positions so I'm nestled between her legs. I position myself at her opening, teasing her for a second before I plunge into her with one thrust.

"You are mine," I groan.

Eve weaves her fingers through my hair and rolls her hips up. "Again."

I pull all the way out before thrusting in to the hilt. "You are mine."

Her moans get louder each time our bodies come together, and when she lets go for the second time, she throws her arms out to the side, lays her head back, and arches into the sensation.

"Yes!" she screams, hooking her legs around my waist.

I realize then she still has her stilettos on, the heels of which are digging into my back. Still, I pound into her. Again and again until she stops trembling and brings her hands up to my chest.

"I said it was your turn," she says, trying to pout though she can't keep the smile away.

I lean forward and kiss her lips softly, nipping at her lower lip. Then, I spin her around and edge her legs apart.

Eve quickly lifts her hips, giving me better access, and I push into her from behind.

"*Now* it is my turn."

Her ass is as perfect as the rest of her, and I palm a cheek in each hand as I work my length into her.

It only takes a few thrusts before I'm close.

And when Eve reaches around, her fingers gripping my thigh, drawing me in closer, I fall apart.

Every ounce of frustration and fear and stress I've felt over the past week. Every moment I spent wondering whether I'd ever see her or feel her or touch her again. All of it pours out of me and into her.

When I'm finished, I collapse beside her on the bed. Eve draws close to me, her head on my chest.

We lie there for a long time.

Just listening to each other breathe.

Trying to enjoy the few minutes of peace we have together before another day dawns at the Crooked Tree Inn.

12

EVE

"We can't spend so much time together today," I say, drawing the blankets up around my chest.

The bed in Luka's room is much nicer than the one in mine, and for a moment, I luxuriate in the high thread count before I fully remember where we are. When I remember, I drop the sheet, exposing my naked body.

Luka studies my breasts, his eyes hungry despite the fact we spent most of the night making love, and then he looks away and nods. "I know."

He sits on the end of the bed and runs a hand through his dark hair. The muscles in his back contract and stretch, and I can't stop myself from crawling towards him and wrapping my arms around his toned abdomen.

He reaches back and strokes my damp hair. We took a shower together, spending much longer than required soaping each other up and finding bliss under the endless hot water.

Now, however, sunlight streams through a crack in the curtains and birds are chirping faintly from the trees around the inn, and our little bubble has burst.

We have to go back to the auction.

"I hate this," Luka groans, turning his face and leaning back so our cheeks are touching. "I fucking hate this."

"Me too."

He spins around and pushes me back onto the mattress, his hands poised on either side of my face. "I don't want anyone else to touch you."

"Me neither."

He strokes his thumb across my forehead, down the slope of my nose, and over my lips. "I don't even want anyone else to look at you. I mean, you should see the way they look at you."

"I do," I remind him, smoothing my hands down his chest.

"You are the most beautiful woman here and they all want you. I want to kill them," he says through gritted teeth.

"You will," I sigh, stretching up to press my lips to his.

Luka curls a hand around the back of my head and deepens the kiss, parting my lips and slipping his tongue into my mouth until I'm liquid in his arms. Until I don't remember where we are or what time it is or who I am. Every nerve ending in my body is focused on his mouth on mine.

And then there is a knock at the door.

We both stiffen, and Luka looks to the door like he will be able to see through it. Then, he plants one more kiss on my forehead, tosses the sheet over my naked body, and moves to the door.

Standing on the other side is Kari. Her blonde hair is pulled back in a limp ponytail today, and she flinches back when shirtless Luka opens the door.

"I'm here for Number Seven," she says softly, looking down at the floor.

"She isn't ready yet," Luka growls, probably frightening the woman even more.

Kari looks up and past Luka to find me sprawled on the bed. Her eyebrows pinch together in concern as she studies me, clearly looking to make sure I'm okay. "I am supposed to take you to your room to shower."

"She is showered," Luka says. "She doesn't need to leave."

"Well, I'm supposed to—" Kari looks from Luka to me, trying to decide if she can handle this on her own.

"Can I change here?" I ask, wrapping the sheet around my chest and sitting up. "That would be easier anyway."

Especially since I don't have a dress to wear. I put the one from yesterday on after my shower, but Luka ripped the shoulder strap in his urgency to tear it off me again.

"I brought a dress," Kari says, holding up a red gown draped over her arm while glancing to the pile of red discarded on the floor. "Just in case you needed it."

Luka holds out his hand for the dress, and Kari hands it to him. "I'll wait outside for you."

I nod, but Luka slams the door shut before I can say more.

"She is scared," I tell him when he throws the dress on the bed.

"She called you Number Seven," he grimaces.

I let the sheet fall away again and move towards him on my knees. When I reach him, his large hands grip my waist, warm and firm. I wrap my arms around his neck and arch my body against his. "That is because she doesn't know who you are to me. She doesn't know that you aren't like the other men here."

Luka looks poised to argue, but when I rock my hips against him, his eyes glaze over. He looks down at where our bodies meet and then bends to press a kiss to the top of my breast. "I'm scared, Eve."

I nod. "I know."

"There are few things in this world that scare me, but the thought of not being with you, of someone taking you from me ..." He grips my waist even harder, almost crushing me. He sounds haunted, like a man woken up in the middle of a nightmare.

"That won't happen," I whisper, curling my finger under his chin and lifting his eyes to mine. "You are going to win every auction. In twelve hours, we'll be back here together and nothing else will matter."

Luka pulls me into one last kiss, letting it linger until there are butterflies in my stomach and my hands are too shaky to dress myself.

He helps me slip into the panties Kari brought and then zips the dress for me. It is significantly shorter than the dress from the day before, but rather than being skintight, it flares out around my thighs in a flouncy skirt. The top is still just as low cut, though, exposing more cleavage than I'm usually comfortable with.

Luka's nostrils flare when he looks at me. "I hate that you look so sexy in that. Everything about this place should repulse me, including the clothes they pick out for you to wear. I should despise you in this outfit."

I shake my head and hug him, laying my head against his chest. "I'm still your wife. You can find me sexy in anything I wear. I give you permission."

"Good," he sighs, kissing the top of my head. "Because you are killing me in this dress."

I pull back and look up at him, mustering as much of a smile as I can. "Just know that no matter what happens today, you are the person I'm imagining ripping this dress off me."

He groans softly, the sound a low rumble in his chest. "How much time do you think we have?"

"Not enough for you to ravish me properly." I smile. "That will have to wait until tonight."

He takes a deep breath and nods. "Tonight."

Kari is waiting outside for me, just like she said, and she walks next to me in silence as we make our way through the maze towards the lounge. Finally, she looks over at me.

"Are you okay?"

I almost admit that I'm great—much better than I was yesterday—before I remember I am supposed to be traumatized. She thinks I was taken to bed by a stranger and tormented all night long. She has no idea that I came no less than seven times in eight hours.

"I'm feeling strong," I say, settling on a partial truth. I do feel strong. After being reunited with Luka, I feel more confident about my chances of getting out of here.

Kari furrows her brow and crosses her arms over her chest. "That's good, I guess."

"It is," I agree, hoping to keep Kari from worrying about me. "I'm one day closer to getting out of this inn."

Another partial truth. No matter what happens with the auction, I will be leaving the inn on Wednesday.

I just hope to God that it's at Luka's side, as a free woman.

Suddenly, Kari grabs my arm and pulls me to a stop. Her eyes are wide, and she looks up and down the hallway nervously before she speaks. "It is in your best interest to accept your fate."

"Kari," I sigh. "I'm not delusional. I know—"

"No," she says, cutting me off. "I've seen so many women come through here thinking their life will be one way when they leave. They are rarely ever right. To protect yourself, it would be best for you to accept the fact that you will always be someone's property. Thinking you'll be free again is a pipe dream."

She stares at me for a few seconds, trying to drive home the point, before she starts walking again.

"How long have you been here, Kari?" I ask quietly.

"Four years."

The two words are cold and devoid of emotion, but they send a shiver up my spine.

When we get to the lounge, the bidders haven't arrived yet, but all of the other women are standing in front of the fireplace like they are ready to take a group picture. The taller women are in back with the shorter in front, and Edgar is standing in front of them like a photographer without a camera. When he sees me and Kari walk in, he waves for me to join the group.

"Number Seven, finally." Then he brushes Kari aside. "Go wait in my room."

Without hesitation, Kari lowers her head and walks back down the hallway.

I move to stand at the edge of the group, but Edgar directs me to the center in the back row. "The best seat for our most expensive girl."

He says it like a compliment, but it feels like a slap in the face.

The other women barely move out of my way as I squeeze in, so I end up jostled back and forth between them, and I can't even be angry. If Edgar is going to show me any special attention at all, it means they will hate me. I understand it.

As I'm moving into position, I glance up at the electronic bidding board and see that there is already a bid for me for the day. I am the only woman who has been bid on this early in the day. I hope it is from Luka, but next to the number is a maroon dot. I didn't notice those the day before, but I guess it signifies who made the bid.

My only theory is that the color of the masks coordinates with the dot on the screen. Luka is black, not maroon. There was a man in a maroon mask, and he bid on me last night.

I suspect he is already bidding on me again, and my stomach flips.

When I make it to the middle of the row, I realize Maddie is standing next to me. She gives me a nervous smile as I approach, and I tip my head.

She looks younger today. She is in another purple dress, but her hair is pulled away from her face in a low twist that cascades down her back, and it highlights the softness of her cheeks.

For her sake, I have to be strong. I have to show her how to get through this week.

And then I have to save her.

"Now that you are all here," Edgar says pointedly to me. "I want to talk about what we expect from each of you."

As if they don't already expect enough. Several of these women were taken to bed by strangers last night. Surely, Edgar doesn't have the audacity to expect more of them.

Unfortunately, he does.

"You need to be friendlier to the guests," he says. "I want more smiles and flirting and enticing these men to want you or you will all be punished."

Everyone seemed friendly enough to me the day before considering the circumstances. They should have all been reacting the way Maddie did, screaming and crying in the middle of the dance. The fact that they didn't openly weep is impressive. But now they have to put on even more of a show.

"And this isn't just for my sake, but for yours, too," Edgar explains. "You see, any woman who is not bid on by the end of the week … will be eliminated."

The word hangs in the air for a few seconds before I register what he means.

Killed.

Any woman left at the end of the week will be killed. Simple as that.

"We do not have the resources here to keep you until next year, so your only way out is through one of our guests."

There are only ten guests.

The realization hits me hard, knocking the wind from me.

There are fourteen women and ten guests. It's sickening, gruesome math.

The best-case scenario leaves four innocent women in unmarked graves.

The women around me come to the same realization, and a nervous whisper rushes through our group.

"I'm sure you are all doing the arithmetic," Edgar says with a sick smile. "The odds are stacked against you, which means you need to be even more friendly. Perhaps, a few of our wealthier guests will buy more than one. It has happened before—though, I must say, not so often."

I look at Maddie out of the corner of my eye. She is staring down at her feet, her breaths coming in shuddery bursts. I want to reach over and lay a hand on her back, but I don't. Not while Edgar is watching us. I want to try and do what Luka asked: not draw any more attention to myself.

Just after Edgar delivers the devastating news, he claps his hands in the way he likes to do before announcing the next activity, and then turns to begin welcoming the bidders as they make their way into the lounge.

Many of them are holding cups of coffee and pastries, clearly having just eaten breakfast, and my stomach rumbles. Apparently, there will be no breakfast for those of us on the auction block.

"Take a seat, take a seat," Edgar says, encouraging everyone to find a spot in the semicircle of furniture that has been rearranged around the fireplace. "We have a nice little show planned for you this morning."

My heart rate ratchets up, slamming against my rib cage. I look for Luka in the crowd and spy him standing off to the right. It calms me for a moment but then I tear my eyes away. I don't want anyone to see our connection.

Edgar moves in front of us, facing the bidders. "Yesterday was all about getting comfortable and mingling, but today, we want to show you that our women are top of the line. So, we have a fun little game planned to show you how obedient these slaves can be."

I'm very confident this game will not be fun for any of the women, and there seems to be a consensus about that. Soft sobs come from the group, and Edgar clenches his hand into a fist behind his back in warning. The subtle hint works and the cries cut off at once.

Edgar then claps his hands in front of him once. "Let the game begin."

The game is simple and sick.

One by one, the women move into the center of the semicircle and for five minutes, they must do whatever the crowd asks of them. The one saving grace is that anything overtly sexual is off-limits, but it only serves to bring out the bidder's creativity.

The man in the fox mask is enjoying this display most of all.

He tells Number Six, a tan woman with wide-set hips and a big chest, to do jumping jacks in front of him, making her continue until she is out of breath and red in the face.

After that, the man in the bird mask asks her to moan the alphabet, which is impressively—if not horrifically—inventive.

When it is Maddie's turn, she freezes up next to me.

"Number Eleven," Edgar repeats, waving her down to the center of the floor. "Come on down."

Then, he turns to the crowd. "This isn't a good start, is it?"

"She needs to be taught a lesson," Fox-Face calls, licking his lips eagerly.

This time, I press a hand to her back and push her forward. She walks slowly to the center of the room, her hands shaking.

The men are harshest on her. Probably because of her meltdown the night before.

Rather than anything sexual, they demean Maddie in whatever way they can.

She licks the bottom of shoes, slaps herself in the face, and tries endlessly to complete a cartwheel, each time landing in a crumpled pile on the floor that looks more and more painful with each attempt, her dress hiked above to expose her lace panties to the beasts gathered closely around her.

When the five minutes are up, Edgar openly grimaces as she passes him. Maddie is near tears.

I reach out to comfort her when she returns, but she pulls away from my touch and wraps her arms around herself. Bruises are already forming on her legs.

After that, it is only ten minutes before Edgar claps his hands and grins at the crowd. "We've saved the best for last." He turns to me and winks.

"Number Seven, come on down."

13

LUKA

Watching Eve walk into the center of the room is like watching her move in front of a firing squad.

Every man in the room sits a little taller, eager for her performance.

The game is sick. The things they've been having these women do are childish and demeaning—of no real use to anyone making a purchase. It is just a way to give these sick men a sense of power over women since, apparently, they can't get it in their normal lives.

But, silly tasks or not, I can't stand by and watch Eve be humiliated.

Eve and I talked this morning about staying away from one another and trying to look less interested, but that was before I knew she'd be at the mercy of these animals.

She doesn't look at me as she moves to the center of the room, and I am certain everyone in the room can feel the tension emanating off me. I'm practically vibrating with it.

I have to stop this. I have to end it now.

"Your five minutes ..." Edgar says, looking down at his watch, "begin now."

Fox-Face opens his mouth immediately, but before he can get a word out, I find myself speaking. "Pretend you're doing a strip tease without taking off your clothes. For one full minute."

Fox-Face snaps around to glare at me, his mouth turned down in a frown.

Eve doesn't look at me, but she begins to sway her hips to an imaginary beat, drawing every eye in the room in the process as her arms lift and she moves gracefully. I want to kill every man looking at her, but it's better than some of the tasks other men gave previous women, and it seems authentic.

Edgar watches the time and the men grow restless as the seconds tick past. I, however, am scrolling through my brain for another task. Anything to keep her from exposing herself to these bastards.

I'm counting along with the seconds and studying Edgar, and as soon as he lifts his head to announce the minute is up, I call out another order.

"Sing something sultry. Provide the music for your earlier strip tease. Make it as good as the dance."

There are audible groans now, and Edgar narrows his eyes at me before nodding for Eve to go ahead and complete the order.

She is not the most incredible singer, but she picks a sexy song and draws out every line slowly and sensuously, once again managing to captivate the entire room. Thankfully, she makes the song last just over two minutes, meaning there are only two minutes left in her allotted time.

As she hits the final note, I try to call out once more, but the man in the maroon mask beats me to it.

"Pose on hands and knees like the dog you are," he says, pointing to the floor directly in front of him.

For the first time, Eve looks at me and a wave of guilt washes through me.

I let her down. I wasn't fast enough.

Then, my guilt turns to rage.

The man in the maroon mask is smiling, watching intently as Eve moves to stand in front of him. Then, slowly, she gets down on all fours.

"Turn around," he says, directing her to move clockwise until her ass is facing him.

The dress is short, just a flouncy little thing that barely covers the top of her thighs. On her hands and knees, it reveals almost her entire ass.

Maroon Mask slides down in his seat, the bulge in his pants obvious, and I want to kill him.

Before I even know what I'm doing, I cross the room to stand between him and Eve.

He jumps back in surprise and then glares up at me. "What is your problem?"

I grab a fistful of his outrageously embroidered suit jacket—today's is gray with red and orange flames down the arms and legs—and pull him to his feet.

"You are my problem," I growl.

His eyes go wide with fear, but he tries to play it off with a cool smile. "She doesn't belong to you yet, friend. I think last night may have confused you."

I want to rip his throat out. I want to beat his face into a pulp until my hand is too bloodied to continue. I want to kneel him down on the floor and kick him face-first into a roaring fireplace.

"Gentleman," Edgar says, needling his way between us. "Tempers are high. Perhaps we could all use a little yoga. She is in downward dog pose, after all."

A few men laugh, and I turn towards them, glaring until they stop, clearing their throats nervously.

I take a step back and see that Eve is looking up at me, her eyes pleading.

I'm drawing too much attention. Way too much attention. I'm fucking everything up.

"You're right," I say as evenly as I can while my heart is still on fire. "I just need a little air."

I turn to leave, but stop when I hear Edgar tell Eve to continue doing as she was told. For a second, I contemplate turning around and doing everything I wanted to do to both Maroon Mask and Edgar, but I take a deep breath and walk out the front door.

I lean against the brick front of the inn and blow smoke against the backdrop of the morning sky.

The sun is up now, the warmth burning through the layer of mist that hangs over the top of the trees. I try not to count the seconds as they pass. I try not to think about what Eve is doing inside. About what they are making her do.

I've never felt this helpless before. So out of control.

Maybe coming here was a bad idea. Maybe I should have rallied the Bratva and attacked the inn with everything we had.

Though, as the thought crosses my mind, two guards march around the corner of the inn, guns at their sides. I look to my left and see two more guards disappearing around the corner to walk the side perimeter.

There are no gaps in their vision. No noticeable flaws in their security.

Inside and out, there are guards or members of the Cartel watching at all times. There is no way in or out. No way out except through following their rules.

The door opens, and I hope it is Eve coming to see me, even though we discussed keeping our distance.

It isn't.

It is the red-headed girl who cried yesterday. The one who inspired Eve to try and save every single one of the slaves. Maddie, I think her name was.

"Thought maybe I'd join you," she says, holding up two cigars with *Crooked Tree Inn* stamped on the side.

I flick the ash from my cigarette. "I brought my own."

She tucks the spare cigar between her breasts slowly and then puts the other in her mouth, puckering her lips around the end. "Care to give me a light, then?"

The end isn't cut. This girl has no idea what she is doing with the cigar or with men.

"You aren't supposed to be outside."

"I'm supposed to make sure the guests are having a good time," she purrs. "So, that's what I'm here to do."

I tuck my lighter in my pocket, and her shoulders slump, the cigar slipping to the corner of her mouth.

"You weren't so eager to please yesterday," I remind her.

She hastily pulls the cigar out of her mouth, twiddling it between her fingers. "I was seriously reprimanded for my breakdown yesterday, and now I see that I was wrong. Now, I know my place."

If Eve could hear her now, she would be even more persistent about saving these women. This girl has been brainwashed and it only took them one day.

"I also see," she says, batting her eyelashes and moving closer to me, her hips swaying with every slow step. "That I was wasting my time on the wrong sort of men."

"I see nothing has changed, then." I glare down at her, but it does little to curb the enthusiasm in her eyes. She reaches out and strokes one finger down my arm. I shift away from her touch. "I'm not the kind of man you want taking you home."

"You don't know what I want," she says quietly, her blue eyes blinking up at me. She looks down at herself, pushing her chest out further. "I know I'm in this purple dress and there are women in red who are more experienced, but none of them are as eager as I am."

I look away and curl my lip. If the girl wasn't so pathetic, I'd push her aside for her shameless begging.

She tosses her red hair back over her shoulder. "None of them want to please you as much as I do."

I hold up a hand to stop her from taking another step towards me. "I'm only going to say it once more: go find someone else."

The girl steps forward until her chest is pressed against my hand. I yank my hand back quickly, narrowing my eyes at her, but there is no sign of fear or shame, just yearning. "There is no one else. Not after the way you treated Number Seven inside."

It takes me a moment to realize she is talking about Eve. I shake my head. "What do you mean?"

"The way you went easy on her during the obedience event," she says.

"All of the other men were cruel, but you were gentle. I want a gentle man."

My behavior was rather obvious, I suppose. I should have stayed quiet and let Eve do whatever she had to do to maintain our ruse. Instead, I allowed my jealousy and protective nature to take over. And now I have a girl chasing me around like a lost puppy.

"I'm not gentle," I snap. "I just don't like for my slaves to perform for others. Believe me, when we are alone, Number Seven does whatever I tell her to."

Without missing a beat, the girl steps forward and rolls her body against my side. "I'll do whatever you tell me to. Right now. You don't even have to pay."

I sigh. "Go away. That's what I want you to do."

She hesitates for a moment, and I wonder whether she isn't going to go back on her word and continue pestering me to buy her. Instead, she quickly throws her arms around me before I can stop her, and then spins away and walks back into the inn.

The rest of the day is less organized than the morning's event. It is more like the day before, the bidders and women mingling together.

Rather than join the crowd, I stand along the edge of the room with the two female bidders. Overall, they seem to act as though the entire week in the inn is an inconvenience. During the obedience training this morning, they stayed quiet, rolling their eyes when the women were performing. I have the sense they would be happy to have the entire week over with so they can simply make their bids.

The men, however, seem to be growing more eager with every hour that passes.

The first day, everyone—aside from Fox-Face, perhaps—was on their best behavior.

Today, though, the men are letting their cruder instincts into the light.

There are rules against the women doing anything explicitly sexual before being purchased, but several of the men are pushing the boundaries as far as they can. Women are straddling bidders as they sit around tables drinking and playing cards. It is obvious most of the women are not having a good time, but a few of them are putting on a real show—Maddie included.

I try to keep my distance from her, but she continually pops up whenever I turn around.

She keeps bringing me drinks, sitting close to me when we gather for meals, and hiding behind me when other men start to approach her.

I want to push the girl away and demand she keep her distance, but when Eve sees me sticking close to her, she makes a point to get close to me and whisper a quick thanks.

"She needs someone to look out for her."

Otherwise, Eve keeps her distance the way we discussed this morning.

She talks with other men, doing what she needs to do to keep them happy. I know it is our plan, but it doesn't make it any easier to watch her curled against another man's side while his arm is wrapped around her lower back. Knowing she is my wife and loves me doesn't make it any easier to watch when the man in the maroon mask corners Eve in the lounge and practically pins her against a wall to talk to her.

When I see his leg shift between Eve's, his knee brushing against hers, my vision goes red.

Every single one of my instincts demands that I stand up and defend the honor of my wife.

Just as I start to charge towards them, however, Eve catches my eye over the man's shoulder and lightly shakes her head.

It does nothing to douse the fire raging in my chest, but it does keep me across the room from them.

When I don't think I can take another second, however, I storm out of the room and into the hallway for some fresh air. When the door behind me opens, I assume it is Maddie coming to beg me again, and I throw a dismissive hand over my shoulder.

"I'm not in the mood for company."

"That's understandable," a male voice says. "These events can be taxing."

I turn and see Edgar standing in the doorway, his hands folded behind his back. "I only wanted to make sure you didn't need anything. But if you are fine, then I will just—"

"Actually," I say, stopping him. "I do have a question."

Edgar turns to me, a blank smile on his face.

"Is there a way that any of the guests can leave the inn for a short period of time and then return?" I ask. "No more than a couple of hours."

All morning, while I watched Eve move around the inn and talk to other men, I distracted myself by planning.

If I can leave the inn even for an hour, I can find a phone, call Grigory or someone in the Bratva, and give them more information on where to look for Milaya. That way, I can tell Eve that the men are doing something while we are trapped in here, and it will assuage a small amount of the guilt eating at me.

But before the idea even has legs, Edgar swats it away.

"I'm sorry, sir, but no one is allowed to leave the inn. Not even me," he admits. "It is a safety issue. I'm sure you understand."

Disappointment settles in my stomach like a stone, and I shrug. "I suppose I don't have any other choice."

Edgar's face is sympathetic, but I've seen enough of the man to know that it is an act. Everything the man does is a performance.

"It is simply an unnecessary risk. If someone leaves, they could go to the authorities with their firsthand account of our operation, and we would all be arrested. There is also the risk that a guest could use their knowledge of our proceedings and the inn's layout to alert their cohorts on the best way to infiltrate our operation. And beyond threats of arrest or violence, there is the chance that a desperate bidder would leave the estate to procure more money to bid on his woman of choice, which while great for our business, is bad for the integrity of the event."

"There are a lot of threats to your life and business," I say.

"Unfortunately, yes," Edgar says. "It is a burden I have learned to live with."

Sensing I have no further questions, Edgar tips his head slightly before turning to go back into the lounge.

But then he stops and looks back over his shoulder. "I don't need to worry about you, do I, sir?"

"Me?" I ask, rolling my eyes and smiling. "Of course not."

I can't tell if Edgar is more or less confident because of my answer, but he goes back into the lounge and leaves me alone in the hallway.

I stay there for ten minutes before rejoining the party.

We eat dinner all together, Eve sitting between Fox-Face and one of the female bidders and across from the man in the maroon mask.

While I have kept my distance all day, the man in the maroon mask has made his intentions quite obvious. He wants Eve, almost exclusively. And I realize how much he wants at the bidding that night.

The price soars to over eight thousand before the man bows out and lets me leave with my wife. As we pass, however, he bows at the waist.

"I hope you two have a pleasant evening," he says, his exposed mouth pulled back in a wicked smile. "With the way you are spending your money, it may very well be your last."

With that thought burning a hole in my head, I lead Eve up the stairs to my room.

14

EVE

Luka doesn't talk to me as we walk to his room, and even once we are inside, he walks straight into the bathroom, pulls his mask off, and rinses his face in the sink.

The day was long without being able to talk to him.

I could feel the tension rolling from him all day, dark and ominous like an impending storm cloud. I expected him to release his rage in a torrential downpour at any moment, but he managed to keep it together.

Still, it seems to have worn on him.

When he comes out of the bathroom, I am sitting on the edge of the bed, my hands folded in my lap. I want to reach out and touch him. I want things to feel the way they did this morning when we could barely function without our bodies being pressed together. But things feel different now, and I don't want to push Luka if he isn't ready.

He stands a few feet away, looking at me with his head tilted to the side.

"Today was shitty."

I laugh out of surprise. "It really was."

"Not being near you felt like torture," he says. "Plus, your little friend wouldn't leave me alone."

"That was the only thing that made me feel better. Seeing you taking care of her left me with one less thing to worry about," I say. "Thank you."

Luka pinches his lips together and looks down at the floor. "She wants me to buy her."

"What?" I ask, trying to imagine Maddie wanting anyone at all to buy her. The day before, she nearly had a breakdown at the idea. "Did she say that?"

He nods. "Several times. Quite explicitly."

I shrug. "Well, I mean, who can blame her? You are obviously the best man in the room. She'd be foolish not to try for you."

"I don't want to get her hopes up."

I know what he means. We won't be saving her. Luka won't pay for her, not if it means he won't have enough money to buy me. And since Maddie is earlier on the roster than I am, Luka won't risk bidding on her at all.

I want to talk more about saving the rest of the women so it won't matter how much money Luka has, but I know there is no point. We won't reach an agreement. Not right now. Before we can have that discussion, I need to ease the tension building between his shoulders. We both need to be reassured in who we are together before I can press him to give anything more of himself.

"It is just stress," I say, standing up and moving towards him. I gently lay a hand on his shoulder, loving the hard feel of his body beneath my fingers after a day without it. "She is doing whatever she can to make this situation bearable for herself, and part of that is trying to ensure she is sold to a man who, at the very least, isn't a monster."

Luka wraps an arm around my waist and draws me close to his body. He looks down at me, his lips parted in a breath. "The rest of these men are monsters."

"No argument here," I say softly, unable to catch my breath. Even after being together so long, touching Luka and being pressed up against him never fails to make me feel weak in the knees.

He curves both arms around my back, arching my body into his. "Especially the man in the maroon mask."

My cheeks flush, and I look away. "He is persistent."

"He is a pain in the fucking ass," Luka growls. "When he told you to act like a dog, I thought I was going to have to kill him."

I smooth my hands from his shoulders down to his chest, loving the thump of his heart beneath my palm. "There is no need. Believe me when I say, there is only one man I want to get on my knees for."

A playful spark lights in Luka's eyes, and I could almost cry when I see it because it is so normal. It is an expression I have seen on his face hundreds of times before, but not once since we've been trapped in this place. I had begun to worry I was never going to see it again.

"Is that right?" he asks, one eyebrow raised.

I swipe my tongue across my lower lip and nod my head slowly. "That's right."

Luka's eyes are glued to me as I drag my hands lower across his chest and grab a handful of his shirt. I pull it free from the waistband of his suit pants and unbutton them with a flick of my finger.

I press my fingers against the hard muscle of his abdomen and lower until I feel the cut of his 'V' leading me down. Luka doesn't hesitate to help when I begin pushing his suit pants down around his knees, and when I pull his underwear down, he springs free, already at the ready.

"I was obedient this morning because I had to be," I whisper, drawing circles in the thin trail of hair across his lower abs. "But now, I'm going to be obedient because I want to be."

Luka licks his lips as I slide to my knees in front of him, my hands resting on each of his hips.

"So, what do you want me to do?" I ask, working my lips together before pouting them out.

"Take me in your mouth." His voice is husky, close to losing control before we've even started.

I nod and then do as I am told.

He moans as soon as my mouth wraps around him, and when I press onto him as far as I can go, he tips his head back and curses at the ceiling.

I wrap a hand around his base to work him from both ends, and Luka curls his large hand around the back of my head, giving shallow thrusts into my open mouth. I accept him readily, sucking and swirling my tongue around him until his legs begin to shake under my fingers.

"Goddamn it, Eve," Luka growls, grabbing a handful of my hair and tipping my head back slightly.

I can tell he is close already, and if he wants to finish this way, I'll gladly help him. I wasn't lying when I said I wanted to obey him. Tonight, I want to give Luka whatever he wants. And if he wants my mouth, he can have it.

Luka moans when I swirl my tongue around his tip, but before I can take him fully in my mouth again, he pulls away.

I wipe my mouth with the back of my hand and look up at him.

His green eyes are lost to the dark of his pupils. He is half wild already, barely able to instruct me to lie down on the bed.

I lie back on the center of the bed, but Luka grabs my ankles and pulls me towards him until my ass is almost hanging off the side. He reaches under my dress and yanks my panties down in one fluid motion.

"Legs up," he says, motioning for me to put my legs over his shoulders. I do, and the moment they are in position, he finds my opening and presses inside.

I'm ready for him, and he sighs with relief as he slips inside of me. "You are so wet."

"I told you I wanted to obey you," I moan as my body adjusts to his size. "It makes me hot."

Luka's body slaps against mine, and he pauses to look down at me.

We are both still mostly clothed, which somehow only adds to the moment. The idea that he wants me so badly he can't be bothered to strip his shirt off or unzip my dress is sexy as hell.

He grips my waist with strong hands and drags me onto him again and again, his hips thrusting into me, slapping together until it is the only sound in the room. That and the sound of our ragged breathing.

When Luka slips his hand between my legs to swirl a thumb over my center, I come fast and hard, unable to hold myself back any longer.

Luka comes soon after.

He collapses next to me, breathing heavily, but only a few minutes later, he unzips my dress, rolls me over, and takes me from behind.

In the morning, my body is sore in the best way possible.

We slept more than the night before. Both of us were exhausted from days of little sleep and stress. But whenever Luka woke up in the night, he would reach for me and pull me close to him, making sure I was there. And several times, that led to us finding comfort in one another's bodies, clinging to each other until we found release from the fear that has become a near-constant in our lives over the last week.

After I shower, Luka has me again, this time pressed against the bathroom wall. The steam from the shower is still heavy in the air, settling on my skin like a fine mist. Our bodies slip and slide together. Luka holds onto me with a crushing grip that I'm sure will leave bruises on my waist, but I don't care.

I wrap my legs around his waist, tip my head back against the wall, and stifle a cry as pleasure rips through me like a bolt of lightning. Luka comes and buries his head in my neck, pressing kisses to the sensitive spot beneath my ear.

When the knock comes at the door, he hugs me tighter and shakes his head. "I'm not going to let you go."

"We have to," I say, listening as the knocks grow more insistent the second time. "Just three more days."

Luka growls, "Three days is a lifetime."

I grab his face and kiss him long and hard, our lips soft yet urgent on one another. His tongue sweeps into my mouth, threatening to steal my sense, but when a third set of knocks raps against the door, I peel myself away from him, wrap a towel around my body, and go to the door.

It is Kari, looking just as nervous as the day before and once again holding a red dress for me to wear.

This one is closer to the one I wore the first day—tight and mid-thigh length—except it is strapless and the top cuts across the middle of my chest, exposing an incredible amount of cleavage.

"I look like I'm wearing a corset," I complain, trying to stuff myself back in the dress. Kari is waiting outside, so I don't have time to try and tape down my chest or do anything to keep myself from busting out of the seams.

"You look incredible," Luka says from behind me. His hand is on my waist, but his voice is sad. Because he knows I look this way for the other men to appreciate. I am dressed this way for their eyes to devour me.

I spin around and arch my body into him, wrapping my arms around his neck. "I love you."

He kisses me, making my stomach flip and my knees go weak, and when I leave with Kari, I turn and look at him one more time. He smiles, but the emotion doesn't reach his eyes. I can't blame him.

Kari studies me for any signs of a breakdown as we head to the lounge, but I'm too focused on finding the energy to make it through another day to care.

Just like the day before, the women are lined up in front of the fireplace with Edgar in front of them, hands folded behind his back. When he sees me approach, he beckons me with a wave and then waits until I'm in position to clear his throat.

"Today is about showing the men that you can handle more than just pleasure," he says. "For the first hour of the day, you are all going to complete a different chore. However, let's not forget the lesson from yesterday. If anyone asks you to stop or take on a different chore, then you must listen. Be obedient."

My sense of self-respect almost demands I refuse to take the duster Edgar thrusts into my hand, but just at that moment, the bidders began to arrive, and I see Luka walk into the room.

His black mask covers the most beautiful parts of him, but it lends him an alluring air of mystery. His suit today is coal gray and crisp, and his black shoes are perfectly shined.

Edgar claps his hands, announces to the bidders what the first event today will look like, and then waves for all of us women to begin our work.

Several of the girls in purple dresses are tasked with cleaning out the fireplace, others are sent to the kitchen to take care of the breakfast dishes, and the rest of us set about dusting and mopping and cleaning windows all around the first floor of the inn. The bidders split up to watch whichever woman they are most interested in, which leaves Luka, Fox-Face, and the man in the maroon mask lingering close to where Maddie and I are working.

Maddie's purple dress is a loose shift today with thin straps that crisscross around her neck and across her chest. It barely brushes the tops of her thighs, so every time she leans forward to put some weight behind the mop, she flashed a peek of her backside, which the men can't seem to ignore.

Fox-Face and Maroon Mask take up position directly behind her, though far enough away that we can't hear their commentary. *Thank goodness.* And Maddie doesn't seem to notice she is being watched at all. Her eyes are focused on the floor and nothing else.

"How are you doing?" I ask her quietly as she mops closer to where I am dusting picture frames and knickknacks on a long buffet table.

"Fine." The word is clipped and harsh.

I narrow my eyes and move closer to her. "I know this has been hard on you. Understandably so. I just want to let you know that you can talk to me if you need—"

"I don't need anything from you," Maddie says, glaring at me. Her thin top lip is pulled back and her blue eyes are vibrant and shining with emotion.

The first night, Maddie seemed to cling to me. She was frightened, and I did my best to comfort her.

Now, however, she is being openly hostile and treating me like her enemy.

"You and I are on the same team," I remind her. "Don't let the Cartel manipulate you so easily."

She huffs out a laugh. "You think I'm the one being manipulated? Please. You're the one who looks relieved to spread your legs at the end of every day."

Her words hit me like a physical slap, and I rear back from the blow. "Excuse me?"

Maddie smiles, happy to see her words found their mark, and then shrugs. "I'd almost think you like being Luka's slave."

I don't know what to say or how to defend myself. I can't tell Maddie that Luka is my husband. It is too risky, especially since she is clearly upset with me. There is no telling who she would tell the information in order to help herself.

In the end, it doesn't matter because Fox-Face draws closer to us and begins openly enjoying the sight of Maddie mopping the floors. I slowly slip away, dusting down the length of the buffet and then moving towards the hallway so I can have a second away from everyone's eyes.

Before I step into the hallway, I turn and see Luka at the far end of the room. He is standing next to one of the female bidders, arms crossed over his chest, eyes on a blonde woman who is on her hands and knees in front of the fireplace.

My heart squeezes with jealousy.

I know it isn't fair. Luka doesn't want to be here anymore than I do. However, even the thought that he would look at another woman the way I only want him to look at me leaves a sour taste in my mouth.

Suddenly, I'm even more eager to get away from the others.

Edgar finds me soon after I step outside and instructs me to clean a nearby bathroom if I have nothing better to do with my time.

The bathroom is small—just a few paces wide in each direction—and noticeably spotless, but that is fine with me. I set to work pretending to clean the already clean room, glad for a few minutes alone. I'm so deep in thought that I don't hear anyone walk into the room. I only look up when the door closes.

It is the man in the maroon mask.

He is smiling, his teeth glimmering in the single light above the vanity. He looks like a wolf before pouncing on his prey. I stand tall and press myself flat against the wall.

"Would you believe me if I said I was surprised to find you in here?" he asks, tilting his head to the side.

I want to speak. To say something light and breezy—anything to let him know he isn't scaring me.

Except, he is.

My throat is suddenly so dry, and I can't formulate any words. All I can focus on is the thrum of my heart in my chest and my desperate desire to slow it down.

He licks his bottom lip and then turns towards the toilet. I'm certain he isn't doing what I think he is doing until he lifts the lid and unzips his pants.

I grimace and face the wall while the sound of his urine hitting the water fills the small room.

"Feel free to look," he says over his shoulder. "Take a little peek at what lies in your future."

A shiver rolls down my spine.

When he finishes, I finally manage a haggard breath, hoping I've just endured the worst of this encounter.

He moves to the sink to wash his hands, and for the first time, I notice his limp. It is slight enough that he can usually play it off, but in the enclosed space, he doesn't have as much room to move and maneuver.

"One of these nights, the man in the dark mask is going to run out of money, and I'm going to win you," he says. He dries his hands and crosses his arms over his chest, staring down at me. "I don't want you to think I don't have money. I do—plenty of it. I am just not willing to throw so much away on a woman who might not be worth it."

My instinct is to be insulted, but then I remember that I want this man to think I'm not worth it. He has been Luka's stiffest competition every night so far, and he apparently has plans to continue that trend.

"Though," he says, bobbing his head back and forth. "The fact that he is willing to spend so much on you two nights in a row means the first night must have been good for him."

He takes a step towards me, and I want to evaporate. I want to disappear into the wall and escape this moment. But there is nowhere to go.

The only way out of the room is past him, and he doesn't seem willing to let me through right now.

"What say you?" he asks. "Did you show him a good time?"

I blink, staring at him like an animal caught in the headlights, feeling more helpless than I've ever felt in my life.

He takes another step towards me and reaches out, laying a hand on my shoulder.

His touch repulses me. His hand is warm, but it might as well be a snake tongue caressing my skin for how much I enjoy it. I pull away from him.

"It is none of your business what happens between me and—" *my husband.* That is what I want to say. Instead, I swallow the words. "Between me and another guest."

"It's okay. You can tell me if you enjoyed it," he says softly. "I'm not a jealous man. Just ask my friends. I always share."

My stomach turns.

Luka has to get me out of here. I've known that since the moment he arrived, but this man is driving the idea home for me. I can't go with someone else. There is no telling how long I'd survive being passed between this cretin and his friends.

Then, he brings his hand up to my neck, rubbing his thumb down to my collarbone. "Or maybe you don't want to admit that it was bad. That's okay. I'm sure it was no fault of your own. I mean, how could a woman like you ever disappoint? If he didn't treat you right, I promise I will. I'll make sure you have a good time."

This man has no idea exactly how good it is with Luka. He has no idea how good it can be with someone because, clearly, he has never known what it is to be in love.

If he did, he wouldn't be here at this auction to buy himself a good time.

"Perhaps," he says, moving in even closer until there is just a breath between us. "You can give me a little taste of what I'm missing. A little encouragement for the auction tonight."

I close my fist, ready to knock him in the nose, but I can't. As much as I want to, it will only cause more trouble for me later.

He closes his eyes and leans down, expecting me to listen to him. To do whatever he asks because he would rather have a sex doll than a real human woman.

Instead, I do the only thing I can think to do and grab the cleaning bottle from the countertop and spray the stream directly at his crotch.

I only realize when he yelps because he never put himself away after using the restroom.

Apparently, he wanted much more than a little bit of encouragement. He wanted a free sample. And instead, he just received a chemical mist to his most sensitive member.

The man jumps back and begins fanning his crotch, unsure what to do, and I take the opportunity to dart past him and back into the hallway.

I can still hear him mumbling and bumping into things in the bathroom, and I book it down the hallway, walking as fast as I can without breaking into a full-out run. When I reach the end of the hallway, I turn towards what I hope is the lounge area, but I stop short at the sight of two people standing close together at the end of the hallway.

I see Maddie's wild flames of red hair first. She left it loose around her shoulders today rather than pulled back. It looks nice.

Then, she moves slightly, and I recognize Luka standing next to her.

He has his mask on, but I can see the firm set to his mouth. He is frustrated and doing his best to hold it in.

My heart trips at the idea of him sneaking around in hallways with Maddie, but as soon as the idea pops into my mind, I push it away.

He wasn't sneaking. He told me Maddie talked to him the day before. He told me what she wanted and how he felt about it. Luka has been open with me, so there is no reason for me to doubt him.

With that in my mind, I walk down the hallway towards them, waving when Luka looks over Maddie's shoulder and sees me.

Relief washes across his features, and I chastise myself for ever doubting him.

When Maddie sees his attention is elsewhere, she turns around and narrows her eyes at me.

"I thought you were supposed to be dusting," she bites.

"Finished." I smile, hoping to soften her anger, but it seems to only sharpen it.

When I stop next to their group, Luka takes a silent step towards me, and Maddie notices.

"I was just having a conversation with our guest here," she hints, nodding her head towards the lounge. "Maybe we can catch up with you inside."

"I think we were about done," Luka says. His tone is harsh, but the words are gentle. He is trying to be kind to her. For me.

"No," Maddie argues, eyes widening in desperation. "I had more I wanted to say about—"

"There is plenty of time to talk the rest of the day," Luka says, moving back towards the lounge. "We'll finish up then."

Maddie moves to follow him inside, but I reach out and grab her arm, gently pulling her back towards me.

She wrenches her arm out of my grip. "Don't touch me."

"What is the matter?" I ask quietly. "You've changed so much in the last couple days, and I'm trying to understand what has happened."

"Nothing," she growls, rolling her eyes.

I reach for her hand, but she rips it away from me, and a thought I can't shove away appears.

"Has someone hurt you?" I ask, stepping closer to her. "You are a virgin, so the rules should preclude you from being purchased throughout the week, but if someone hurt you, you can tell me. Lord knows rules don't actually apply to the bidders."

My mind flashes back to the man in the maroon mask cornering me in the bathroom. Did he or someone else do something similar to Maddie?

"I'm not telling you anything," she says.

"Maddie, we are in the same position here."

She barks out a laugh and pushes a finger into my chest. "By the looks of it, I'm going to be sold to one of the gross men that commands women to smack their own asses or moan the alphabet. I am going to be sold to a man who will look at me as nothing more than a place to put his dick. But you? You somehow spread your legs wide enough to hypnotize the nicest man here into caring for you. So, no, we are not in the same position."

I want to argue with her, but I can't. Not really.

While we are both on the auction block, I have someone here who loves me and is fighting for me.

Maddie is alone.

"You want Luka to bid on you," I say softly.

Maddie looks up at me, eyes wide. "His name is Luka?"

I curse internally for giving anything away, but it is too late now. I nod. "It is."

She smiles softly, the anger in her face dissipating slightly, and another wave of jealousy washes over me. She wants my husband. She doesn't know he is my husband, but she wants him. And by the looks of it, she thinks he is more than just the best option available. The moony look in her eye tells me she has a crush on him.

I'm trying to find the words to explain to her that I'm doing everything I can to help her without giving our plan away, but before I can, there is a gunshot.

Followed by screams.

Maddie looks at me, eyes wide. "What was that?"

I grab her hand and pull her down the hall towards the gunshot. This time, she doesn't pull away from me.

We run down the hallway, past the bathroom where the man in the maroon mask tried to assault me, and into the entryway. Guests and slaves are moving cautiously out of the lounge and ballroom, looking around to find out what is going on. But Maddie and I have a front-row view.

The front door is wide open, the lawn and parking lot of the inn visible, and just outside the door is a guard with his gun raised.

I follow the line of the barrel to a purple shape on the grass.

One of the virgins.

I can't see her face, but I see that she is moving.

She is dragging herself across the grass, but it is useless. The guards are approaching her from every direction now, highlighting the futility of even thinking about escaping. Luka and I would be no match against that many armed guards.

"What happened?" Maddie whispers.

"She ran!" Edgar bellows, his face stern. "She ran through the open door and our guards did their jobs. Did I not warn you?"

I watch in horror as the guards get closer to the woman, each of them with their gun raised as though her pitiful crawling figure is a danger to them.

Then, one of the guards extends his gun arm, presses his barrel against the back of her head, and pulls the trigger.

The shot echoes through the lawn outside and into the inn, reverberating through the walls until I feel like they will come crashing down on us.

Maddie slouches against my side, momentarily forgetting our feud, and I wrap an arm around her waist to keep her standing.

She already angered the Cartel once, so I don't want her to make another scene. Especially since we've just seen what happens when you piss them off.

They kill you in cold blood.

15

LUKA

The bidding board is still in the lounge Sunday evening, but there is one notable difference: Number Five has been crossed out with a thin black line.

The change is slight, but it hangs like a dark cloud over the entire room. At least for me. Many of the other bidders don't seem as bothered. Fox-Face is still chatting with the brown-skinned woman he has almost exclusively set his sights on, and the man in the maroon mask keeps making eyes at Eve, winking at her whenever she happens to look his way.

I can see in her face that she is trying not to cry. Ever since the woman was killed this morning, she has been on the verge of tears, and I want nothing more than to take her back to my room and wrap her in my arms.

There is just another night of bidding that stands in my way.

Just like the two days before, the man in the maroon mask has already bid on Eve, marking his interest in her. Tonight, he has started with three thousand dollars, following the same trend as the last two nights of increasing the bidding.

One by one, the women in red dresses are handed out to the highest bidder. Some of the women who aren't bid on receive death glares from Edgar and then fall back in line looking terrified.

Eve told me any woman not bid on at the end of the week will be murdered. As scared as they all are, a few of them must be relieved that Number Five was killed.

Less competition.

Eve tries not to look at me as it gets closer and closer to her turn, but there is little point in trying not to show our interest in one another. I've bid on her the past two nights. Everyone here knows she is the woman of my choice. Still, I do my best to follow her lead and look ambivalent, at least.

When Eve steps forward, the man in the maroon mask wastes no time making his interest known. He walks through the crowd, eyes pinned on her. And for the first time, I notice his limp.

It isn't obvious, but his right leg stutters slightly with each step.

I study him, trying to understand why this matters.

His suit today is the same shade as his mask. The jacket has a shimmer to it that catches the light with black silk lapels. The pants are a similar material, though in a darker shade.

Everything about him screams *showman*. He isn't someone afraid of being recognized, which is why I'm surprised when I realize how long it has taken me to recognize him.

I know who the man in the maroon mask is.

His name is Joel Foli.

Known for his extravagant clothes and a limp in his right leg from a much-publicized motorcycle crash a few years before, Joel Foli is an infamous hacker. He is a hot commodity in the criminal underworld, receiving offers from every crime ring in the city, including my own family.

If anyone needs to crack security codes or steal credit card information without being caught, Joel Foli is the guy to call.

He is expensive, though, which means I have even more reason to fear him in this auction. His finances could rival or exceed mine.

My only hope is that, unlike me, Joel won't be willing to give up everything to save Eve.

"Five thousand dollars," Edgar calls, nodding when I raise my hand and then turning to Joel, assuming he'll increase the bid. He does.

It moves up one thousand dollars at a time until we hit ten thousand, and I think Edgar might pass out from excitement. We are only on night three and one of his women has moved into the five-digit zone.

I hate Joel a little more every time he raises his hand to increase the bid, but I also can't help but think that he could be useful to me. If we weren't both fighting for Eve, I could talk to him about helping me track down Milaya. If anyone can get into the Cartel's accounts and figure out what they may have done with her, it is him.

Finally, at fifteen thousand, Joel looks longingly at Eve and then steps back and bows out. "That is my limit," he says, turning to me with a smile. "For now."

I grit my teeth and try to look at the larger picture.

If he can help me track down Milaya, I might let him live after this week is over.

For a few days, at least.

Edgar wraps up the proceedings for the day, and Eve moves quickly across the room towards me, relief obvious in her face. I want to pull her against my chest, but it has to wait until we are in my room. Not here in front of everyone.

Despite my restraint, I still notice Maddie cast a dirty glance in our direction. As if she can feel the darts flying at her, Eve turns to look at Maddie. The girl's glare grows even darker, eyebrows pinching together, and Eve quickly turns back to me.

"What the hell was that about?" I ask, placing a hand on her lower back to lead her from the room.

She shakes her head, but I can tell it is bothering her.

"Tell me." It is a gentle command. She is dealing with enough right now that petty fights between her and other women don't need to weigh on her mind as well.

We are some of the last people out of the lounge, so the hallway is nearly empty, everyone disappearing into their rooms with their winnings or going back to the slave quarters at the back of the inn.

I grab Eve's hand and pull her back to face me. "Tell me what is going on."

"It isn't a big deal," she says, eyes going glassy with tears. "Really. In the face of everything else, it is just some basic drama. But suffice it to say, you were right about Maddie wanting you to buy her. I think she has a crush."

My chest swells with protectiveness. "Did she say something to you?"

Eve squeezes my fingers. "Yes, but it hardly matters. She is scared and trying to make this situation as good as she can for herself."

"It matters to me," I say.

There have been so few ways in the last week that I've been able to help or protect Eve. I couldn't keep her from being kidnapped, I couldn't save our daughter, and I couldn't keep her from being put on the LeClerc auction block.

But this? I can handle.

I can stop a mean girl from tormenting her, especially when Eve has done nothing but try to help Maddie. She doesn't deserve this, and I can fix it.

"Let's just go," Eve says, grabbing my hand.

I pull away from her hold, lifting a finger to tell her to give me a moment. "I forgot something."

Before Eve can argue, I duck back into the lounge and am relieved to see Maddie is still hanging around.

She has taken off her heels and is holding them by the straps, circling her ankles to stretch them. She doesn't see me enter.

"Hey," I call.

When she sees me, her eyes go wide, and then she beams at me. Eve is right. This is more than just an auction for Maddie. She legitimately has a crush. Or a hope, at least, that maybe there is a light at the end of this tunnel for her.

"Hey," she purrs.

I shake my head to cut her off before she can say anything else. "Give it up."

Confusion clouds her smile. "What—"

"I'm never going to bid on you," I say. "You are wasting your time flirting with me and tormenting Eve. I don't want you. And it isn't Eve's fault, either. She wants me to be nicer to you, but as long as you are throwing daggers at her from across the room, I'm not going to be nice, do you hear me?"

Maddie's eyes are filling with tears, and she bites her lower lip.

"*Do you hear me?*" I repeat.

She nods, looking down at her bare feet.

Without another word, I turn and leave.

Eve turns on me as soon as I close the door to my room.

"You shouldn't have said anything to her!" she yells. "I told you it wasn't a big deal."

"It looked like it was a big deal," I argue.

"But it wasn't."

"Tell that to your face." I run a hand down my face and shake my head. "I'm sorry, but you were clearly upset, and I figured I could take care of it."

"That is what you think about everything," Eve says, spinning around and pacing towards the bed. When she gets there, she turns on her heel and charges back towards me. "I can take care of myself."

"So you've said."

My tone makes her raise an eyebrow, and I sigh. "I'm sorry, but—"

"She is scared. She is scared and alone, and I don't want to alienate her."

I reach out and lay my hands on Eve's shoulders. She tries to wriggle free, but I hold on. "And I don't want her to screw up your chances of getting out of here."

Eve shakes her head. "She wouldn't."

"She could. She already got herself in trouble with the Cartel once, and the closer you stick to her, the more you put yourself at risk."

Eve opens her mouth to argue, but I cut her off. "You saw what happened to Number Five today."

She closes her mouth, chewing on her bottom lip, and then nods. "I did."

"Seeing how heartless they were towards that woman only reinforced the fact that I would let every single one of the women here die before I would ever let anything like that happen to you."

Her cheeks go red, and her brown eyes go hard. "That isn't right, Luka."

"I don't fucking care if it's right!" I roar. "It's the truth!"

She drops down on the edge of the bed and folds her hands in her lap. "You always do this. You always come to my rescue when I don't need rescuing."

"I know. And I won't apologize for it, either."

She looks up at me, clearly surprised that I agree with her. I shrug. "I know that I micromanage everything when it comes to your safety and Milaya's, but I can't help myself. My life has always been dangerous, but I've never had anyone in it that I cared about as much as I care about you and Milaya. I guess I'm still getting used to what that looks like for me."

Eve holds out her hand to me, and I grab it, letting her pull me onto the bed with her. She lays her head on my shoulder. "I'm still getting used to what it feels like being loved by someone like you."

I kiss her temple. "We are both going to have to find a good balance, but until we are out of here, I'm going to err on the side of caution."

I feel her unhitch her breath to argue, but I squeeze her fingers and continue. "Because in here, any slipup could mean you get hurt. And if you get hurt, I'm going to kill whoever did it, probably getting killed in the process. And if we both don't make it out of here, there is no telling what will happen to Milaya."

Eve is silent and still for a long time before she finally crawls away from me and moves to the top of the bed, sliding beneath the blankets. She pulls back the comforter, inviting me in, and I crawl in next to her without argument.

We fall asleep that way, tangled in one another, trying to forget our troubles for a few hours.

I manage a solid forty-five minutes before I wake up to restless legs and a restless mind.

I can't lie in bed for another minute, so I gently pull away from Eve and get up.

After rinsing my face in the sink and changing into a soft pair of pajama bottoms, I pace back and forth across the room, trying to figure out what I'm going to do next.

The plan has always been to win Eve in the auction, but what after that? We can't just go home without our daughter. Not when her nursery is sitting there empty. Not when her swing is in the living room and her bottles are on the countertop.

Eve won't be able to go home until we have a plan, and I won't either.

Since I can't call anyone on the outside or leave the inn, my options are to try and get someone on the inside to help. Which, right now, means Joel Foli. So, I wrack my brain trying to figure out how I can get him to help us.

Aside from paying his fee, I'm not sure what other way I could persuade him. Especially since we are in a silent feud over my wife.

Plus, I can't even tell him Eve is my wife. Not while the auction is still going. Not while I'm weaponless and trapped inside the Cartel's inn. He could use it to have me kicked out or killed, ensuring he wins Eve.

Somehow, I have to talk him into helping me without Eve being part of the bargain.

"Luka?"

Eve is sitting up in bed, her eyes squinting against the shaft of light coming from the bathroom.

"Sorry," I whisper. "I didn't mean to wake you."

"You didn't," she says. "I had a nightmare."

I sit on the edge of the bed and hold her hand in both of mine. "Are you okay?"

She nods. "Are you?"

"Yes."

"Liar." Eve smiles, but it doesn't reach her eyes. She repeats my words from earlier. "Tell me."

I explain to her what I know about Joel Foli and what I've been thinking about how to get Milaya back.

"I noticed his limp in the bathroom earlier," she says.

I frown. "The bathroom?"

Her cheeks flush and she tries to move past it, but I insist she tells me the story. So, she does.

"He cornered you?" I growl.

She squeezes my hand when I try to stand up, as though I'm going to dart out of the room and knock on every door until I find his. "I got out. It was fine."

"It's not fine. He shouldn't have scared you like that."

"In some sick way, I think he believes I want him," Eve says. "He was trying to seduce me."

I grit my teeth, biting down on my lower lip hard enough that I think I might draw blood.

"Maybe it isn't all bad," Eve says. "Maybe we can use it to our advantage."

"What are you talking about?"

She runs her fingers nervously across the comforter. "Well, we need his help and clearly ... we have something he wants."

Her meaning hits me all at once, and I rocket to my feet, shaking my head. "Absolutely not. No fucking way."

"But if it means getting our daughter back?" she asks.

I hesitate. "Of course I would do anything to get her back, but—"

"No buts. Either you'd do anything or you wouldn't. Which is it?"

I growl at her wordlessly, and she gives me a sad smile.

"I know you don't like it, but we have to consider that it might be the only option."

"The last option," I say, wagging a finger at her. "Using you is the absolute last option. I will figure something else out."

She opens her mouth to argue, but I don't let her. I've conceded enough tonight.

Instead, I lie next to her, spin her around so her back is against my chest, and I wrap an arm around her middle. Then, I kiss the back of her neck and whisper against the shell of her ear. "Go to sleep."

"You too," she teases, bumping her ass back into me. "You need the rest."

Eve's breath goes slow and even again, but I can still feel the tension in her shoulders, as well as in my own. We are together, but each night, our troubles seem to crowd in closer and closer until there isn't room for much else besides the fear of what is to come.

16

EVE

Knocks on the door pull me from sleep. I feel Luka stir next to me, and then we both curse at the same time.

"I overslept." I grab the clock next to the bed and groan when I see that it is already 8:00 in the morning.

Luka opens the door and invites Kari inside. "She is running a bit late this morning."

Kari presses her back against the door, looking like she would rather be anywhere else in the world but here.

Luka, still half asleep, walks back to the bed and kisses my forehead. "Give me a second in the bathroom and then it is all yours."

Kari's eyes widen at our affection and ease, and I stiffen. Such a stupid, careless mistake. I can only pray she won't say anything to anyone else. I don't think she will.

When the bathroom door opens, she holds out a red silk robe and a pair of black thigh-high boots. "How fast can you be ready?"

I run a hand through my hair and decide there is enough hairspray in it from the day before that I don't need a shower. "I can get dressed and clean up in the sink. Ten minutes, maybe."

She nods and then turns away while I dress. "You two seem comfortable together."

"Yeah," I say hesitantly, not sure how much to give away. "I suppose we are."

She hums, clearly disapproving. I wonder how many times she has seen something similar happen at these auctions. "He *seems* nice."

"If you don't mind me asking, what is your experience with the Cartel?" I ask. "I know you said you have been with them for years, but how did it happen?"

She stares down at the floor.

"You don't have to tell me if you don't want to. I have just been curious."

"No, I can tell you." She takes a deep breath and tucks her pale blonde hair behind her ear. "I fell in love with a man as soon as I moved to the city. I was young and had only been here a month. I didn't know anyone, so we spent all of our time together. He was so sweet to me. And fabulously wealthy. He showed me a life I had never known before—fancy restaurants, nice cars, beautiful hotel rooms. I was pampered more than I ever had been in my life."

"Sounds nice," I say, waiting for the catch.

"It does, doesn't it?" She stares straight ahead as though she is looking at a movie screen I can't see. Then, she blinks and shakes her head. "I thought he loved me, so when he told me I should be more open to public affection when we were together with his friends, I listened. It was the least I could do after everything he'd done for me."

"Affection?" I ask. "What does that mean?"

The silk robe barely comes to my mid-thigh, and when I tie the belt around my waist, the slit goes high enough that you can see the black lacy underwear I have on. I try to adjust the material to cover more of my body, but it is useless.

"Kissing," she says. "At first. Then sitting on his lap, massaging his thighs, straddling him. When I tried to refuse, he would tell me that I'd do anything for him if I loved him. He would question my devotion."

"That isn't fair," I say.

Kari nods and opens her mouth to say something else, but just then, the bathroom door opens and Luka steps out. A billow of steam wafts from behind him, and I realize he took an incredibly fast shower. I was so distracted by Kari's story that I didn't even notice the water turning on or off.

"All yours," he says, stepping aside to wave an arm into the bathroom.

Kari clams up as soon as Luka is in the room, pressing herself against the wall.

Luka dresses slowly, and I clear my throat. When he turns around, I nod to the door. He gets the message.

"Let me get dressed and then you two can have the room to get ready," he says, quickening his pace.

Kari is a silent statue until Luka pulls me in for one chaste kiss on the lips and then leaves to head down for breakfast. As soon as the door closes, she turns to me. "You two are *really* comfortable together."

I gesture for her to follow me into the bathroom. "Keep telling your story while I get ready."

"Well, I did everything he asked, but over time, his demands grew more and more uncomfortable," she says, leaning against the bathroom doorway. "First, he wanted me to have sex with him in our bedroom while we had guests over. Then, we had sex in front of people."

I gasp. She nods sadly. "I know. But at the time, it all felt so normal. I knew it was strange, but everyone around me acted like it was commonplace. I thought maybe I'd just gotten involved with a relaxed group of people."

"He was grooming you?" I ask, taking a guess.

Instead of answering, Kari keeps talking. "Then, he wanted me to have sex with his friends. I tried to refuse, but he told me it was rude to walk around in the skimpy clothes I wore and tease them without offering them a little taste. I wanted to deny him, but he threatened to leave me. And by that point, we were living together. I didn't have a job or a house or any money. And I was afraid what my family would think of me if I told them. So, I did it. I thought maybe it would just be the one time, but it happened over and over again. Sometimes, multiple times in the same night."

Tears well in the back of my eyes, but I try to hold them in. I have a feeling Kari doesn't want my pity.

"By the time I realized Edgar was part of the Cartel, I was already in too far and—"

"Edgar?" I gasp, clapping a hand over my mouth.

Kari's face turns a deep red, and she nods. "I guess I gave it away."

"Edgar was your boyfriend?"

She nods. "I thought so, at least. Now I realize I was just a stupid girl who he fooled into loving him. He never cared for me. Our relationship was all for the Cartel."

"And you can't leave?" I ask.

She lowers her chin, looking up at me from beneath pale eyebrows. "You saw what happened to the woman who tried to leave yesterday.

Do you think I want to end up facedown in the lawn in a puddle of blood?"

"Good point." I twist my hair back in a low bun and smudge eyeliner around my eyes, stepping back from the mirror. "I'm ready."

When I get to the bathroom door, Kari stops me. "I'm telling you this because I want you to be careful."

"Too late," I say. "I'm already up for auction."

"Be careful with your guy," she says, pointing to the bedroom. "He may be sweet now, but things can change in an instant. Protect your heart."

I want to tell her the truth—give her some sliver of hope that maybe Luka and I will be able to do something about the Cartel once we are on the outside. But I can't risk it. So instead, I thank her.

"I do have a good feeling about him," I admit. "But I won't forget your story."

"That's all I ask," she nods. Then, she leads me out of the room.

Instead of taking me to the lounge like every other morning, Kari takes me to the back of the inn where the servants' quarters are. When we get there, the slaves are all gathered in one central room with concrete walls. Edgar is counting heads and then nods when he counts me and realizes we are at thirteen.

"We are meeting here today because I want to give you all a moment to gather yourselves and perhaps even practice a little bit."

I look around and realize everyone is wearing the same thing today. The virgins are still in purple and everyone else is in red, but we are all wearing the same short robes and high boots.

"Today is about performing," Edgar says. "Every day has been a performance, but now that the week is nearing the end, you want to do whatever you can to ensure these men want to bid on you."

Or else you'll be killed.

The words hang unspoken over the room.

"You need to show these men how willing and eager you are to please them. So, one by one, you are going to do your best to please me."

Up until this morning, I knew Edgar was a monster simply because he was involved with the Cartel, but he was a strangely sexless part of the operation. Now, however, I can see the lust in his eyes as he scans the women in front of him.

He nods for Number One to step forward as he sits down in a chair. He directs her movements until she is straddling him and circling her hips on top of him.

It is obvious how much he is enjoying it when the girl stands up. The bulge in his pants is hard to miss.

Just as he said, one by one the women come forward and do whatever he says. Some of them kneel in front of him and massage his thighs as Kari mentioned. Others suck on his earlobe and kiss his neck.

The rule all week has been to avoid anything explicitly sexual, but clearly that rule does not apply to today's activity.

When he gets to Maddie, she steps forward on trembling legs.

"Hurry up," he commands, waving her forward impatiently.

He commands her onto her knees, which she obeys, but then he tells her to unzip his pants.

All of the air seems to escape from the room. I feel frozen, and Maddie must feel the same because she doesn't move. She doesn't even appear to breathe.

"Now," Edgar demands.

Maddie jumps and then reaches for his crotch. When her hand brushes along the front of his pants, Edgar groans slightly, and Maddie pulls back, covering her face with her hands and whimpering.

"Not again!" he shouts, flinging his arms to the side in frustration. "You haven't pulled yourself together yet? There are only two days left in the auction. Do you want to be the last woman left standing after everyone else is gone?"

Maddie's shoulders begin to shake. Her sobs start quietly but grow in volume as her emotions take over.

Edgar stands up and kicks at her, softly at first. But just like Maddie's crying, his anger only grows. His second kick is a lot harder, and it sends her splaying across the concrete.

"I'm sorry," Maddie sobs, wiping at her eyes with the backs of her hands, smearing her makeup. "I'll do it. Sit down, and I'll do it."

"I give the orders," Edgar says to Maddie and the rest of the room.

He grabs her by the front of her shirt and pulls her to standing only to pull his hand back and crack it down hard across her cheek. She slumps to the floor again, and I can't watch another second.

I dart from my spot in the line and reach for Maddie, but before I can, Edgar hits me too.

The slap stings across my cheek, and I barely have time to react before he wraps his hand around my arm so tightly I wince and begins dragging me back into line.

"And you," he growls through gritted teeth. "You are worth a lot of money, but I've had enough of your insubordination."

He pushes me back into position and lifts his hand like he is going to hit me, but he doesn't. He takes a deep breath and then lowers his hand to his side, smoothing down his shirt and vest.

"You deserve a more thorough punishment, but you are as good as another man's property at this point," he says, glaring at me. "I wouldn't want to damage you before the purchase is final."

Edgar turns and stomps towards Maddie, hauling her to her feet. She winces, thinking the same thing I am, that he is going to continue hitting her, but instead he pushes her towards me. "We are done here for today. I'm sure I've given you all a good enough example of what will happen if you don't perform the way you are expected to."

He turns and leaves without another word, leaving us all standing in the small room, wondering what to do next.

Maddie stumbles towards me and throws her thin arms around my waist. "I'm sorry for the way I treated you. I'm sorry about—"

I shush her, smoothing down her hair. "It's okay. I understand. I'm sorry he yelled at you."

She looks up at me, and I can tell she understands I'm talking about both Edgar and Luka. Tears gather in her eyes and spill across her cheeks.

I help her clean up her smudged makeup. When Edgar returns to lead us to the lounge, Maddie is standing by my side and looking as good as new.

The morning is spent doing different versions of what Edgar wanted done. Unlike the previous mornings, the men don't need to be creative during this task. They get to ask for exactly what they want, though overt sex acts are still off the table.

Lap dances.

Strip teases.

And heavy petting that fills the room with soft moans and labored breathing.

As soon as he realizes what is going on, Luka claims me without hesitation. Part of me wants to tell him that we need to maintain our ruse, but perhaps that ship has sailed. Edgar as good as admitted I belonged to Luka—though Joel Foli is certainly still making his interest known.

Luka has me sit in his lap, straddling him so we are face-to-face and free to talk. He presses his lips to my neck and whispers in my ear.

"Who bruised your arm?"

I look down and realize there are dark lines of fingers forming across my forearm. "I'm not going to say."

Luka's hands tighten on my waist, and I circle my hips against him to relax him again. He hesitantly allows me to.

"I don't want you losing your cool on anybody and ruining our plan so close to the end," I say, grinding down into him. I am performing because I have to, but with Luka, it is hard to keep that line straight. His body pressed against mine will always be like a drug. I lose myself in him.

He kisses a line down my chest and between my breasts, moaning as he goes. "I'll keep control."

"Yeah, right," I tease, arching into him. "You can barely keep control now."

His hand slips around my thigh and brushes across my center. "That's because you are so fucking hot."

I smile and rock my body on top of his.

Over his shoulder, I see Joel Foli receiving a dance from Number Six. He tears his eyes away from her wide hips and thin waist to look at me and smile.

I shiver.

Luka begins to turn to see what made me uncomfortable, but I capture his lips with mine before he can. "Do you want a drink?"

He shakes his head. "I just want you."

For a moment, we kiss and cuddle and find solace in one another. But it can only last a short time before we have to be practical.

"I think I'm going to try to convince Joel to leave the inn," Luka says.

"What?" I ask, glancing back at Joel who is now grabbing Number Six's hips and grinding himself against her backside. He looks like he is having too much fun to even think about leaving.

"I can't leave because then I won't be able to bid on you," he explains. "But maybe I can convince Joel that there is no way he is going to get you, so he might as well leave. Maybe I can pay him to look for Milaya. That way, while we are in here, he can be looking for her. When we get out, we could go save her."

I nod, trying to be supportive. "Maybe."

"I just need to get him alone," Luka says.

I think he needs to do a lot more than that. Joel doesn't seem like the kind of guy who will give up easily.

Suddenly, Luka tenses. His hands are like stone around my waist and his entire body is clenched and ready to either run or fight.

"What is it?" I whisper.

Even with his mask on, I can see that his face is pale. I follow his eyes and feel myself go stiff as well.

Rian Morrison is standing in the entryway.

She is wearing the same uniform of a pencil skirt and starched button-down shirt she had on the day she kidnapped me. Her blonde hair is pulled back in a severe ponytail. But unlike the scowling woman I met at her family's mansion, she is smiling at Edgar as though they are old friends.

Luka picks me up off his lap, sits me back down in the chair, and moves to the minibar.

I don't need to ask to understand what he is doing. We can't be seen together. Luka is wearing a mask, but Rian isn't an idiot. If we are cuddled up together on a chair, she'll realize who he is. She'll ruin our plan and have Luka killed.

I sit frozen as Rian walks into the lounge and takes a look around. Her eyes fall on me almost instantly, and her smile widens.

My stomach turns. I want to run and grab onto Luka, afraid Rian will drug me again and drag me somewhere else. But I can handle her on my own.

I have to.

She approaches with a cocky strut. "Eve," she says, tipping her head to me. "Or, should I say, Number Seven? It looks like you are doing quite well on the bidding board. Congratulations."

"What are you doing here?" I ask, not bothering to hide my disdain. Rian isn't one of the bidders. She won't affect whether Luka purchases me or not. Unless, of course, she finds out Luka is here at all.

Rian lifts her chin and shakes her ponytail out. "I was granted special access to the auction because I supply the Cartel with a fair amount of … inventory."

"Isn't this the kind of activity someone in your position is supposed to be cracking down on?"

She shrugs. "I'm still cleaning the streets of crime in a way. I offer up drug addicts and other criminals I come into contact with through my job as an agent. I pick women no one will notice and make a little profit along the way. Win-win."

"For you," I spit. "Not for the women you trade."

"Well, we can't all win," she says. "I guess you are learning that the hard way."

I sit tall and ball my fists, ready to fight. Rian simply takes a slow step back and shakes her head. "I hope you are behaving better for the guests. I have a reputation to maintain with the Cartel and offering up a troublemaker won't help."

I open my mouth to argue, but she holds up a finger to stop me. "May I remind you that a baby could sell for a lot of money on the black market?"

My heart lodges in my throat, blocking all air to my lungs and words from my lips.

Rian smiles. "That is what I thought."

I clear my throat and swallow back the unshed tears. "If you let Milaya go home—give her to Luka's parents—I won't hold a grudge. I will tell Luka to let you live."

Rian stares at me for a second and then scoffs. "You are something else. You are about to be sold as a slave and you still think you have any kind of control over me? Stupid woman."

She walks away before I can say anything else, but I decide one thing in that moment:

When the time comes, I'll kill her myself.

17

LUKA

I overhear a very small portion of Rian and Eve's conversation, but sticking too close is a risk I can't afford. While they are talking, I grab a drink from the bar and move to the opposite side of the room, hoping if I stay low and avoid getting too close, Rian will be too distracted with Eve to pay any attention to me.

I'm standing in the corner when I see Joel push aside the woman he was grinding against and move into the entryway. I take my drink and follow after him.

I don't see him immediately when I walk into the entrance hall, but then I hear a muffled voice coming from a closet to my left. I press my ear against the door.

"And that number is firm?" Joel asks, humming to himself. "Good. I can work for that. They are paying up-front, right? Even better. Yeah, I'm at the auction now. I have my eye on a damn fine prize, and she might cost me a pretty penny."

It sounds like he is on the phone, but cell phones are supposed to be off-limits inside. Clearly, like so many other things, Joel found his way around the rules.

He wraps up the call quickly, and when he opens the door, I'm standing just outside with my arms crossed over my chest.

His eyes go wide, and then he visibly relaxes, his shoulders easing back. "I guess I've been caught," he says wryly.

"You are breaking the rules," I say. "I could have you thrown out for that."

His lips twist to one side. "Are you going to?"

I shrug. "That depends."

He sighs. "I suppose you want Number Seven all to yourself?"

My instinct tells me to say yes. Ensuring Eve is mine no matter what would save me so much heartache, but if things go well with this conversation, I can both ensure that and save Milaya.

"I do, but that isn't what I'm asking for," I say honestly. "I need a favor."

Joel shifts his weight to his good leg and tilts his head to the side, studying me. "Why would I do a favor for you?"

I take a deep breath and then reach up and pull down my mask. Not all the way off. I twist it to the side so he can see my face while still blocking myself from view of everyone else in the lounge behind us.

Joel's eyes widen in surprise and he takes a step back before recognition flickers in his eyes. "Luka Volkov."

I slip the mask back on and nod towards the door. "Care to have a smoke outside?"

Whether Joel will help me or not, I don't know. But he is interested enough to follow me outside.

"Do you know who I am?" Joel asks after he lights a cigarette.

I blow smoke and nod. "I do."

"What gave it away?"

I gesture to the snakeskin suit he is wearing today. "Your clothes certainly helped."

He curses under his breath. "I had them sent ahead so the Cartel could make sure I wasn't hiding anything. I don't wear another man's suits."

"Plus, your limp and your obvious wealth." I shrug. "It wasn't hard to follow the clues."

He nods. "I suppose I should have hidden my tracks better. After all, that is what I do for a living. We all leave trails here and there, don't we? Little things we think don't matter—a harmless picture, a childhood pet's name in a tweet. It's all there, if you know how to look."

I shake my head. "And you're the man to find it, it seems."

"Indeed. Anyway," he sucks on the cigarette and blows out a thin stream of smoke. "What is this about? What do you need from me?"

I hate laying myself out on the line like this. I hate that I have to make myself and Eve vulnerable to this man when I don't know if I can trust him yet, but there is no other option.

Not when Rian is inside, and I have no clue when she'll leave and see us out here talking.

Not when Milaya is out in the world, alone and without her parents.

I don't have another choice. So, I lay it all out for him.

"My daughter has been taken," I say quietly, staring straight ahead at the lawn. Almost the exact spot where the slave was murdered yesterday. I fantasize that I can still see the bloodstains, but I know that's not true. The Cartel had cleanup crews out here for hours, touching up every blade of grass. "I don't know where she is or who has her, and you are the only person I can think of who can help. I don't have a phone or a weapon or any way to contact the outside world, but you've made your living getting around obstacles like that. For the right price, I think you could help me."

Joel stares at me, eyes narrowed. "I can help you, but I have to wonder why, if your daughter is missing, you are at this auction."

I pinch my lips together, hoping Joel won't put the pieces together. Or, if he does, that he won't care.

"I can't tell you that right now. But I'll pay you whatever you want," I say, hoping to persuade him. "You'll have to leave the auction, but I'll make sure you are compensated."

He stares at me and lifts his chin, looking down the nose of his mask at me. "You know, someone hired me to look into you before."

My attention snaps to him, and he grins, amused by my reaction.

"The Irish hate you," he laughs, shaking his head. "Whatever you did to piss them off, you fucked up. They hired me to look into your background. In the end, they weren't paying enough for my services, but I did some perfunctory digging, and you know what I found?"

He leans towards me, one hand poised next to his mouth. His next words are said in a stage whisper: "A marriage license."

I resist the urge to curse under my breath. This was a mistake. I know that now, but it is too late to take it back.

"You know what I think?" he asks, taking another puff of the cigarette and blowing the smoke directly in my face. "I think Number Seven is your wife. I think that brown-haired bombshell is your *Eve*."

"How much do you want?" I ask. I need to get this conversation back on track. I've lost control, but I can get it back. "Like I said, I'll pay you anything."

He twists his mouth to the side and hums, but it is all for show. He isn't really thinking, and we both know it. "With this information, I can have you killed. All I have to do is walk inside and tell the Cartel who you are, and you'll be shot on sight. Then I can have what I really want, no?"

I snub out my cigarette and finish the last swig of wine in my glass. "And what is that?" I growl.

He laughs and moves past me, hand on the doorknob. "I want to fuck your wife."

Before the words are even out of his mouth, I shatter the wineglass against the brick face of the building and stab the stem into his carotid artery.

I know I only have one try. If I miss, the stem is liable to break, and Joel will be wounded but not mortally.

Thankfully, I don't miss.

The stem sticks from his neck, pulsing up and down with the weakening pumps of his dying heart.

Blood slicks down my arm, running underneath my suit jacket, and coats the front steps.

Joel falls backwards just behind a large bush growing next to the front steps, and I quickly step over him, move into the entryway, and hustle up the stairs.

I have to get rid of my clothes before anyone finds his body.

When I return to Eve's side, I'm in a black suit that is similar to the one I had on before, though these lapels are silk. I pray to God no one will notice.

Rian is across the room getting a drink, but Eve still looks at me, eyes wide, and tries to push me away.

"Have you left this room since I've been gone?" I whisper.

Eve's brow furrows. "No, I've been here."

"You have lots of witnesses?"

She waves her arms around the room. "Everyone. Why? What is going on?"

I shake my head and wrap an arm around her waist. "Act casual."

She lays her head on my chest and then pulls back, grabbing my lapel. "Did you change?"

I stare down at her, saying as much as I can with one look as possible, and Eve gets it. She knows that something bad is going on and I can't talk about it. She lays her head on my chest, and we sway to the soft music playing in the background.

Compared to a few other couples in the room, we are hardly noteworthy.

Fox-Face has Number Thirteen's hand down the front of his pants, though he is trying to disguise this fact with a strategically positioned pillow in front of his crotch. And a few of the other couples are damn near having sex in the lounge.

Rian seems distracted enough watching them that she isn't paying much attention to me or Eve, but Edgar is my real concern.

I see him counting heads, his head bobbing as he counts each slave and then each bidder. When he stops, he frowns. He does it again and has the same reaction.

He realizes that one of the bidders is missing.

Edgar turns and walks into the entryway, and I go rigid. This is it.

Fuck. Fuck. *Fuck.*

"Luka, what is it?" Eve whispers, her voice trembling. "What is going on?"

I shake my head and hug her even tighter against my chest. I hug her like it might be the last time.

Because it might be.

The thought feels like a torpedo in my brain, slicing through everything else until I'm useless, desperately clinging to my wife because I don't know what else to do.

Then, Edgar returns.

There are two large guards on either side of him, and when he lifts his hands above his head to clap for everyone's attention, I know what he is going to say before he says a word.

Eve looks up at me with nervous eyes before turning to Edgar.

It is good I didn't tell her. Because when Edgar announces that Joel Foli is dead, she looks genuinely shocked.

"Someone broke the rules," Edgar says. "And for it, they will be executed."

18

LUKA

"Someone has been killed?" Fox-Face asks, gripping the waist of Number Thirteen even tighter. "Who? One of us?"

Us. As opposed to *them.*

No one cared much when a woman was shot in the head in front of them the day before, but suddenly they are terrified.

"Joel Foli," Edgar says, his eyes moving slowly across the room. "He was the man in the dark red mask. And a rather loyal patron of the Cartel, which only increases our desire to catch whoever did this to him."

"He was the one making bids for Number Seven," Peter Struthers says.

He has kept a rather low profile all weekend, sticking to the women lower on the bidding board and not making a scene, but apparently he is ready to change that.

He turns to where I am standing next to Eve. "He was giving you a fair amount of competition."

I want to punch the man in his ruddy face and pile him on top of Joel in the entryway along with anyone else who dares stand in the way of Eve and I making it out of here alive.

That isn't possible, though. So instead, I shrug.

"Yes, he was, but that is hardly reason to kill the man," I say. "How did he die? No one here has any weapons, so surely that could narrow down the search. Perhaps Mr. Foli angered one of your guards and found himself in over his head."

Edgar whispers something to the guard next to him and then addresses the room. "Joel Foli was stabbed in the neck with the stem of a wineglass."

Eve clutches at her chest and turns her face into me. A rumble of shock moves through the room.

"Then I guess that doesn't narrow it down," I say, shaking my head. "How horrible."

Edgar narrows his eyes in my direction. "Not that I am accusing you, sir, but where were you exactly?"

"Exactly when?" I ask. "Do we have any way to know how long the man has been dead? I spoke with him an hour ago, but haven't seen him since then."

"You spoke with him?" Edgar asks.

I nod. "As many of you have this morning, as well. Believe me, if I'd known he was going to be murdered, I would have kept my distance to help maintain my innocence."

The guards on either side of Edgar take a step forward, and Eve tenses beside me. I didn't tell her what is going on, but I'm sure she has guessed by now.

"His body is still warm," Edgar says. "The blood hasn't congealed yet."

A woman whimpers behind me.

"I can't say where I was the exact moment he was killed since we don't know when that was," I say. "But I was talking to Number Eleven before coming to see Number Seven."

I see Maddie's attention snap towards me from the corner of my eye, and then everyone is looking at her.

It is to my advantage that she is naturally nervous already because it doesn't raise any eyebrows when she bites her lip and twiddles her fingers.

I would have used Eve as my alibi except Edgar must think I killed Joel to keep him from bidding on Eve. So, they could think Eve was in on the murder. I have to find another witness, and Maddie seems like the best bet.

I can only hope she'll play along.

"Is that true?" Edgar asks, looking at Maddie from beneath dark brows.

Maddie glances over at me and Eve and then nods quickly, eyes wide. "Yes. I spoke with him."

Eve shifts closer to me, nudging my arm, and I don't need to look at her to know she is upset with me for bringing Maddie into this. For whatever reason, she has a soft spot for the young girl, and I am putting her at great risk by involving her in my crime. Though, she was already in great risk. At least this way, if she backs up my story, I'll be a lot more inclined to try and save her once Eve and I get out of here.

If we get out of here.

"I was talking with Number Eleven," one of the female bidders against the back wall says. "For the last twenty minutes, at least."

Edgar pulls his top lip back in a snarl and looks from me to Maddie. "Are you lying to me?"

"No," Maddie insists. "I really did talk with him. Maybe I'm confused about the timing."

The soft-spoken man who showed me to my room and promised to take care of any of my needs the first day I arrived is nowhere to be seen as Edgar rounds on me. "What are you not saying? Where were you?" he hisses in a venomous voice.

Eve wraps her arm around my elbow, clinging to me, and I pat her hand.

"I'm telling you everything I know."

Edgar nods to the guards behind him, and they move forward. But they've only taken a few steps when Eve suddenly pulls away and moves to stand in front of me, acting as a guard between me and Edgar.

"He isn't telling you everything," she says.

The room goes perfectly quiet, and I'm too surprised to say anything.

Is she going to reveal our secret? Is she going to tell them I was the one who killed Joel?

At this point, anything could happen, so I'm not really sure.

"Then please enlighten us," Edgar snarls.

Eve takes a deep breath, her narrow shoulders rising and falling. "I killed Joel."

"No." The word is out of my mouth before I can stop it. I lunge forward to grab Eve, but she moves out of my reach.

"I killed him," Eve said. "Because he tried to assault me, and I didn't want him to own me. He was a horrible man, and I'd kill him again if I was given the chance."

My chest feels like it has been cracked open. The world around me is chaotic and unrecognizable, and I have no way to bring it back into focus.

Edgar is yelling something and the room is a flurry of voices and movement. Then, my vision clears, focusing on the only thing that matters: two Cartel guards are moving towards Eve.

One of the men clamps his hands on Eve's arm, but before the second guy can, I run forward and pound my fist into his nose.

Blood spurts out and the man yells, falling back.

The second guard lets Eve go to focus on me. I kick him in the stomach and am about to crack his kneecap backward when Edgar claps his hands the way he has all week long. I turn and see him with his arm around Eve's throat.

"Touch anyone else, and I'll kill her," he says.

Just to be sure I know he is serious, he pulls a concealed weapon from inside his jacket.

I stumble away from the guard and back into the crowd. They step back to form a large circle around me.

I only realize when I reach up to wipe the sweat from my forehead that my mask is gone. It is lying on the floor near the bloody guard. It must have fallen off during the fight.

Edgar instructs the bloody guard to call more soldiers to keep watch over the room and then leads Eve towards the entrance hall. I move to follow, but three fresh guards appear, weapons lifted and at the ready.

Eve looks back at me once as she is dragged from the room, and then she is gone.

Hopelessness spreads in my chest, along with a kind of gnawing desire to do something, anything.

I can't watch her be taken from me again.

I can't let this happen.

I spin in a circle, trying to understand my options. I've been mapping the inn since the moment I arrived, memorizing windows and exits and potential weapons, but all of that information seems to be inaccessible to me now. Now that Eve is gone and our entire plan is in jeopardy, I'm panicking.

I don't usually panic. Years of training have taught me to remain cool under pressure. But right now, I'm losing my shit.

That is when I see Rian Morrison standing in the corner.

Her eyes are wide, mouth hanging open.

My mask is gone.

I understand the importance of that now.

Rian Morrison knows who I am. She recognizes me, and she knows who Eve is to me, and she knows why I'm here.

She darts from the corner to a nearby guard. He looks at me as she speaks, and the fog in my brain seems to lift for a moment.

The guard gestures to his friends by the door and they all move in at the same time. But just as the men get within arm's reach, I spin around and grab the fireplace poker from the stand behind me. I plunge it through the nearest guard's chest, grab his weapon, and kick him back.

Time feels like it is moving in slow motion, but I know I only have precious seconds before I'm killed. I lift the man's gun to my shoulder and take aim at the second closest guard, hitting him straight between the eyes. The man drops to the floor, dead.

I know people around me are screaming and hiding, but I don't hear them. Don't see them.

I'm only focused on the threats to my life and, by extension, Eve's life.

My second shot hits the next guard in the chest and takes him down. The third guard, however, lowers his weapons and raises his hands.

"Don't shoot," he begs, looking down at his feet. "This is just a job for me. I don't care about any of it. Don't kill me."

I gesture for him to drop his weapon, and he does. I take it and the guns from the other two guards, as well.

When I turn to find Rian Morrison, I realize she is gone, having slipped out sometime during the fighting.

That is fine. I'll find her soon enough.

But first, Eve.

I make it to the entryway, following where I saw Edgar take Eve, before more guards flood in.

I shoot at them in an orderly fashion at first, but my aim quickly grows erratic.

There are too many guards coming from too many directions for me to keep up with.

I pass the main hallway and move towards the dining room and a narrow servants' hallway I've never been in before; all the while I can hear more guards approaching from behind.

Then, suddenly, there is a guard standing in front of me.

I fire, hitting him in the shoulder, but not before he gets me in the leg.

Adrenaline is pouring through me, dampening my senses until the shot is nothing more than a burning sensation. Just heat. That's all it is. I can handle heat.

I fire again, this time hitting the man in the neck. Blood paints the wall next to him. But then there is another explosion behind me. And fire.

Not real fire, but a deep, throbbing heat coming from my side, and I don't need to look down to know I've been shot a second time.

I spin and fire at the man who shot me, but he darts behind a wall. I turn and keep going.

That is when I see an open door ahead of me. It is dark, and then I see guards coming up a set of stairs.

That must be where Edgar took her.

So, into the basement I go.

I move towards the stairs blindly, firing shots at random, hoping some of them hit their mark because I don't have the time or energy to aim.

My vision is going black around the edges, and my legs feel heavy and wooden. I try to put one foot in front of the other, but it feels like my right leg is dragging behind me, and before I realize what is happening, I'm face-first on the floor.

I know I need to get up. I know I need to stand and keep moving and fight, but darkness clouds my vision and pushes back my fear. It eases my worries until I let my eyes fall closed and sink into the thin carpet of the hallway.

19

EVE

Edgar's hand cracks across my face, snapping my head to the side so hard I worry about my neck breaking under the pressure.

"What happened between you and Joel Foli?" he asks for the tenth time.

"I told you." I spit blood on the concrete floor. "He tried to sleep with me without paying and wouldn't take no for an answer. I panicked and stabbed him with my wineglass."

Edgar sighs and paces around the room, his hands folded behind his back.

The space is small. It looks like the servants' quarters I was first brought to after arriving at the inn, but the furniture and carpeting are gone. If there ever was a window, it was long ago boarded up with cracking plaster. There are only two doors; one that leads to the bathroom and a second that leads to the hallway.

I heard a commotion coming from the front of the inn earlier, but I haven't heard anything in a while.

I try to convince myself that Luka is fine.

"And you acted alone?" he asks.

I nod. "The other man only confessed because he didn't want me to get in trouble. He thought he wouldn't be punished for it in the same way I would be."

"Luka, you mean," Edgar says, his mouth tilting up in a half smile.

My heart stutters, and I nod.

"I saw his face when he first arrived and suspected his identity, but once he showed such a great interest in you, I was certain."

He knew all along.

I can't believe we were both so naïve to believe we were actually fooling anyone.

"Why didn't you do anything?" I ask.

"Because he was paying for you," Edgar said. "Large amounts of money. By every account, it seemed as though Luka Volkov was going to play by our rules, and that was fine by us. Regardless of what Rian Morrison wanted, if he bid on you and won, we would honor that purchase."

I drop my chin to my chest, exhaustion taking over all at once.

Our plan would have worked. If we could have just kept our heads down and finished out the last two days, it would have worked.

"But you two had to go and fuck it up," Edgar said, clicking his tongue. "By killing one of our largest contributors, too. Big mistake."

"It was me," I say. "Only me. I told you."

Edgar sighs and tilts his head to the side. "You look sincere, but I'm not sure I believe you. I didn't have constant eyes on you, but I think I saw you in the lounge all morning."

"I was only with Joel for a few minutes before he attacked me," I say. "It was fast."

"Are you sure you're telling the truth?"

If they kill me, that's fine. Luka can still get out. He can still find Milaya. They can still have a life together. And that is all that matters.

I nod. "Yes."

Edgar moves towards me, stopping when he is just a breath away. He grabs the front of my robe and lifts me up until we are standing nose to nose, looking into each other's eyes.

Then, his fist buries itself in my stomach.

The air rushes out of me, and I gasp, trying to fill my lungs.

Edgar lets go of my robe, letting me drop back down into the metal chair. "I still don't believe you."

Just then, the door opens and a guard steps inside. There is blood splattered on his face, and even Edgar's eyes widen when he sees him.

"We've lost men," the guard says. "Not sure on numbers yet."

"And Luka?" Edgar asks.

I'm still fighting for air, but I pause, hanging on every word.

Please be alive. Please be alive. Please be alive.

"Shot," the guard says. "Several times."

My world narrows. My heart shrivels in my chest, and it takes every ounce of strength left in my body to stay seated and not slide to the floor.

I thought I couldn't breathe a minute ago, but that was heaven compared to this. Compared to the vise-like grip of despair wrapping around my ribs and squeezing me with a crushing force.

I won't survive this. I won't. I can't.

"Is he still alive?" Edgar asks.

The guard nods. "Unconscious, but breathing."

A mixture between a sob and a laugh tears out of me, and I lean forward, pressing my palms into my knees and focusing on the floor between my feet. I have a bad case of emotional whiplash, and I feel like I could hurl. I take slow, deep breaths through my nose and out of my mouth, trying to stabilize my jagged heartbeat.

Edgar turns to me. "You hear that, Eve? Your husband is alive. Good news, yes?"

I don't look up. I'm focusing on keeping my wits about me.

"Make sure he stays alive," Edgar says to the guard. "There are plenty of people who would pay good money to torture and kill the leader of the Volkov Bratva. Or use him as a slave. Hell, I myself would pay good money for that."

All at once, I understand why Luka came to the Crooked Tree Inn to save me. I was angry with him for not going after Milaya, but now I get it. Thinking about him being sold to someone and tortured and used, possibly even killed—it is too much. Too horrific.

If the roles had been reversed, I would have gone after him.

He didn't know where Milaya was. Neither of us did. So, he did what he could. He used the information he had and tried to save me, and now more than ever, I wish I could kiss him. I wish I could apologize and tell him that I understand.

When the guard leaves, Edgar turns back to me, arms crossed over his chest. "So, now that your identities are out in the open, you might as well tell me your plan."

I shake my head. "We didn't have a plan."

His hand burns across my face before I realize it is coming, and the blow sends me slipping off the chair and falling to the floor.

My knee cracks against the concrete, and I wince. But there isn't time to recover. Edgar is moving towards me again. I try to scoot back across the floor, but he kicks my feet out from under me and then presses his foot against my chest until I'm flat on the cold floor.

"Does anyone else know you are here?" he asks.

"No."

He presses harder until all I'm capable of are tiny, shallow breaths. "Tell me."

"I am!" I cry, tears rolling down my cheeks. "I didn't even know Luka was coming for me until he showed up. He didn't want to anger the Cartel, so he came alone."

Edgar shakes his head. "The leader of a Bratva wouldn't go anywhere alone."

"Luka would," I assure him. "If he did bring someone, don't you think they would have stepped forward to help when he was being attacked by guards?"

The thought seems to ring true, and Edgar contemplates it for a moment before he presses down harder on my chest until I'm sure my ribs will crack under his heel. "I was surprised he came for you at all, honestly. Men like Luka? They always have mistresses. Plenty of women they can turn to whenever the desire to get their dick wet strikes. And while you are sexy, you hardly seem worth all of this trouble."

I want to grab his foot and knock him on his back for questioning Luka and insulting me, but my body is tired. The Cartel takes great care of their guests, but they keep their slaves weak on purpose. Dinner has been the only substantial meal we've had all week, and even then it was bland and seasonless.

Lying there on the floor beneath Edgar's foot, all I can think about is baked macaroni and cheese. I make it with breadcrumbs on top and three different kinds of cheeses. It was one of Luka's favorite meals, especially when I added grilled chicken.

Edgar lifts his foot, allowing me a breath, and then kicks me in the ribs.

Pain explodes in my side, but I think about dinner with my family. I can see Luka in the kitchen, eating from the pan before the meal is finished, Milaya tucked in his arms.

Edgar kicks me again, but this time, I smile.

I'm barely paying attention when Edgar finally has me dragged from the room and taken to another.

The only way I could endure the torture was to focus on my family. To focus on Luka getting better and saving Milaya.

The only way to survive was to imagine a future in which I would be with them again and cling to the memories I still have. The memories that no amount of pain can take away.

The guard pushes me through a door and then slams it shut hard enough that the walls seem to rattle. I close my eyes and press my hands over my ears, trying to keep my brain from rattling around inside my head.

"You need to lie down."

I open my eyes and squint against the light from a lamp in the corner. The voice is familiar but it takes me a minute to place it.

"Kari."

She doesn't look up, her head bent over a bed in the room. "There are ice packs here for your bruises. I'll look you over in a minute when I'm done here."

"Is this your room?" I ask, lifting myself slowly to my feet.

"No, it's yours," she says. "At least for now. Until you two are better."

You two.

I look up and notice there are two beds.

And next to Kari is a table covered in medical instruments. And blood.

My heart realizes Luka is nearby before I do. It lurches in my chest as though it wants to leap out and cross the room to be with him.

"He is doing okay, but he needs time to rest," Kari says. "And I'm not sure the Cartel will give him much time."

I tiptoe to the edge of his bed and look down at him.

It is so nice to see him without his mask on. I could see him without it at night, of course, but during the day, all I could see was his square jaw and his mouth. Now, though, I get to take in all of him.

His face is still handsome, but pale. So pale.

"Has he lost a lot of blood?"

"Three bullet wounds will do that," Kari says.

When I gasp, she winces in apology. "Two of them are grazes, so it isn't quite as bad as it sounds."

I grip the side of the bed to keep standing, and Kari reaches out and pushes me back towards the second bed. "Sit down before you collapse. Like I said, I have to take care of him first before I can tend to you."

I'm too tired to argue. I sit on the hard mattress and watch her work. She cleans and disinfects and then grabs a suture thread and needle.

"Are you qualified to do this?" I ask. Not that we have any other options.

Kari nods and pulls aside the flaps of Luka's suit pants to reveal the wound in his thigh. It is gaping and bloody, and I can't look. "I was a surgical student. I transferred to the city to pursue better educational opportunities. It is part of the reason Edgar was interested in me at all. The Cartel needed in-house medical assistance."

Her hands are steady as she works and that is enough reason for me to trust her. In her position, I would be shaking like a leaf.

"There are ice packs in the cooler," she says, tipping her head towards the door. "If you need something for your bruises."

Mostly for something to do other than try not to pass out at the sight of my husband being operated on, I go to the cooler and pull out an ice pack.

The cooler is also full of blood bags.

"Will you need these?" I ask.

"He lost a lot of blood."

My stomach turns and I close the lid quickly, dropping down onto the mattress.

Now that I am out of immediate danger, my body is starting to ache. Bruises are forming across my arms and legs and deep muscle aches are starting to make themselves known. I can already tell that it will be excruciating by the morning.

"I guess you are dying to tell me you were right," I say. "That it was pointless to fight against the Cartel. That I should have just gone along with their rules and done my best to get out of the inn."

Kari doesn't answer me for so long that I think she must not have heard me. She snips the black thread coming out of Luka's leg and then runs an IV.

I don't want to think about the many different ways this operation could be unsanitary. I don't want to consider the possibility that Luka could survive a gunfight only to die of an infection. I have to trust that Kari knows what she is doing.

She rolls over a metal stand with little arms and hangs a blood bag from it. I look away as she begins the transfusion. When she is finished, she turns to her table and begins organizing her supplies, shifting things around. Finally, she crosses the room and stands in front of me.

I look up and see that she is holding something out to me. A scalpel.

"What is—"

Kari presses the blade into my hand and folds my fingers around it. "End them, Eve."

It takes me a minute to realize who she's talking about.

The Cartel. She wants me to take them down.

I shake my head. "I don't understand. You told me you've been here for years, that it would be better to just go along with them. What about our sorry state has made you change your mind?"

"Love," Kari says, rolling her eyes. "It sounds corny, but I have never seen two people more willing to fight for each other than the two of you. Edgar told me the truth about who you are to one another before I came in here. If you'd told me you were husband and wife from the start, I might have started supporting you sooner."

"I wish I'd known that," I say.

She shrugs. "After everything I've been through, I've learned to keep my expectations low, but after you survived a beating at the hands of Edgar and Luka was willing to take on every single Cartel guard to save you—well, there is a glimmer of hope."

I take the scalpel and lay it on the bed next to my thigh.

A girl and her scalpel versus the world. What could go wrong?

20

LUKA

There is pain, but mostly there is darkness.

Tiny blips of light make it through to me, but they are lost in another wave of nightmares and pain.

I see Eve and Milaya waving to me. I don't know where I am or where they are. As I walk towards them, they don't get any closer. I begin to run, but they remain out of reach. When I call out their names, begging Eve to walk towards me, my voice is swallowed up like I'm in the vacuum of space.

The only sound is my ragged breathing.

In and out.

In.

Out.

I sound like an old car chugging up a hill. Or a half-broken washing machine during a spin cycle.

There is a mechanical whirring noise that seems out of place, and no matter how hard I try to scream, nothing can drown out the sound.

Except the shots.

Gunfire cracks through the air, and I hit the ground, ducking from the shots.

I call out for Eve and Milaya, but again, they can't hear me.

When I search for them, they are gone. Where they were standing is only a puddle of blood.

"How is he doing?"

The deep voice comes from above me and around me, and I spin but can't find it.

Then, suddenly, I'm back in my body.

My eyes are still closed, far too heavy to open, but I know I'm awake because of the pain.

It is everywhere, rippling through my body in a constant current but also coming from somewhere deeper. Somewhere in my core, like the pain is being created there and sent to the rest of my nerves. I try to move, but my legs are strapped down. Even if they weren't, I don't think I'd have the strength to pick them up.

"He'll live."

Through the haze of pain, I'm able to recognize the voice of the woman who has been helping Eve every morning. Kari, I think.

"He is lucky," she says. "The shot to the leg is the worst. The others are grazes."

"Our guys need to work on their aim," the deep voice says. He is probably a Cartel member. One of the guards who shot me, maybe. Or one who dragged Eve away. "Hey, buddy, wake up. Edgar wants to see you."

I hear shuffling footsteps. I want to get up and chase after them, demand to know where Eve is. What happened to her?

Did they kill her?

The thought hurts worse than any of my wounds, but still I can't move. Can't speak. Can't do anything but lie here feeling useless.

I hear the door open and close, and I know I'm too late. The opportunity has passed.

Then, I slip back into the darkness.

When I wake up again, I'm shivering.

I'm cold everywhere. So cold most of my body feels numb, and for a second I have the terrifying thought that I'm dying.

Eve and Milaya are gone, maybe dead, and I'm dying in a room at a shitty inn under the watch of Cartel members who want to skin me alive.

Then, I feel the cold shift down my back like it is a living thing, crawling down my body. I flinch.

"Luka?"

The sound of her voice, even scratchy and sleepy, is like music to me. For the first time in I don't know how long, I open my eyes and turn towards the sound of it.

Eve is lying next to me. Her face is splotchy and bruised, one of her eyes swollen until it is almost shut. But she is smiling.

"Luka, you're okay."

I reach out and grab a strand of her hair, more to tell myself that she is indeed real and not a figment of my imagination.

Then, I look down and see the ice pack pressed between our bodies. It is wedged between her ribs, which are clearly black and blue, and my side where a large bloody bandage is taped down.

"Are you too cold?" She pulls the ice pack from between us, showcasing even more of her bruises.

I frown. "What did they do to you?"

She shakes her head. "It doesn't matter. You almost died."

"Just grazes," I say. "That is what Kari said."

"You could hear her?"

I nod. "A little."

"Then you must have heard her talk about the shot to your leg."

I look down and see an especially large bandage across my thigh. I'm still wearing pants, but the right leg has been cut up to my hip.

"Kari thinks she got the fragments out, but it could be fractured. She doesn't know."

"I feel fine," I lie, shifting slightly on the bed. The slight movement sends a burst of pain shooting up my leg and through my core. I tense and Eve sees it.

"You filthy liar."

I smile and then lift her chin with my finger, bringing her towards me. "Why did you lie for me?"

She leans forward until her nose touches mine, shaking her head to brush them together. "Because I love you."

Our lips press together softly as though it is the first time. I reach out and cup her face, curling my fingers behind her ear. When I drag my hand down her neck and across her waist, she winces.

I pull back and look at her. The bruising is even worse than I thought.

"What did he do to you?" I growl, tracing the swollen purple bruises down her ribs and across her back.

Eve relays the torture, explaining in minimal detail how Edgar abused her. Every slap she narrates is like I'm getting shot all over again. Before she's finished, I'm shaking all over with bloodlust.

I'm going to kill the motherfucker who hurt my wife.

"I'm sorry." I close my eyes and shake my head. "I should have been there."

She grabs my face and kisses me. "You tried to be. That is what matters."

I try to believe her, but my failures seem to be stacking up. Time and time again, I have let my family be hurt, and I can't help but feel like I'm not doing my job.

"You need to rest," she says, lying down on the small bed next to me and draping her arm across my chest. "I don't know when they'll come for us, and we both need to be as strong as we can."

I try to imagine fighting with this broken, battered body, and I can't imagine it. I'm terrified that, once again, I'm going to have to sit uselessly by while my wife is pulled from my arms and dragged away.

Eve sits up, her hand over my heart. "Calm down. Rest."

"Are we going to get out of here?" Perhaps if I was stronger I wouldn't ask the question, but I'm not, so I do.

Eve's eyes flutter, going glassy, and she nods. "Of course we are. We are going to get out of here, get our daughter, and go home. I am going to make steak au poivre with pommes frites while you fill the glasses with our best wine."

She explains the perfect night together, and I can see it all clearly in my head as I drift off to sleep.

Once sleep has me, however, the images shift.

Instead of steak, there is human flesh. Instead of pommes frites, there are bones.

One by one, I'm taking out the Cartel members, all the while recounting everything they've done to my family.

Every horrible thing they've done to deserve this punishment.

I save Rian Morrison for last. I laugh as she screams.

There is no way to know what time it is when I wake up, but I feel better.

Not good. Not even okay. Just *better*.

It hurts as I sit up, and I look over and see Eve asleep next to me. Her face is even more swollen than before. Purple bruises with green around the edges cover her cheek and the skin around her eye.

Still, she is beautiful.

I want to reach out and brush her hair behind her ear, but I don't want to wake her. Not yet. If I did, she would stop me from doing what I'm about to do.

Shoving away my fear of the pain, I swing both my legs off the bed and set my feet on the floor.

It comes like a train speeding towards me, slamming into my chest all at once. Pain explodes inside of me, hot and pulsating.

But then it recedes.

I squeeze my eyes shut and wait as it becomes a dull roar in the back of my mind.

When I stand up, the pain comes again, but the pressure of my foot against the floor seems to stabilize it in a way. It sharpens the pain so it is relegated to just my right leg, making it marginally more bearable.

When I take a step, however, my vision goes black around the edges.

Immediately, I shift my weight to my good leg.

Will I have a limp? Like Joel Foli? In a sick way, it seems ironic.

But a limp is the least of my worries now. Getting out of here alive seems like priority number one.

With every step, I feel more capable. The pain doesn't ease at all, but I grow more accustomed to it. Rather than being surprised by each wave, I'm able to anticipate it, grit my teeth, and move through it.

Not quickly, mind you, but I can do it.

"What are you doing?"

Eve's voice catches me off guard, and it is lucky I'm near the wall because I have to throw out an arm to keep myself from falling over.

Eve is out of bed and at my side in a second. "You should not be walking around. Why didn't you wake me up?"

She took the robe off earlier, leaving her in nothing but a black lacy bra and matching panties. Under other circumstances, I would already have her pinned against the wall, the lacy scraps flying through the air.

I lean down, ignoring the blast of pain brought on by the position, and kiss her forehead. "Because I knew you wouldn't let me walk around."

"You need to be resting," she says.

"I have been. Now, I need to get stronger."

She shakes her head. "It's too soon."

"We don't have time."

I can tell by the furrow of her brow she wants to argue, but she can't. She knows I'm right. Neither of us knows how much longer we have before Edgar or any of the guards come back for us.

I turn to walk back towards the bed and see two water bottles and a hunk of bread sitting on the metal operating tray. "Do you want a drink?"

The water is room temperature and covered in condensation, so I know it was left a while ago.

When I try to hand it to Eve, she hesitates. "What's wrong?"

"At the ranch," she says. "The Morrisons' house. They gave me water but it was drugged. It knocked me out. They held me down and forced it down my throat."

I file that away as another reason why I'm going to rip Rian Morrison limb from limb.

"I'll take a drink first," I say, twisting the cap off. The bottle was still sealed, which seems like a good sign.

Eve watches nervously as I drink half the bottle, and then helps me walk back towards the bed. After several minutes when I'm still awake and feeling fine, she drinks the other half of the bottle.

"It only took a minute or two for the drugs to take effect," she says. "These must just be normal bottles."

"Whatever they have planned, they don't want us unconscious," I say, unsure whether that is a good or bad sign.

We break the bread apart and share it, but Eve insists I take some of hers. "You are bigger than I am. You need more calories."

"But you are hurt," I say.

She points to my leg. "So are you. Worse than me. *Eat.*"

I listen to her and then lie back on the bed, holding out an arm for her to snuggle into.

"You are stronger than I ever thought," I whisper into her hair. "I always knew you were stubborn and brave, but I had no idea you could endure so much. That you could fight so hard."

"Honestly, neither did I," she says. "I didn't know I could do it until I had to."

"You tried to explain it to me at the beginning of the week, but I didn't get it. Not until now." I kiss her temple. "I'm sorry."

Eve shakes her head. "Don't apologize. You are the reason I'm strong at all."

I think back on the last few days. On how weak I've felt. How helpless and small, and I shake my head. "No, you always had it in you."

"That's true," she says. "But I found it because of you. Because of how you lead our family with such strength. You made me realize that I have that inside of me, too. When I needed strength these last few weeks, I thought of you and Milaya. Doing that helped me get through whatever was happening. You two made me strong."

"I love you," I whisper, pulling her close to me. "And I'm sorry you had to be strong."

Eve sits up and tucks her legs underneath her, resting on her heels. "Please don't be sorry. You are here. You came for me and for Milaya and that is what matters. When Edgar was torturing me, all I could think about is that I would have done the exact same thing you did if you'd been taken. You knew where I was, and you came for me. I shouldn't have ever made you feel bad about that."

I don't realize how much I need to hear her say those words until she says them.

I reach out for her, touching her waist tenderly, letting my fingers slip against her bare skin and higher until the black lace of her bra is under my thumb.

She looks down at my thumb and lifts an eyebrow. "Are you serious right now?"

I shrug. "I can't help it. You look good."

"You can barely walk," she says, biting back a smile.

"Luckily," I whisper, walking my fingers around to the clasp on her back. "I can lie down for this."

When I unclip her bra, Eve lets the straps slide down her arms slowly, her breasts pushed together from her position. I try to sit up so I can kiss them, but the pain is too much. Eve presses me back against the headboard and then straddles me, her knees on either side of my hips, hovering over me.

"Are you sure?" she asks. "You are hurt. I don't want to—"

I grab her face and bring her lips down to me, silencing her protests. She goes fluid against me, arching her body into my chest, and I know she wants this as much as I do.

We move slowly, caressing each other with gentle fingers and soft kisses. Eve unzips my pants and wraps her hand around my length, and for the first time in hours, I feel something besides pain.

Pleasure builds in my abdomen like a small fire and with every stroke, Eve adds another log.

I grip her waist, doing my best to avoid her bruises. When I slip my hand between her legs and push aside her panties, she freezes, pouty lips parting so seductively I think it might finish me right here and now. She lets out tiny breaths with each stroke of my finger and it isn't long before she is circling her hips against my hand.

As soon as I pull my finger away, Eve positions me at her opening and slides onto me in one stroke.

Her weight on my lap isn't much, but it's enough for me to remember the wound to my leg. Still, pleasure wins, and I dig my hands into her hips and pull her down onto me over and over again.

It isn't our best sex, but being with her in a way that feels normal and good is exactly what I need.

She circles her body over me, arching her back and riding me gently.

I hold back as long as I can, but when she presses her body close to me, her breath hot against my neck, and moans that she is coming, I let go.

We fall apart together, sweaty and bruised and grasping for the last seconds of relief before reality crashes down over us.

21

EVE

They come for us a few minutes after I put my clothes back on.

I'm sitting on the bed next to Luka. He is bare-chested, his pant leg split up to his hip, and his bandages looking close to needing to be changed when the door bursts open.

Faster than I think should be possible in his state, Luka is on his feet, jaw clenched.

"Don't you all know how to knock?"

The guards clearly have no interest in banter as they walk directly to my side of the bed and grab my arms.

I'm too stunned to move.

Luka and I just talked about how strong I am, but as the guards approach, all I can think about is that this could be the last time I see Luka. That could have been the last time we ever have sex. I might never get to speak to him again.

"Don't touch her!" Luka roars, hurtling over the bed and throwing himself at one of the guards.

I scream and try to help him as much as I can, thrashing my arms and legs to make it more difficult to hold onto me, but the guards barely move. They are so much stronger than me. And right now, they are stronger than Luka, too.

The guard brushes Luka aside like he is nothing. He falls on the floor and cries out when he lands on his leg.

If it wasn't fractured before, it probably is now.

"I love you!" I yell at him over the din of the room. "I love you."

If this is the last time we are together, I want him to know. I want him to know how I feel. That I don't regret anything.

That I don't regret him.

Luka doesn't answer, but drags himself to his feet using the end of the bed and throws himself forward again.

This time, the guard is visibly annoyed. He sighs and lets go of my arm to deal with Luka, but Luka's attack must be more than he expected because the guard stumbles back as Luka collides with his chest.

Then, Luka rears back and throws a fist, and the man doubles over with a groan as the punch hits its mark.

"Shit," the guard still holding me mumbles. He doesn't look panicked, but he is surprised.

I spin around as fast as I can and knee him in the crotch.

His entire body clenches, and his face twists into agony. "Fuck."

I bring my knee back to hit him again, but the guard is too fast. He wraps an arm around my chest, pressing in on a bruise on my arm, and crushes me against him. Then, I feel the cool kiss of metal at my temple.

"I'll fucking shoot her right here."

The noise in the room goes quiet.

Luka and the guard separate.

Luka is breathing heavily, his arms hanging down like he doesn't have the energy to stand up—he probably doesn't. And the guard is adjusting his uniform and checking that he still has his own gun hidden at his hip. He pulls it and points it at Luka.

"Stay back or we'll kill you both."

When Luka looks at me, I see heartbreak in his eyes.

It is unlike anything I have ever seen on his face before. It is a level of agony I've never witnessed, and I can only imagine it is the expression he wore the night he realized Milaya and I had been taken.

I hope to never see the expression again.

And then I let a sob wrack through my chest, realizing I very well may not. I may not see any expression on his face again.

Not the tilt of his brow when he is amused, or that half smirk he wears when he is trying to pretend he is angry but is actually fighting a smile. I may not see the flare in his eyes as I walk towards him naked. I may not ever again see the smile he saves for Milaya when he's singing her to sleep every night.

I may never see this beautiful man again, and something in my chest cracks wide open.

"I love you," Luka finally says. "I love you so much."

The guard kicks him in the chest, sending him sprawling back on the floor and writhing in pain.

As the two men pull me out of the room, I try to look back and see him one more time, but I only catch a glimpse of his legs sprawled next to the bed before the door slams closed and is locked from the outside.

I'm led to the entry hall of the inn where Edgar is waiting.

He has on a crisp black suit, looking like he is headed to a funeral.

For all I know, he might be.

The men stop a few feet from Edgar, and when he nods to each of the guards, they let me go and step away at once.

"Prepare the slaves for transfer," Edgar says.

I can't believe I ever thought Edgar was a small man. A weak man.

He *is* small, but only physically. Now, after everything he has put me and Luka through, I realize how tall he holds himself. Edgar's shoulders are broad, chin lifted, body relaxed. He is the kind of man with obvious power, but I missed it before. I underestimated him before.

I won't make that mistake again.

"Good news," Edgar says, clapping his hands together in front of him. "Despite your little show yesterday, you have been purchased."

My heart sinks like a stone in my chest, but I do my best not to let him see.

"Arnold McGowan," he says, answering the question I didn't have the voice to ask. He nods his head towards the lounge, and I turn to see a middle-aged man in a dark green mask staring at me.

I remember seeing him, but he never stood out the way the other men did. He never expressed any interest in me, so I paid him no mind.

I can see the interest now.

Even with his mask on, I can see the hunger in his eyes.

I wonder how much he paid for me. Though, really, I don't want to know.

Somewhere in the back of the inn a door opens, and I hear the whisper of tears and sobs.

The women are back there, getting ready to be transported. That is what Edgar sent the men to do.

The auction is over.

I didn't save myself or anyone else. It still happened. The women were sold. I was sold.

It is over.

I expect hopelessness to press in and wash everything else away, but instead, I'm just angry.

Angry that these people think they have the right to pluck people from their lives and make a profit from them.

Angry that my family was broken apart and separated because of an embittered feud.

Angry that Edgar looks at me like I'm no more than a dog who should learn to behave.

"You will go with him without fighting," Edgar says. "If you do fight, it will only bring more heartache for you. The Cartel does not offer returns, but Arnold has been instructed that should he wish to be done with you, you cannot be freed."

The front door is still open, and a gentle breeze rolls in over the grass.

It seems unfair that such horrible things could be happening on an otherwise beautiful day. I look past him to the rolling grass behind him and the tree line beyond that.

I wonder when I will see the sky again or feel a breeze. Will Arnold be a kind master? Will I be allowed to go outside and see the world? Or will I be trapped in a basement and left to waste away?

How long will it take before I lose my hold on sanity?

As Edgar continues outlining the many different ways I could be disposed of to ensure I do not run and tell the police of my experience in their custody, I see a shadow separate from the tree line behind him.

Like a large bird, the black figure pulls away from the trees and it takes me several seconds to recognize the creature is not a creature at all, but a vehicle. A black SUV.

And behind it is a similar vehicle. And another.

A line of SUVs drives through the trees and up the dirt road that leads to the inn.

And they are driving fast.

Edgar's brow furrows. He hears the sound of the tires crunching across the gravel, but he wasn't expecting anyone. Certainly not this many people.

He turns around and curses under his breath, and I realize all at once who it is.

Luka told the Bratva we would be at the inn for five days. It has been just over the one hundred and twenty hours he told them to wait, and he still hasn't been in touch.

So, here they are to save us.

While Edgar is staring at the cars, Arnold McGowan moves from the lounge into the entryway. "Who is that?"

"Guards!" Edgar yells over his shoulder.

While he is distracted, I reach down and run my finger along the hem of my robe. When I feel the touch of cool metal against my fingertips,

I wrap my fingers around the blade and tug. The suture thread Kari used to sew the blade into my robe tears easily.

Edgar turns back to yell down the hallway again—the sound of the women crying in the back room is loud enough that the guards must not be able to hear him—but before any sound can come out, I take a deep breath, lean forward ...

And plunge the scalpel into his neck exactly where Luka taught me to.

His flesh gives way easily beneath the sharpened edge. Blood pumps from the wound in rhythmic pulses, drenching me up to the elbow.

Edgar's mouth opens and closes like a fish desperate for air, and then he drops to his knees. His hand comes up to his neck, but it is far too late to stop the bleeding. Even if an entire surgical staff was standing in the room, they wouldn't be able to help him.

In a few more pumps, he will have lost most of the blood in his body.

A few weak pumps after that, and he'll be dead.

I feel a sick pride. Even if they kill me now, at least I'll have fulfilled my promise.

I step back to avoid the blood pooling on the wood floor, and Arnold McGowan yells and jumps back. "What in the fuck did you do?"

The SUVs are lined up in the grass outside the inn, and men I recognize—men without masks on—are moving towards the inn, guns raised.

I move to step out onto the porch, but there is a hand around my neck, holding me back. I sputter for breath as Arnold McGowan yanks me back inside.

"You are mine. I bought you," he growls. "You are coming with me."

He tries to take me back down the hallway, but I can see Grigory moving towards the front door of the inn. I am so close to being rescued. I can't stop fighting now.

I thrash, throwing my entire weight in every direction so Arnold has to use both arms to hold onto me.

He wraps his arms around my middle, picking me up off my feet, but he doesn't have my arms pinned to my side, and I still have the scalpel.

He realizes this after it is already too late.

I slash the blade across his neck just as he lets go of me.

I drop to the floor, pain roaring through my tailbone, but it has to be better than Arnold feels. Blood is spurting from his neck, not quite as lethally as it did from Edgar's, but it still isn't good.

Arnold stumbles away, clutching at his neck, but his hands grow slippery with blood.

"Eve."

I turn and see Grigory and four other men standing in the entryway. He gestures me aside with his weapon, lifts it, and pulls the trigger.

Arnold drops to the floor behind me, lifeless.

I run towards my friends, my family. "Luka is in there somewhere. And there are a bunch of women in red and purple dresses. They are innocent. Don't hurt them. But find Luka."

Luka, Luka, Luka.

His name is my heartbeat, my only purpose.

I understand how he felt now. When I asked him to save the other women, when I insisted it was important, he told me he cared about nothing but me. I couldn't understand it in the moment, but I see it now. I feel it.

If I left this inn with just Luka, it would be okay. I would survive.

Without him, though? I'm not sure. I can't imagine how my body would go on if he wasn't in the world.

"I need a gun." I spin around and hold out a hand to the men. "Now."

Grigory looks from me to the men around him and then back. "We have guns. Stick close to us and—"

"My husband is your leader, and I just gave you a direct order," I hiss. "So give me a fucking gun."

Grigory stiffens, then half bows before nodding to the skinny man on his side. I recognize him as a newer recruit. This is probably one of his first missions. He looks disappointed as he hands me his gun and heads back out to the SUV, but I don't mind. He'll have plenty more.

As for me, I hope it will be my last.

I tiptoe through Edgar's blood to grab the keys from his inside jacket pocket. Then, Grigory goes in front of me, listening as I direct him to the small room in the servants' quarters where Luka and I were being held.

As soon as the door opens, Luka lunges forward, holding the metal table over his head. He swings it, and I see the moment he recognizes the men in front of him as his own.

He throws his weight to the side quickly, barely missing Grigory, and nearly falls over.

"Shit, it is good to see you," he says, limping to a standing position. "Where is Eve? Is she—"

I step forward, and Luka wraps me in his arms.

I can hear the men moving further down the hallway towards the sound of the women screaming. There are gunshots and cries of both pain and terror. But it all fades away as I stretch onto my toes and kiss him.

"We're going to get out of here," I whisper against his mouth, tears pooling in my eyes.

I blink them back and hold my gun with two hands.

He nods and echoes my words. "We are going to get out of here."

Luka makes like he is going to grab my gun, but then he thinks better of it and asks another of the Bratva members for his. He hands it over immediately.

"We have to get out of here," Luka says.

I follow him for a second before I stop and pull away. "I need to go see if the women are okay."

"Eve," Luka groans. "Let the men handle it."

I shake my head. "They are terrified. But if they see me, they may come with us. They will trust us more. I have to go check on them."

"We need to make sure every member of the Cartel left in this building is dead," Luka says.

"Then go. I will meet you when it is over."

He stares at me, his green eyes wide and searching.

I pray I'm not going to have to fight him on this. That I'm not going to have to tell him once again that I can handle this. By now, I hope I have shown him that I can.

Luka steps forward, wraps a hand around my neck, and pulls me to his lips. The kiss is quick but fierce. He presses his forehead to mine once and then pulls away. "I'll meet you when it is over."

On his way out the door, he tells Grigory and a few other men to stick close to me, and I don't mind. I want the backup.

Luka turns left and heads back towards the entryway while I go right, towards the sound of the dying gunfire.

By the time we get to the main holding room where all of the slaves were held the first day we were brought to the inn, the men in the Bratva are making small circles and checking corners for anyone they could have missed.

The women are nowhere to be seen.

With Grigory just behind me, I go through the back door and out onto the gravel behind the inn.

It is not meant for guests—just a loading and unloading zone with white vans scattered around, several of which have bullet holes in the sides.

I bend down, looking under the nearest van and then the one after that.

Have the guards already delivered all of the women? Are they gone? Am I too late?

Then, I hear a shift of the gravel. It could have come from me or Grigory walking around, but my instincts tell me otherwise. I walk around the corner of the building and see one final car parallel parked along a shallow curb. Peeking over the hood I see a flash of curly red hair.

"Maddie?"

The girl jerks upright, her blue eyes peering at me from behind the car. And then, in an instant, Maddie is running towards me like I'm the last life vest on a sinking ship.

She slams into me hard enough that every single one of my bruises complains, but I ignore it and hug her back with my free arm. "How many of you are left?"

"Some of the women were already gone when the men arrived," she says through a cascade of tears. "We didn't know who they were, but they were killing the guards, so we just ran."

"They are good guys," I say.

Technically, they are criminals, but in this situation, they are heroes. Absolute heroes.

Three other women crawl out from behind the car, crouching low. They are numbers ten through thirteen.

Four women out of thirteen.

It is better than nothing, but not what I hoped for. I wish I could have done more.

"Stay with them," I say to Vito, a short, bald man with a tattoo of a snake across his neck. "I'll send someone back to have you bring them to the front when it is clear. Protect them."

Maddie is reluctant to let me go, but as protective as I feel over her, I have my own daughter to worry about now.

Luka and I might get out of here alive, but the Cartel still has our baby girl.

I have to make sure Luka is okay, and then we have to get her back.

There is no other option.

22

LUKA

Dead bodies are scattered across the hallways and the stairwell. Blood drips down the walls and saturates the carpets, filling the air with the scent of iron.

We move slowly through the inn as we have a thousand warehouses, drug dens, and stash houses before, but there is no movement. No sound.

I think the Cartel members may all be dead.

Then, as I move to leave the lounge, I hear the sound of a wooden cabinet door closing.

It is a soft thud, just a whisper, but in the silence, every noise is amplified.

I turn and see the bar cart behind me. One of the half-full bottles resting on the edge is sloshing slightly. Enough to let me know it was recently disturbed.

I hold my finger to my lips and limp towards it.

Silently, I count to three, and then wrench the doors open.

Kari's pale blonde head is the first thing I see, but it is enough. Her hands are held up in surrender, and she is shaking all over.

I lower my gun and kneel down on my good leg. "Kari?"

She looks up, blinking. "Luka?"

I'm not even halfway through reassuring her she is safe and we won't hurt her before she scrambles out and clasps her hands together as if in prayer. "I'm sorry. I want out of here. I worked for the Cartel but only because I had to. I'm not one of them. Please take me with you. Please."

She is talking so fast I can hardly understand her, but I understand enough. She wants out.

"You saved my life," I say, laying a hand over hers. "I don't blame you for anything that happened here."

She nods but still pulls away from me.

I can understand that. After everything she has been through, I wouldn't want to be too close to a man, either.

Eve had such compassion for these women, and while I still find it difficult to fully empathize, I'm trying. I want to take care of Kari the way Eve would. The way Eve would want me to.

Kari stays close to me as we finish our sweep of the first floor. A few men come from upstairs and tell us that floor is clear, too.

The Cartel is dead.

Or gone, at least.

Edgar is lying in the hallway, a gaping wound in his neck, and I have a feeling it's from Eve. Part of me is disappointed, but part of me is proud, too. If I couldn't be the one to kill him, I wanted it to be her.

Suddenly, there are footsteps coming down the hallway, and I turn to see Eve, Grigory, and a few other Bratva soldiers jogging down the hallway. When Eve sees me, she visibly relaxes.

"Thank God."

We embrace quickly, and then she turns to Kari. "Are you all right?"

The woman wraps her arm around Eve, clearly more comfortable in her presence than in mine. "I'm fine. I think I'm free."

"You are," Eve says, grabbing her hands. "You are free."

Eve leads us all back down the hallway. I follow along, but my leg is starting to hurt more and more with every step. Soon, I won't be able to go on. I need to sit down and soon.

We pass the servants' quarters and go through a back door to a gravel alley behind the inn.

Maddie and three other women are standing there with Vito. He has an arm around a trembling Maddie, comforting her so effectively the two of them don't even look up as we approach.

"The Cartel is gone," Eve announces.

Maddie squeals in happiness and turns to embrace Vito. He awkwardly pats her on the back, shrugging at Grigory, but he leans into the hug when he thinks no one is watching.

"What do we do now?" Kari asks.

"Do whatever you want," Eve says. She digs in her pocket and finds a ring of keys. "Take one of the cars and get out of here. All of you."

"I can go home?" Maddie asks.

Eve nods gently. "You can. If you want. But you don't have to."

"What other option do we have?" a brunette woman asks.

Eve asks a member of the Bratva for a pen and uses the back of a business card from one of the cars to scribble our number on the back of it. "Call me if you need anything. But there are resources in the city for you. Safe houses and charities. There are organizations that will help you find a job and keep you off the streets."

I walk over to the building and rest on a wooden crate, stretching my injured leg out in front of me while Eve talks to the women. After a few minutes, they all seem eager to leave. Kari hugs Eve, waves to me, and thanks the other men for saving them. Then, she leads the other women to the SUV.

Eve watches the dust settle behind where the SUV disappeared through the trees, and then she comes to find me.

"What now?" she asks.

I nod to the back door. "Unfortunately, we have to clean up."

"I thought there were people for that kind of thing."

I think of Rick Koban and how he would feel about the Volkov Bratva taking down this cell of the LeClerc Cartel. As a past attendee of one of their auctions, I'm not sure he'd approve. Besides, I have a better idea.

Eve and I walk into the building hand in hand. When my limp worsens, she loops her arm around my waist and helps me to the entryway. I nod to where Edgar is going cold on the floor.

"Was that you?"

She nods, her face pale. "It was. Both of them."

I notice the second man lying in the doorway between the entryway and the hallway. I don't recognize him until I see his green mask lying on the floor next to him. He stayed pretty quiet all week, but that doesn't mean he didn't deserve to die for what he wanted to do to Eve.

"This entire place makes me sick," Eve says. "I know the Cartel was only using it for the weekend, but it feels tainted now."

"Well, it won't be here for long."

She looks at me, brow furrowed. "What are we going to do?"

I dig in the pocket of my ruined pants and pull out my lighter. "We're going to burn it down."

It makes the most sense. Not only do I want to torch the building that represents a week of hell for my family, but getting rid of all of these bodies will be a headache. This way, we can take care of two birds with one fiery stone.

"Won't someone call the police?" she asks.

"Not if we call in a favor with our contacts at the emergency call center. Plus, this place is far enough out that anyone who sees the smoke will think a farmer is burning his fields."

Eve spins in a circle, looking around the inn. When she turns to face me again, her jaw is set. "Let's do it."

Just then, the Bratva members come in with a few jugs of gasoline and fire starter from the maintenance shed. Eve takes one of the containers, I take another, and together, we walk through the inn and douse the place.

Eve covers the servants' quarters, splashing a little extra across the backs of the fallen Cartel members. I douse the floor of the lounge where we spent four days playing along with the Cartel's sick games. And Eve and I both pour out the last of our containers in the entryway, the last drops falling on Edgar's back.

Once everyone is outside, I flick my lighter and toss it through the front door of the inn.

The flames catch immediately in a whoosh of heat and air, and I hurry off the porch, not wanting to risk second- or third-degree burns on top of gunshot wounds.

Eve is standing in the grass, looking up at the inn, and I'm amazed once again at how strong she is.

When I married her, I knew she was stubborn. I knew she stood up to me more than any other woman ever had, and I knew she spoke her mind.

I didn't know, however, that she could carry so much. I didn't know she could shoulder the burden of protecting our family. I didn't know that when I was at my weakest, she would rise up and battle our demons.

And more than anything, I didn't know it was possible to love her more than I did a week ago.

As I approach, she turns to me, eyes bloodshot and tired. "Are we done?"

"A few of the men will stay to make sure the flames don't go out," I say, offering her my outstretched hand. "Let's go find our daughter."

As soon as we are in the SUV and driving away from the flames, I borrow a random Bratva phone and begin making calls. To everyone and anyone who could help.

I reach out to every brigadier and tell them to put all of their men on high alert. They need to be on the lookout for any possible child trafficking by the Irish or the LeClerc Cartel, and someone needs to get eyes on Rian Morrison immediately. She left the inn before the Bratva arrived, and I don't want her to skip town before Eve and I have our chance to get revenge.

While I'm on the phone, Eve fidgets with the skimpy robe and the fashion boots the Cartel forced her to wear. She looks like she is about to crawl out of her skin, but she also looks exhausted.

Dark circles are pressed under her eyes, and she is slumped forward like it is too difficult to hold herself upright.

When I hang up the phone, I slide carefully across the seat to sit next to her, my leg warm against hers. "Why don't you go back to the house?"

She opens her mouth to argue, but I lay a hand on her leg and continue. "I know you want to help, and you can, but maybe you should rest first."

"You're the one who is hurt," she says.

"So are you. Plus, you did so much back there. You fought hard, and no one would blame you if you rested. Even just for a few hours. I have every single resource at our disposal out looking for Milaya. If she can be found, we'll find her."

Eve shakes her head. "If?"

"Bad choice of words," I correct. "She is out there. I know it."

Eve turns to stare out the window, her long chestnut hair draped over her shoulder. The ends are tangled, and I think I see a bit of dried blood in the ends, but I don't want to check.

When she turns back to me, her forehead is wrinkled in thought. "Rian told me something yesterday—or a few days ago, whenever it was. It is hard to keep the days straight."

"What?"

"She said ..." Eve pauses, tilting her head to the side before looking up at me. "She said a baby would sell for a lot on the black market. Which means she hadn't sold her yet. She still had her."

"Or she was just trying to torment you?" I offer.

Eve shrugs. "Maybe, but if that was the case, why wouldn't she tell me Milaya had been sold or killed?"

The idea makes both of us shiver with dread, and then Eve shakes her head. "No, I think she let a little bit of her plan slip. I think they still have Milaya."

I want to believe Eve more than anything. I want to believe that Milaya is fine and well, simply being looked after by strangers. But that kind of hopeful thinking is dangerous. If I let myself or Eve believe Milaya is perfectly unharmed, it will make it even more devastating if something has happened to her.

Still, I can't bring myself to question Eve's theory. "Maybe."

Eve sits up a bit straighter. "Rian's comment makes it seem like she has direct say over what happens to Milaya, but she is far too busy to take care of her herself. There is no way Rian would bring Milaya with her to the auction. So, someone else has to be watching her. Someone close to Rian."

I nod along, growing slightly more convinced the more she explains. "So, Milaya would be near Rian, but being taken care of by someone else? Maybe someone within the Irish?"

"Maybe," Eve nods, leaning forward, elbows on her knees as she thinks. Then, suddenly, she sits bolt upright and turns to me, brown eyes wide. "I know where she is."

"Okay, hold on." I lay a hand on her back. "We can't jump to conclusions. I have my guys out looking for any signs of her. If you have a theory, I'll pass it along and have someone else follow up on it. Then, we can go from there."

Eve shakes her head firmly. "No, I know where she is, Luka."

Again, I don't want her to get her hopes up, but I also can't bear to douse the fire I see in her eyes. "Where is she?"

"Rian would have wanted Milaya close to her, but wouldn't want to take care of her," Eve repeated. "Well, when I was being held before the auction, I was kept in the Morrisons' ranch. Rian and her father both came in at different times to give me water and drugs, but I never saw her mother."

"Rian's mother?" I ask.

Eve nods. "I asked about her once, but Rian's father told me it wasn't any of my business. Well, what if she's the one taking care of Milaya?"

I think about it for a few seconds, but Eve leans over and grabs my arm. "What do you think?"

"I think it's a theory," I admit. "Not flawless, but we aren't exactly spoiled for good ideas right now."

"It's a good one," Eve says. She squeezes my arm harder. "Are we going to go there now?"

I sigh and turn towards her, wincing as my leg twinges. "I think you should let the Bratva handle it from here. You've been through a lot and—"

"And my daughter is still out there with our enemies," she says, face blank. "She is being held prisoner, and I am going to be the one to save her."

I want to argue. I want to tell Eve that she should go home and wait for word. That she should sit back and let me and the other men handle it.

But then I remember how fierce she was at the inn. How in control and calm under pressure she was. How ruthless she was towards our enemies.

I can't deny her the opportunity to save her daughter. I certainly wouldn't allow myself to be locked away in our house while she or anyone else went to find Milaya. I can't ask Eve to do the same thing.

Finally, I nod.

"Yes?" Eve asks, sitting at the edge of her seat.

"Yes," I say. "You are an asset, and I want you there with me."

Before I can finish the sentence, Eve throws her arms around my neck. Then, she collapses against my chest and begins to shake with sobs. "We are going to get our daughter back."

I rub her back and hope to God she is right.

23

EVE

Cole's parents wanted grandchildren.

I remember them mentioning it the first time I was at their house.

Rian is so busy, I'm not sure she'll ever settle down and give us grandchildren, his mother said. *But I knew our Cole would find himself a pretty wife to start a family with.*

That is why his family could sell me off to the Cartel the way they did. To them, I was nothing more than a pretty woman meant to bear children. And even worse, I failed to do that for their family, so why not chain me up and strip me of my freedom? I deserved it in their eyes.

Rian's dad mentioned something about grandchildren when I was at the ranch before being taken to the inn. *You could have given us the grandchildren we always wanted.*

The more I think about it, the more obvious it is.

Of course, Rian's parents would take Milaya. While I disappointed them and disrespected them and took their son away from them,

Milaya was innocent and perfect and beautiful. Of course they would take her from me as payment for what Luka and I did to Cole.

Luka has the driver of the SUV pull over so he can organize our men. He sends every Bratva member we have to the ranch, and I can't express how grateful I am to him for taking me seriously. For letting me come with him.

If anything good came out of the last week at the inn, it is that I feel more capable now than ever to stand up to the villains in my life.

I spent my entire childhood and most of my adulthood being terrified of my father's wrath. Being afraid of disappointing him or earning his anger. Now, however, I am free.

I believe in myself. I trust my own mind and opinions. And more than anything, I trust my own strength—both mental and physical.

I am capable of more than my father ever thought possible. More than I ever thought possible.

And I don't intend to ever be held back again.

When Luka gets off the phone, he turns towards me, and I see the flare of pain in his face as his leg shifts.

I'm worried about him.

About infection, about whether he will be able to walk into the ranch and walk out again with injuries so extensive.

But just as he isn't doubting me, I have no intention of doubting him. Our relationship has to be built on mutual trust or it will never last.

"What is the plan?" I ask.

"Everyone is on board," Luka says. "They've been looking since the minute I left for the auction. But they didn't find anything. Not even a whisper. They agree that your idea has the most merit."

"So, we are going now?" I ask, leg bouncing with nervous energy.

Luka told me I should go back to the mansion and rest, but there is no way I could sleep.

I'm exhausted. I feel it deep down in my bones in a way I've never felt tired before. But there is no way I could sleep. Not when my baby is far away from me and with strangers.

I won't be able to sleep until she is home.

Luka nods. "We are going now. Everyone is headed there. We are going to meet on the old highway just outside the ranch and just like they did at the inn, we are all going to approach together. The Morrisons won't have time to run even if they do see us coming."

I reach across the seat and squeeze his hand, gripping his fingers to help ground myself as we drive towards the ranch. Towards the place where we will hopefully find out daughter.

The mission is rushed and disorganized, but there isn't time for more.

Rian could be receiving word right this minute that the Cartel at the inn was decimated. She might guess that Luka and I have escaped and are coming for her. There is no time to waste formulating a plan of attack. If we do, we might get there to find the Morrisons and Milaya are already gone.

I pray they are still there.

I pray Milaya is with them.

As we drive towards the meeting spot, I squeeze Luka's hand and offer up one more prayer to whoever is listening:

I pray that my family will make it back together.

Once everyone is in position, we decide to walk.

Driving down the long dirt road to the house is too noisy and will draw too much attention. Walking is better because we can stay in the tree line until the last moment when we need to cut across the large lawn that surrounds the house.

Plus, on foot, men can actually take up position at every point around the house and ensure that no one inside can escape without us knowing it.

The only problem is that walking, especially across uneven ground, puts a lot of pressure on Luka's leg. He puts on a brave face, clenching his jaw and walking tall, but I can tell he is uncomfortable. And the closer we get to the house, the worse his limp gets.

"Are you ready?" I ask him. What I really mean is, *Are you okay? Can you do this? Will we make it out?*

But I don't say any of that.

Luka looks down at me, grabs my hand, and smiles. "We are ready."

Just as a shadow of peace begins to creep over me, the crack of gunfire fills the air.

Luka yanks me behind him and stops moving, his entire body rigid and on high alert.

"Where did that come from?" a man yells.

We all look around, but aren't sure.

Then, it becomes obvious.

Bullets fly from the second floor windows of the house. They whiz past us, exploding into tree trunks, wood shrapnel flying.

Luka throws me on the ground and sprawls over me. "They were ready for us."

"Who?" I ask. I can't imagine Rian Morrison and her parents taking up position in their bedroom windows to shoot at us. They wouldn't fire; they would run.

"The Irish," he growls. Then, he turns back to his men. "Fire back. But restrain yourself when you can. We don't know where Milaya is."

My heart stutters in my chest at the thought that Milaya could be caught in the crossfire. Surely the Morrisons would be smart enough to keep her far away from this shootout, right?

"She is fine," Luka whispers into my ear, lifting himself up to his good leg.

I scramble up quickly and help him up. "We need to get in there and make sure."

Luka nods and then positions himself in front of me as a human shield. I want to argue, but I know it would do no good. That is one battle my newfound independence will never win. There is no chance Luka will let me take a bullet for him.

The Bratva spread out behind us, taking up position behind trees and small outbuildings around the ranch. They fire up at the house, and based on the frequency of return fire, I guess some of their shots are finding their targets.

Unfortunately, the Irish are finding their marks, too.

When I look back over my shoulder, I can see several Bratva members facedown in the grass.

I turn away and try to push the thought from my mind for now. There is nothing we can do about it.

Mourn later. Fight now.

Luka waves a few men ahead of us, instructing them to lead the way into the house. As soon as they run past us, we pick up our pace and follow after them.

"We stick together!" Luka yells over the shots ringing out. "We get inside and search room by room until we find them."

I begin to nod, but then I see something at the far-right corner of the house between the sunporch and the garage.

A flash of movement.

I freeze and pull away from Luka, trying to get a better look.

"Eve," he says, grabbing my hand.

"I saw something." I slip out of his grip and move towards the corner of the house. Then, I see her.

Rian Morrison.

She runs from the garage and is crossing the open grass to get to a side door on the sunporch.

She is here.

When I turn back to Luka, I know he has seen her, too.

"I have to go," I yell.

Before I can, Luka grabs my hand. "We can follow her once we are inside. We can go ahead with our plan and find her then."

"She could escape back through the sunporch. I have to go through that door now."

Luka's eyes narrow. He looks from me to the corner of the house, and we only have a few precious seconds for him to make his decision before Rian gets inside and disappears in the vastness of the house. Or finds another door to escape.

"Our men aren't in position like we wanted," I say, moving backwards towards where I last saw Rian. "There are too many holes in our plan now. We don't have time to waste. Trust me. Please. For Milaya's sake."

Suddenly, Luka grabs my hand and pulls me against him, pressing his lips to mine firmly and quickly.

Then, he spins me back towards the corner of the house. "Run, and I'll cover you."

I don't hesitate. I just take off running for the corner of the house as fast as my body and my high-heeled boots will let me.

With every step, the heels sink into the ground, but I keep going, ignoring the burning in my thighs as I push myself.

I hear Luka behind me, but then there is a shout.

I turn and see him on the ground.

For a moment, my heart is lodged in my throat, making it impossible to breathe. I freeze, staring back at his form on the ground.

Then, he struggles up and waves me on.

He lifts his gun up and pulls the trigger. A man on the roof shakes as the shot hits, and then he tumbles forward off the roof, landing ten feet to my left.

"Go!" Luka yells at me again.

This time, I don't hesitate. I hold my gun close to my chest and run.

Luka is okay. For now.

Luka is alive. For now.

And now is all we have.

I run through the sunporch door and into a small sitting room, but I don't see Rian anywhere.

The house is dark, but otherwise ordinary. It looks like any normal living room in any normal house anywhere in the country.

Except for the sounds of footsteps and gunfire coming from the other end of the house.

Except for the shattered living room window.

Glass is sprinkled across the floor like confetti, sparkling in the last rays of sunlight breaking through the trees.

The house seems to be vibrating around me with noise and movement and violence. It is so intense I almost feel seasick.

But I grab the corner of the couch and listen, trying to pick out any sound that will lead me to Rian or Milaya.

Then, through all of the din, I hear a cry.

At first, I think I must be imagining it. It is just my mind playing tricks on me, letting me hear what I want to hear.

Then, I hear a tiny cough and another desperate cry.

I remember nights spent sitting up with Milaya in her nursery when she wouldn't go to sleep. When she cried and cried, and I wasn't sure what to do to make her feel better. All of those moments that, at the time, felt endless and frustrating, were moments I looked back on while I was being tortured and held prisoner and forced to do things I would never do of my own free will.

And now, I know without a doubt my baby is upstairs.

I sprint to the nearest stairs and up them with tunnel vision.

Nothing else matters.

I don't see anyone else or hear the gunfire. Every single one of my senses is focused in on Milaya and her cries and her needs.

I'm so close to her. So close.

I reach the top of the stairs and pause long enough to figure out where I need to go next.

When I hear her cries again, I barrel towards them, not even bothering to stay quiet.

Then, a door flies open and someone shoots.

The crack of gunfire is so close it makes my ears ring. I drop to the floor, losing my gun in the process, and I don't realize until I roll over that my back is roaring in pain.

I've been hit.

I don't have time to worry about that, though, because Rian Morrison is standing over me with a gun.

I've barely recognized who she is before I swing my legs to the side and kick out at her.

My ankle swipes the back of her knee, and like a tower of wooden blocks, Rian topples onto the floor next to me.

I spin and grab for the gun, but Rian is faster than I am. She pulls it back, sits up, and takes aim. Just as she pulls the trigger, I knock the gun to the side, but it isn't enough.

Heat courses through my thigh followed by flashes of pain so blinding I can barely see.

I scream and want nothing more than to grab my leg and curl up in the fetal position, but at that very second, Milaya begins to cry again.

I hear it. Her tiny voice cries out, followed by dainty little coughs.

My helpless baby is in the room just a few feet away from me, and I can't die here.

Not like this. Not when I'm so close.

My gun is too far away and the likelihood that I'll be able to get Rian's gun out of her hands is slim. So, before Rian can recover and get into shooting position again, I reach down into my boots and pull free the scalpel I hid between the boot and the inner lining when we were riding in the SUV. I didn't know when or if I would need it again, but I wanted to be prepared, and now I'm happier than ever for that preparation.

I slash the blade clumsily at Rian's leg and manage to find purchase. The blade, while small, was created for carving through human flesh, and it does its job, gouging a deep wound in Rian's ankle.

She screams, her tidy blonde ponytail flailing out behind her like a possessed spider, and jumps away from me.

I slash out again and again, crawling after her and carving up her legs until blood is coating the bottom half of her shins and dripping onto the floor.

Rian is so desperate to get away from me she slams into the wall. She inhales sharply, and I realize she has knocked the wind out of herself. As quickly as I can, I spring to my feet and grab for the gun.

She fights, gritting her teeth and trying to pull it back, but I slam the heel of my boot on the top of her foot, and she screams and loses her grip.

"Please." She falls to her knees. The carpet is saturated with her blood, and it squelches under her weight. "Please don't kill me. Not where Milaya can hear."

Hearing my daughter's name on Rian's lips sends me into a blind rage. A kind of primal protectiveness rises up in me, and I lift the gun and pull the trigger.

The shot hits Rian in the chest.

She falls back against the wall, her legs folded awkwardly beneath her like a broken accordion.

When she looks down at her chest, I can tell she is surprised. She dabs at the bloodstain growing on her shirt and then stares down at her hand. Finally, she slips to the floor, her cheek against the carpet.

Now that the immediate threat is gone, I can feel my conscience breaking through the cloud of rage. I should save Rian. I should try to get her some help, maybe mend a fence between the Volkov family and the Morrisons. I could end the longstanding feud between the Russians and the Irish with this hand of mercy.

But then I hear Milaya cry.

My sweet Milaya. My little girl.

My daughter, who was snatched from her crib because of this woman's doing.

My precious baby, who has been without her mama and papa for almost ten days. And this bitch threatened to sell Milaya on the black market if I disobeyed her.

Just like that, the tiny seed of empathy inside of me is squashed.

Rian tries to lift her face, reaching a hand out to me as though to touch my boot.

I pick up my foot and drive the heel of my shoe into her hand. Then, I walk past her and into the bedroom.

I go to get my daughter, and I leave Rian Morrison to die.

Milaya is lying in the middle of a crib, her arms and legs thrashing, face red from crying. As soon as I pick her up, she begins to ease. When her little face is pressed against my neck, she whimpers and then settles entirely.

Love and relief like I've never known wash through me.

It feels like I've been without a key body part and it has finally been returned to me. At long last, I can function normally.

Almost.

But I still don't know where Luka is or if he is alive.

"It's okay, sweet girl," I whisper, rocking her against my chest. "Mama is here."

I look around the room and realize there is more than just a crib in here. It is an entire nursery.

There is art hanging on the wall, a mobile above the crib, and a changing table stocked with diapers. A white dress sits in the corner, every drawer filled with pink frilly outfits and tiny baby shoes. The closet is stocked with extra sheets, bottles, and pacifiers.

The Morrisons were preparing to keep Milaya. To raise her.

They were going to get rid of me and Luka and keep our daughter as their own.

The thought makes me sick, and suddenly, I can't spend another second in this room. In this house.

We have to get out.

I press Milaya closer to my chest, shielding her eyes from the blood and chaos of the hallway.

She is in the same position on the floor as when I left her. If she isn't dead yet, she will be soon.

Just as I'm about to step over Rian, I hear footsteps pounding up the stairs.

I freeze, clutching Milaya to me, and then quickly grab the gun and hold it out, ready to shoot my way out of this house if I have to.

Then, I hear the lull in the steps. One loud thud and then a drag. One loud thud and then a drag.

I realize it is Luka coming up the stairs just as he rounds the corner.

When he sees the two of us standing in the hallway, his eyes go wide, and he lets out a sigh of relief that is close to a sob.

"Thank God," he says, holding out his arms to catch me as I throw myself against him.

"You're okay," I whisper tearfully against his neck.

"I'm okay," he whispers. Then, he pulls away and snuggles the back of Milaya's head, kissing her tiny neck. "And you're okay, too."

"She's perfect." My lip trembles, and I drop the gun to wipe at my eyes. "She is perfectly safe."

Luka looks past me and winces. "The same can't be said for Agent Morrison."

Even hearing her name floods my senses with the same rage I felt before. I wonder how long it will be before I can think about her without wishing I could kill her all over again.

"Can we go?" I ask. "Is it over? I want to go home."

There is a commotion behind me, footsteps and shouting. Then, two shots and silence.

"Now we can," Luka says. "The Bratva just took out the last two gunmen."

Milaya yawns and then lays her cheek against my shoulder, and that mixed with the relief of this—the last week and a half of fear and torture and terror—finally being over makes me weep.

I lay my head on Luka's shoulder, our daughter cradled between us, and cry with relief and happiness and exhaustion.

Luka smooths a hand down my back and then kisses me on the forehead. "Let's go home."

With one arm around his waist and the other around Milaya, I walk down the stairs and into the night.

It is over. Finally, it is all over.

EPILOGUE I
LUKA

Eve looks so at home in our kitchen, and I lean back against the counter and watch her work, taking in the sight.

It has only been three days since our escape from the Cartel, but I have logged a lifetime of memories in that time.

I've watched Eve sleep as the sun rises, casting our room in golden morning light. I've studied Milaya's dimpled hands reaching for me. I've sat in the hallway and listened to the soothing sound of Eve singing our daughter to sleep and kissing her good night.

In three days, I have remembered and memorized every single thing I am grateful for in this life. Without fail, every single one of those things involves Eve and Milaya.

My girls. My family.

"Are you paying attention?" Eve asks, peering over her shoulder, one eyebrow raised.

Her face is still bruised, and I can't wait for the reminder of our experience to be gone from her skin. My own wounds will leave scars, but Eve will carry her scars internally.

I've seen them show up already.

The way she gets up in the middle of the night to stand outside Milaya's door. The way she checks the security system again and again and again before we go to bed.

Hopefully, with time, those scars will fade, too.

I limp over to her, a hand pressed to her lower back. "Yes, I'm listening."

"Good," she says, dropping a hunk of butter in the cast iron skillet. "Because this is the important part."

"I thought cooking the steaks was the important part," I say. "It is called steak au poivre, after all."

"Yes, but a badly made pan sauce can ruin the entire dish," she says. "Now, pay attention."

I grab her waist and press my body against her backside, nuzzling into her neck. "I love it when you boss me around."

Eve circles her hips, grinding back into me, and then bangs her spoon against the pan loudly. "Eyes forward."

I stand to attention, grinning. "Yes, ma'am."

I watch and listen as she drops shallots into the butter, letting them brown, and then adds a broth.

"That comes to a simmer," she says, turning away from the stove to grab something on the counter.

When she is mid-reach, I wrap my arm around her middle, spin her into me, and kiss her.

"Luka," she moans against my mouth. She is doing her best to sound annoyed, but her hands are gripping the backs of my arms, holding me against her. "I'm in the middle of things here."

"The soup needs to simmer," I say, waving a hand towards the stove.

"The *broth*," she corrects, rolling her eyes. "Clearly, someone wasn't paying attention."

I kiss her again, nibbling on her lower lip. "Clearly, I just need a less distracting teacher."

When I finally let her go, she grabs a bottle of Cognac from the bar and adds it to the pan, stirring as it begins to bubble and reduce.

Milaya screeches happily from her high chair, and I walk over to her, grabbing the large wooden spoon she was playing with.

"I believe you dropped this, madam," I say in my worst British accent.

As soon as I hand her the spoon, she screeches and throws it again, sending it skittering under the sink.

"She's hungry," Eve says. "I'll feed her as soon as I'm done with dinner."

"She could have played in the other room while we cooked," I say.

Eve looks at me from the corner of her eye before turning her attention back to the pan. "I know. I didn't mind, either way."

I limp back over to her and kiss her cheek. "You flinched when I suggested it."

One by one, she grabs the steaks and places them in the sauce, flipping them over to ensure they are all evenly coated and cooked through.

"I'll get better," she says softly. "It will just take time."

"Is it the security system?" I ask. "The company told me it is the highest quality package they offer, but I can find another company. We can get second and third opinions."

"No, it's fine," she says. "Though, I have been thinking about a dog."

"A dog?" I ask, eyebrows raised. "I never took us for dog people."

"Me neither," she admits. "But since ... everything. I don't know. I think it could be nice to have a dog around. Something to bark at strange noises and scare people away."

"And drool on our furniture and tear up our leather shoes and knock Milaya over when she learns to walk," I finish, counting off my reasons one by one.

"We'll make sure it is friendly and good with kids," Eve says.

"That only solves one of the three issues I brought up."

She turns, stretches up on her toes, and kisses me with her entire body.

Her chest arches into me, her hips circle against mine, and she drags her fingernails through my hair and down my neck, sending shivers down my spine. When she pulls away, she smiles up at me.

"How about that?" she asks. "Did that solve your other two issues?"

In a daze, I nod. "I can buy new shoes and furniture."

She laughs, and I kiss her again, picking her up for a second until she kicks in protest. "You shouldn't be picking me up on your bad leg. It is never going to heal if you keep that up. Put me down, mister."

I slap her butt as she walks back to the stove. "Worth it."

Eve carries out a board of steaks in a row, and I grab Milaya. The doctor told me I couldn't carry anything heavier than our daughter for a few days, so I have to leave the heavy lifting to Eve.

In the dining room, Eve is swatting Grigory's hand, telling him to keep away from the steak until everyone has been served. And the women from the auction, plus Kari, are grouped together at the far end of the table, looking nervous but happy.

"Let me get the sauce and potatoes before these men go rabid," Eve teases.

As she passes me to go back into the kitchen, I see her luminous smile. The one she saves for when she is truly happy.

It is the same smile she wore the day she got the phone call from Kari.

After sending the women away from the inn, Eve kicked herself for not finding a way to contact them. She gave Kari her number, but she couldn't reach out to any of them or find out where they were. She insisted she was fine, but I could tell she worried.

When Kari called last night, Eve almost cried with relief. She invited all of the women over for dinner, as well as Grigory, Vito, and a few of the other Bratva members who helped with the escape.

"Everything looks delicious," Maddie says, wafting some of the steam from the steak in her direction.

Vito is sitting next to her, staring at Maddie like I've never seen him stare at anyone. "It does," he agrees, though I'm not certain he is talking about the steak.

Eve tells everyone I helped her cook the meal even though it isn't remotely true. Unless standing around and lusting after her while she cooked counts as helping, in which case, I was essential to the operation.

"I'm surprised you are cooking, let alone standing up," Grigory says. "How is your leg?"

"Thanks to Kari, it's great," I say. When I turn to her, she is blushing a deep shade of red that makes her blonde hair look even paler. "Have you thought about my offer?"

If possible, her face goes even redder. "I have."

"What offer?" Grigory asks.

"I thought we could use an emergency surgeon. Someone who will work for us and keep us all out of the emergency room."

"That would be a great idea," Vito says. "Maybe Maddie could help her."

Maddie frowns. "I don't know anything about surgery."

Vito shrugs, looking disappointed.

"Well?" I ask, turning back to Kari. "What do you say?"

Eve leans forward, biting her lower lip. "It would be nice to have another woman around."

Kari smiles warmly at Eve and then turns back to me, looking less certain. "I need more time to think about it. I'm not sure yet."

"Of course," I say. "Take your time."

It is a good offer. One of the best Kari is going to get without going back to school. And according to Eve, Kari isn't sure she can handle school. Since working for the Cartel for so many years, she is nervous around large groups of people, which is understandable.

"Well, we would be glad to have you," Grigory says, leaning back in his chair to catch Kari's eye.

Her cheeks flush again, and she quickly looks down at her plate, but I see the smile on her face. I think everyone does.

Eve nudges me in the side, and I nod.

Kari might be smitten.

By the puff of Grigory's chest, he might be smitten, too.

After dinner, we leave the maids to clean up and move into the sitting room.

The fire is lit and the curtains are drawn, giving the entire affair a very cozy, personal touch.

It was planned that way on purpose. Eve and I wanted to arrange this night to give everyone—ourselves included—a fresh start.

Once everybody is seated, Eve nods at me, and I stand and lift my glass.

"Thank you all for coming over tonight. It feels good to be with friends and family after a rather difficult couple weeks."

Grigory raises his glass and then takes a large drink. "That's an understatement."

"We lost good men. Loyal men. So tonight, we honor those men who fought to free me and my wife and my child."

"And me," Kari says softly.

"Me, too," Maddie says.

The other three women murmur in agreement and nod along.

"And all of you, too," I agree.

Everyone stops and takes a drink, but then Eve stands up next to me, her glass raised. "And I'd also like to honor the woman who was killed during the auction. I didn't know her name, but—"

"Angela," Kari says. "Her name was Angela."

I see Eve's eyes go glassy, and she lifts her glass. "To Angela."

Everyone drinks again.

Eve stretches up to whisper in my ear. "Do you mind if I—"

I step back and gesture for her to have the floor. My leg needs a rest, anyway. Standing for even a few minutes at a time makes my muscles spasm.

"I don't want to bring down the mood of the night," Eve says. "But I do want to say thank you for everyone who came to help us. I'm not sure where my family would be tonight if it wasn't for all of you."

We both look to Milaya, who is lying on a soft blanket on the floor, batting at stuffed fish that are hanging from a mobile above her.

"Please don't thank us anymore," Grigory says. "You are our leaders. Of course we came for you."

Eve's lips pinch together nervously, and she looks back at me, trying to gauge my reaction.

Leaders. Plural.

As in, Eve and myself. Together.

In another lifetime, that might have bothered me. Thinking that I don't have the full control of my men. Thinking that I, in any way, had to share their respect, would have bothered me.

But now, I feel nothing but pride.

Eve is strong and respected. More than just my wife, my men see her as my equal. They see her as their leader. And I get to claim her as mine.

My wife, my love. My queen.

I can only see their respect for her as a compliment. As their blessing on us and our marriage and our leadership over the Bratva.

I reach out and grab Eve's hand, kissing her knuckles. Then, I turn to Grigory. "You won't hear another bit of gratitude from either of us on the subject."

He lifts his glass again, downing the second half of it. Judging by the color in his face, that was not his first.

"I'm grateful to all of you for getting me out," Eve says, winking at Grigory when he rolls his eyes. "But I can't push aside the guilt I feel that we are all here and others aren't."

Eve talked to me about this last night when we were lying in bed. I knew the fact that so many of the women had been given over to bidders before we could save them weighed heavily on her. And I also knew there would be no way to deter her once she set her mind to it. So, I am now behind her one hundred percent.

She turns towards Kari and Maddie and the other women. "I am going to keep my job as head chef at Fleurs Vingt, but I'm going to spend as much of my time as I can tracking down the women who were sold and helping them get their freedom back."

"And I told Eve she would have access to any service the Bratva offered that could help," I say.

Grigory and the other members nod in solidarity. "Of course."

"You don't have to help me," Eve says to the women. "But since I think this journey will be so important in my own healing, I thought I would offer you the opportunity to help as well."

"Of course," Kari says, her eyes going glassy with tears. "I would love nothing more than to help."

"Me too," Maddie says. Then, she bites her lip. "I just—I'm not sure I can face the Cartel members again."

Her lip begins to tremble, and Vito reaches out to lay a meaty hand on her knee.

Maddie doesn't bat him away instantly, which he seems to take as a good sign, his mouth twitching up in a half smile.

Eve sets her glass on the mantle and moves over towards where the women are grouped on the end of the couch. The part of the evening where we formally address the guests is clearly over.

I keep my distance while she comforts Maddie and talks through her plan. In fact, it is the furthest apart Eve and I have been in almost three days.

Since getting home, we have stayed close to one another. When we sit on the couch, she sits close enough that her leg brushes against mine.

While she cooks, I am within arm's reach, ready to hug her and kiss her between stages in the recipe. After being forced apart so much at the auction, we can't seem to get enough of having full access to one another.

Milaya is still batting happily at her toys, and I'm watching her when Grigory lifts himself out of his chair and stumbles over to me.

The man is large and can hold his drink, but he is clearly pushing his limits tonight.

"You know," he slurs, dropping down on the hearth next to me. "When you first married Eve, I wasn't certain you were making the right choice. I mean, she is beautiful—"

He lifts his hand in surrender when my attention snaps to him, eyes narrowed.

"She is beautiful, but she was from an enemy family," he continues. "A lot of us thought it would cause way more trouble than it is worth. To be fair, for a minute there it did cause a lot of trouble."

"More than it was worth?" I ask.

Grigory smiles and shakes his head. "No, definitely not. We like Eve."

"She'll be glad to hear that," I say.

"I mean it. We all like her. Even more now that she has shown us her true colors." Grigory tips back his drink, and I consider reaching out and stopping him, but I don't. He can sleep in the guest room if need be. Tonight is a celebration. A time for everyone to relax, Grigory included. "Eve is tough. And kind. She cares about people."

"She cares about all of you," I tell him.

"And we care about her. Maybe even more than we care about you."

He nudges me in the side playfully, and I nudge him right back even harder. "I can see why you married her. You obviously saw something in her from the beginning that we didn't."

Milaya begins to fuss, kicking her little legs, and I reach down and pick her up, balancing her on my good leg.

"I don't think I knew how great Eve was when I married her," I admit. "But marrying Eve is definitely the best decision I ever made."

From across the room, Eve sees me with Milaya and grins. It lights up her entire face, as though a lamp has been turned on inside her eyes, and I feel the certainty of my statement in my heart.

Yes, Eve is the best decision I have ever made.

EPILOGUE II
EVE

Luka is stretched out on the couch, his bad leg elevated on the footrest, when I flop down next to him and bury my face in his chest.

"I'm exhausted," I groan.

"Probably because you insisted on throwing a dinner party for ten people three days after being rescued from a human trafficking ring."

I prop myself up on my elbow and shrug. "Well, when you say it like that, it sounds absurd."

He laughs and pulls me back against his chest, kissing the top of my head. "Dinner was delicious. Everyone seemed to really enjoy it."

"I'm glad. It felt good to be normal for a night."

I wasn't sure if we would ever be able to exist like this again.

So many times over the previous two weeks, I thought my old life was forever lost to me. I thought for certain I would never see Luka or Milaya again. I thought I would never again curl up next to Luka on the couch and bury my face in his neck and breathe in his smell.

But here I am, breathing in the woodsy scent of him while our daughter sleeps upstairs.

A cold panic grips my heart, and Luka must feel me tense because he tightens his hold on me.

"She is okay," he whispers. "There are sensors on her windows, two cameras, and a sound monitor."

I take a deep breath and nod. "I know, I know."

I wonder when the panicking will stop.

I wonder when I'll be able to leave Milaya in her crib and not wonder if she'll be there when I go back in.

"I worry, too," Luka says.

"You do?"

"Of course I do," he says, pulling away from me and sitting up so we can face one another. "I came inside from a smoke on the porch and you two weren't here. My wife and baby were gone, and there was nothing I could do about it. I worry all the time that that will happen again."

I know Luka still carries guilt about the night we were taken. No matter how many times I tell him it wasn't his fault, he can't forgive himself.

Still, I try.

"You know that wasn't your fault," I say, smoothing my hand up his thigh. "Right?"

He shrugs. "I'm not sure if I know it, but I like when you say it."

Then, he twists away from me and grabs something underneath the sofa. "I got this for you. I hope you don't mind."

"I never mind gifts. Gimme," I tease, snatching it from him and tearing the box open. I peel off the layers of tissue paper, tossing them to the floor. When I see what's inside, I stiffen for a moment.

Sitting in the box is a gun.

"It's nothing fancy," Luka says. "Just a standard handgun, but I thought you should have one."

"Thank you." I brush my fingertip across it, and then retreat slightly.

Growing up around guns did little to ease my nervousness about them. And the last few days did little to change that.

While I'm confident with a gun, I'm not comfortable.

"I know you don't like them," Luka says, reaching out to grab my hand, twining his fingers through mine. "But if I am going to make any attempt at being less protective over you, I need to know you have a means to defend yourself."

I put the lid back on the box and lean across the couch to kiss him, grabbing a fistful of his shirt. "Thank you."

When I try to pull away, Luka tightens an arm around my waist and pulls me closer. "Is that how you thank a man for a gift? One measly kiss?"

"I'm not sure if you remember," I say, batting away his advances. "But you never bought me, Luka Volkov. And I do not perform for men who haven't put their money where their mouth is."

I drag my fingers across his lips, shivering at the way his lower lip gives in to my touch.

He crosses his arms over his chest, sitting up straighter. "I'm not sure I've been convinced to invest."

"Oh really?" I ask, eyebrow raised.

"Really."

I grab the gift box and stand up to leave.

"Are you leaving?" he asks, a tiny hint of desperation in his voice. I know he is afraid I've called his bluff.

I nod slowly, biting my lip. "But I'll be back."

"Soon?" His eyes spark with amusement.

"Prepare to be impressed."

I know I shouldn't have kept the collar from the inn.

Or, rather, I shouldn't have *wanted* to keep the collar.

It was a symbol of my enslavement. A way for the Cartel members to differentiate me from all of the other slaves.

The collar was demeaning and degrading and dehumanizing.

But when I look at it, I don't see any of that.

I see a survivor.

I look at the collar and see everything I overcame while at the inn. I look at it and see how far I have come. How much more confident I am in myself and my abilities and my worth.

Ironically, being a slave was the first time I ever felt like I was in control. Like I had the ability to do something more with my life than cook food for someone and be a wife. It was the first time I realized how powerful I really am.

When I wrap the collar around my neck this time, I'm not the same woman who put it on.

I slip the '7' tag from the chain and toss it in the trash. I have a much better idea for what should replace it.

It only takes me a minute to find the necklace in Luka's top drawer. It was a family heirloom passed down from his grandfather to his father and then to him. It is a long chain with a simple gold 'V' in the center. I slide it from the chain and place it on my collar, hoping Luka will notice.

Then, I put on something much sexier than any of the dresses or robes the Cartel had me wear.

The black lingerie is lace and mesh, showing more skin than it covers.

Bruises along my side and legs are still visible, but the swelling is mostly gone. Just a few weeks ago, I would have hidden the trauma I endured. I would have cloaked it under long pajamas and done my best to keep the lights low so Luka wouldn't see.

Now, however, I wear my battle wounds proudly.

I fought. I won. I'm still here.

Luka is still on the couch when I walk back in, but when he sees me standing in the doorway, he sits tall, blinking.

"Like what you see?"

I see the haze of lust cross his face. His pupils dilate and his lips part. "God, yes."

I can feel the temperature of the room change.

When I walk towards him, I do it slowly, crossing one leg in front of the other, allowing him to take in every inch of me before I reach him.

He slides to the edge of the couch and reaches out for me, but I stay just out of reach.

"What are the doctor's orders about having your world rocked?" I ask. "Will it impede your recovery?"

"Fuck my recovery," Luka growls, reaching for me again and huffing when he misses. "I'm gonna die if I *don't* get my world rocked. I want to fuck you."

I laugh, once again realizing this was a moment I didn't know I'd have again.

I didn't know if I'd get to be with Luka this way again. If I would get to see him go wild for me. If I would get to feel the familiar flutter of excitement in my chest when his hands finally land on me, and he begins to worship my body.

I thought our last time would be in the room of that horrid inn, so I promise myself I'll enjoy every second of this.

When he sees the collar around my neck, he frowns. "Why are you wearing that?"

I run my finger across the silk and the gold emblem. "So everyone knows who I belong to."

He leans forward, eyes narrowed. When he sees the 'V' around my neck, he smiles. "V?"

"For Volkov," I say. "Do you like it?"

This time, Luka is too fast for me to dodge. He wraps a thick arm around my waist and pulls me onto him so I'm straddling his hips. His lips flutter against my collarbone and the curve of my breast.

He presses kisses down the center of my body almost to my belly button and back up.

"I like it," he says, his voice deep and husky. "I love it."

His mouth moves up my neck towards my mouth, but I twist away before our lips can touch. His growl of frustration vibrates through my body to my very core.

I run a hand down his chest and across the washboard of his abs to his waistband. My fingers fidget with the button, but I don't undo it.

Not yet.

"Are you impressed?"

"Huh?" he asks, eyes focused on my finger curling in the hair that disappears beneath his pants.

"Are you impressed?" I whisper, lowering my body over his so I barely brush over him.

He lifts his hips to meet me, but I pull away before he can.

"I'm impressed," he says, wrapping his large hands around my hips and pulling me down on his lap.

"So, I'm yours?" I ask, circling my body over his until he tips his head back, eyes closed.

He nods. "Yes. You are mine."

I curl my hand around his neck, my thumb brushing along his earlobe, and lift his head up until our lips meet. Until we are a collision of tongues and lips and breath. Until I've melted into him, and I'm not sure where I stop and he begins.

Suddenly, I'm not playing a game anymore.

I'm not pulling away when Luka reaches for me or dodging his hands.

I'm surrendering. Giving him everything I have and everything I am because I need this.

I need him.

"I need you, too," he groans against my mouth.

I didn't realize I was speaking out loud, but I barely know what I'm doing with my hands. We are moving so fast that I can't keep up.

Luka pulls my shoulder straps down my arms, exposing my breasts. He buries his face against my skin, licking and kissing and teasing.

He swirls his tongue around my nipples until they are sensitive and pebbled.

I unbutton his pants and slide my hand inside, wrapping around his considerable length.

Our foreplay is rushed and clumsy because we are both ready. We've been ready for hours.

When our guests were finishing the last of their drinks and moving towards the door, Luka and I could hardly keep our hands off one another.

He followed me into the kitchen when I went to fetch a tray of desserts and pinned me against the refrigerator, capturing my mouth in a kiss that made it difficult to walk in a straight line when I returned to the living room.

Our entire evening has been building to this moment. Every second of the last four hours has been foreplay, and now the physical act of it seems unnecessary.

"I want you inside of me," I moan against his neck.

Luka curses under his breath and pushes me back on the couch. I know he shouldn't be putting unnecessary pressure on his leg, but he is peeling my clothes off me inch by inch, and I don't have the heart to tell him to stop. The sight of him hovering over me satisfies something primal inside of me. I may be a proud, fierce mob queen now, but I still can't resist being dominated.

Using my hands and feet, I push his pants off his hips, and Luka helps, sliding his good leg out and then, more carefully, his injured leg. He throws his clothes in the pile with mine, and then it is just his skin gliding over mine.

I open my legs to him, giving him access, and he kisses his way down my body and towards my inner thigh.

I feel his breath on my center before his touch, like a shift in the wind before a storm. Still, when his tongue swipes across my center, I'm not prepared.

My entire body arches with surprise, bucking against his mouth. Luka pins me down and does it again. And again.

He licks and sucks until my body is liquid beneath him. Until I'm afraid I'll sink between the cushions of the couch and never be found again.

I tangle my fingers in his hair, pulling him against me, but Luka resists. He pulls away, leaving my body aching and wanting and needing.

"Please," I beg, feeling myself teetering on the edge, desperate to tip over the side and fall.

"Not until I'm inside you," Luka says.

All at once, he grabs my hips, lies back, and pulls me over him so he is underneath me on the couch.

I'm crazed with desire to the point my vision is blurry, so I don't question it or hesitate. I simply wrap my hand around him, position him at my opening, and sink onto him.

"Fuck," Luka moans, his hand warm on my backside.

I'm close.

Already so, so close.

"Come, baby," he whispers, his hand encouraging me to rock and ride and use him the way I need to.

So, I do.

I rock my hips over him faster and faster until I can't catch my breath. Until I don't need to catch my breath.

All I need is Luka's body pressed against mine.

Heat explodes in my belly, sending tendrils of warmth to my extremities and clouding my head.

I cry out, head thrown back, body arched over him.

My muscles spasm and release, and I am helpless against the pull of my orgasm. I have no choice but to ride it to completion. But to follow the wave down, down, down.

When the last shakes of it move through me, I collapse on his chest, breathing heavily.

"That was incredible."

"It really was," he agrees. "Watching you is almost my favorite part."

I lift my head weakly. "Almost?"

He quirks an eyebrow and then lifts me up and off him. Luka lays me out on the couch and licks my still-twitching muscles.

He spreads me in front of him like a buffet and samples a little of everything, somehow managing to stoke a fire in the ruined shell of my body.

By the time he is between my legs and sliding into me, I want it just as badly as I did a moment ago.

It doesn't seem possible to want someone this much. To be constantly in need of them. But here I am, desperate and clinging to him, my hands clawing at his back.

Luka thrusts into me again and again.

I lift my legs up and curl myself around his body, trying and failing to get close enough to him. To have enough of him.

I feel when he begins to lose control.

His breath catches, and his thrusts become more forceful, more staccato. Rather than a rolling melody, they are the bass line.

I circle my arms around him and hold on as he falls apart. As his muscles tremble and shake.

When he is done, he lays his head on my chest, and I smooth my hands down his back.

For so long, I didn't know if I would have this. If I would have this kind of familiarity with someone.

Even when I married Luka, I worried we would always be two strangers forced into proximity. I worried we would always lack intimacy and understanding. That he would never see me and vice versa.

Yet, here we are.

Naked and at ease with one another.

In the last couple of weeks, we were stripped bare of everything except our love for one another, and we came out on the other side stronger.

After a few minutes, Luka gets up and holds a hand out to me. Moving slowly to accommodate his leg, we walk up the stairs to our bedroom and slide between our sheets, wrapping up in one another.

Just as my breathing begins to even out, he reaches up and pulls the silk collar from my neck, throwing it on the floor next to the bed.

"Buyer's remorse?" I tease, tucking my back against his front.

"Never," he whispers, kissing the back of my neck. "It was just a lie, is all."

"A lie? How?"

I feel him hard and ready against my lower back, and my body tingles with anticipation. Luka rolls me onto my back and crawls over me again, his body a shield against the outside world, blocking out everything that isn't important. Everything that isn't him.

"The collar makes it seem like I own you," he says. His finger drags down my body and settles between my legs, drawing sensual circles at my center. "We both know it's the other way around. I am yours."

"Mine?" I moan, eyes rolling closed.

He plunges his finger inside and caresses me. "All yours."

Want more of the Volkov Bratva? Click here to get Milaya's story in BROKEN SINS: A Reverse Harem Dark Mafia Romance.

Or just turn the page for a juicy sneak preview!

BROKEN SINS (A REVERSE HAREM DARK MAFIA ROMANCE)

SNEAK PREVIEW

My father's enemies have claimed me for revenge.

Life as Luka Volkov's daughter is hell.

I live in a gilded cage.

I want out.

But not like this.

His enemies came for me in the night.

Four of them.

Vito, Mateo, Leo, Dante.

Each is darker and more savage than the last.

The Bianci brothers plan to use me for their vengeance.

But not before they use me for their pleasure.

In their hands, I will be bent. Broken.

And after each midnight session, they promise me this...

By the time it's all over, I'll be begging for more.

I'm running for my life.

My lungs are screaming at me. They're filled with fire, acid, lightning. My body wants me to stop. It's practically begging at this point. I don't know how long I've been running. I don't know how much longer I'll have to run if I want to escape. I don't know if escape is even an option anymore.

The men pursuing me aren't heroes. They aren't nice or caring. They're protective, yes, but not in the way you'd normally think of it.

They only want me so they can break me.

They've come close to doing that already. All the days and nights I've been under lock and key in their fucked-up mansion of shadows and secrets have pushed me close to the edge. This is my last chance to get away before they finish what they've started.

They told me I'm their princess. They said that *they* serve *me*.

What a load of fucking bullshit.

For a while, they almost had me fooled. As whips turned to caresses and cruelty turned to kisses, I started to believe the lies they were feeding me. *You're safer with us. We want what is best for you. We are on your side.*

Lies, lies, and damned lies. I've been a pawn since the beginning.

I almost preferred the way things were at first, on those first few nights after they kidnapped me. Back then, I could understand their savagery, their hatred for me. I could understand why they wanted to make me scream and scream and scream until my throat was raw and my voice gave out.

We were enemies, plain and simple.

But nothing is plain and simple anymore.

One thought runs through my head on repeat, a broken record: *Don't stop. Don't stop. Don't stop.* If I stop, I die. Simple as that. There are no second chances in this game I was born into. The men on my trail will kill me with their bare hands.

And the sickest thing of all… is that part of me believes I deserve it.

Maybe I didn't choose to become an expendable piece on their chessboard. It was just my birthright. The blood in my veins is what brought me here.

But I've made all my own choices since then—that is, if choosing between death or captivity can even be considered a "choice." So perhaps I've earned this ending. Perhaps I brought it all upon myself in some sick, twisted way.

The alley is long, damp with rain, cloaked with shadows. My feet pound the pavement. I don't have much longer. My body will simply quit on me sooner rather than later. It has been through so much already. I have been stretched and bent and broken during my nights in the Bianci castle. Who knows how much fight I have left in my bones? In my skin? In my soul?

I can hear the breathing of the men behind me. Their footsteps are heavy and pounding. Four men, almost one thousand pounds of hot muscle and seething rage, have spread themselves out in the night to encircle and ensnare me.

Getting this far was a miracle.

And, as I'm beginning to realize, getting any farther will soon be an impossibility.

I go left, then right, winding through the labyrinth of interconnected alleyways. I run, run, run—until I'm aware that suddenly, I don't hear my pursuers anymore.

There is a rectangle of light at the end of the alleyway I've found myself in. I go towards it. My bare feet splash through puddles, crunch broken glass, step past rats and cockroaches skittering around the dark concrete. I'm bleeding, crying, sweating—but I can't slow down.

Don't stop. Don't stop. Don't stop.

I reach the mouth of the alley, burst out onto the street, and race halfway across without even bothering to check for oncoming traffic. I don't care anymore. If I die smeared across the grill of a taxi—well, so be it. Just another cruel twist of fate from a cruel and uncaring universe.

The night around me is silent and oppressive. It feels like the very air itself wants to suffocate me with its weight. Humidity and darkness combined are like a hand pressing against my chest, stopping me from drawing in a full breath. Time—brief, precious seconds—meanders past at the pace of a predatory shark trawling the dark ocean waters.

I don't have much of it left.

I freeze in the middle of the road. There is a streetlight at the intersection fifty yards to my left. The lamp casts a cone of orange light that looks far too warm and friendly for what's happening to me right now. I think, with the same dark sarcasm that has stuck with me throughout this entire nightmare, that whoever designed this world fucked up. That light should be a cold, vicious blue. Fluorescent. The kind that exposes everything and spares nothing.

I remember fluorescent lights. The first night I woke up in the men's castle, that was what greeted me. Harsh light. Cruel light. Illuminating faces that looked just as harsh and cruel, all sharp angles and deep shadows around the eyes—but God, those faces were beautiful, too. They made me understand why angels chose to follow Satan. Darkness can be beautiful. Darkness can be tempting. Darkness can swallow you whole and make you love every second of it.

The cone of light is empty. It reveals bare sidewalk, nothing more.

Then I blink.

A man steps into the light.

He is tall, almost impossibly tall, with shoulders as wide as a doorframe. He is too far away to make out much of his face. But I don't need to be close to know what he looks like. I have seen it plenty. Up close and personal, just inches away from mine. How many nights have I seen that face? Too many to count. In real life, in my dreams—it won't leave me alone. That proud, aquiline nose. Those verdant green eyes, like an ancient forest underneath the canopy of his thick, dark eyebrows.

This can't be real. I'm dreaming. I have to wake up.

But I know I'm not.

How many times over the last few weeks have I tried to pretend I was Dorothy in Oz? How many times did I click my heels together and say, "There's no place like home"? Too many to count.

But here's the other thing I've learned:

Home isn't heaven, either.

Home might even be worse than this hell I've found myself in. At least, in this messed-up nightmare, the demons announce themselves as such. They don't hide who they are and what they want.

Home... home is where the devils dress up as angels and say they're here to save you. Home is a thicket of lies. Home is a hell of its own making, too.

Funny that I should be thinking of home right now. Because the man standing underneath the light was the one who ripped back the curtain and showed me the ugly underbelly of everything I once knew and loved.

He sees me now. I can tell he does, though he doesn't move or acknowledge me at all. He simply stands under the light, awash in orange. He's wearing a dark navy suit over a crisp white shirt. Both are torn to shreds and stained with blood. One of his hands is bloody, too. It drips from his fingertips and puddles on the sidewalk beneath him.

His other hand is holding a gun.

I freeze like a deer caught in the headlights. He won't fire. At least, I don't think he will. But there are no rules left to be followed. The game has been broken wide open. Up is down and left is right. The good guys are the bad guys and the bad guys are—fuck, I don't know what they are. Or who they are. Or what they want.

As I watch, another man materializes next to the first. Just as tall, just as broad. His hair is shaggier, hanging almost down to his shoulders. I can see the glint of an ear piercing. I know from firsthand experience that the rest of his body is similarly riddled with piercings and tattoos. The angle of the streetlight throws his five-o'clock shadow into sharp relief. He looks dirty, savage, like a wild beast merely pretending to be a man.

I didn't know it was possible, but at the sight of him, my heart sinks even lower.

I'd known that he was with his brothers, of course. They were all after me, moving as one, as a pack of wolves, of hyenas. But somehow, seeing him here and now, in the dead of the night, is even more haunting than it was the first night I woke up.

He was the first one of them I saw. He sat there in the corner of the room they held me in. I heard him before I saw him, actually. The sound of a blade sliding against a whetstone, again and again.

Rasp. Rasp. Rasp.

When I opened my drug-addled eyes, I saw him there, casually leaning backwards in a stool propped against the stone wall like this was no big deal. Like he did this all the fucking time. Like sharpening his knife and looking at his bound captive girl was no big deal. Just another day in the life.

I knew instantly that he was unhinged. His eyes told the whole story. Pain swam in them like molten lava. He had honey-colored irises—if honey had a lethal aftertaste.

I see now that he is holding that same knife. His hands, like his brother's, are stained with blood.

I start to back away. I want to be anywhere but here.

As I watch, a third man steps into the light. He is jaw-droppingly beautiful. Even now, in the midst of all this whatever-you'd-call-it—chaos? nightmare? hellscape?—I sense his beauty and let out a soft sigh. His jaw is sharp enough to slice you wide open. His lips can say and do such beautiful things to me. I know this because he's said them. He's done them. Hell, I asked for it. I *begged* him to trace his lips down the curve of my neck, between my breasts, past the hollows in my hips, and down, down, down... I wanted it so badly. And he gave it to me—in a manner of speaking. But like an evil genie, the wish he granted was somehow everything I wanted and nothing of the sort, all at the same time.

The third man's eyes are cold, blue, and clear, like a husky's. Right now, they betray nothing. Not an ounce of emotion. A mountain lake, undisturbed by even the tiniest ripple. Like the first man, he is wearing a suit. The slacks, at least. The jacket must have been lost somewhere in the mayhem that all of us left behind. His white dress shirt is crisply ironed, the first few buttons rakishly undone.

Somehow, he made it through everything with only one drop of blood staining the collar.

I count the men again. One, two, three. Green eyes, blue eyes, honey eyes.

But the fourth is missing.

The one who started it all.

The one whose voice, whose touch, whose very essence is seared into my soul like a cattle brand.

Where is Vito Bianci?

I turn and find out immediately.

Vito's chest is as solid as granite when I turn and collide into him. How he snuck up behind me without making a sound, I'll never know. There are many things I'll never know about Vito, actually. He is like an ocean of oil, hiding so many secrets beneath his surface.

But I have seen some of them. There is a beating heart behind that chest. It is buried underneath pain—so much pain—but I have seen it in one beautiful, unforgettable glimpse. He may regret showing it to me. In fact, I know he does. It makes what he has to do next so much harder.

I take a deep breath and swallow past the knot in my throat. It's over for me now. I am back in the brothers' possession. Perhaps it was foolish to think I ever had a chance of becoming free again. That hope—that shattered, broken hope—is stabbing me in the heart right now like shards of glass that once made up a delicate sculpture. I shouldn't have ever hoped. It will make the ending that much worse.

I look up at Vito. He is not as tall as his younger brother, but he is the most muscular. He has the same nose that they all do. Strong, straight as an arrow, leading up into a proud forehead. Those eyes—I used to swear they were black all the way through, pupil and iris alike. I don't know anymore. I don't know anything anymore. What's real, what's fake, what's a lie, what's true?

Who the fuck knows?

"We have found you, Milaya Volkov," he growls in a voice deeper than sound, rasping like a metal edge on stone. "You cannot run anymore."

I don't say anything. There's nothing to say. He's right—I can't run anymore.

We stand there and stare at each other for a few long moments. My breath has slowed from short, sharp gasps to a soft inhale, exhale, inhale, exhale. He doesn't blink, doesn't move, doesn't say anything else.

Is it insane that I notice his smell? Blood and sweat and cologne all mixed together. It's as intoxicating as it was the very first time. I must be deranged. My time in their castle drove me mad. "Stockholm Syndrome" doesn't even begin to cover it.

Maybe I was wrong about being near the breaking point.

Maybe the truth is that I broke a long, long time ago.

I can sense the others drawing close around me. They step in and join me in a circle of darkness. I am surrounded now by a wall of men. They all have a similar smell. The same blood and sweat as Vito. But each of them bear a unique musk that is entirely their own.

Like a ballerina figurine in a toy box, I do a slow pivot and drink in the sight of each of them. Even now, I can see that my killers are gorgeous. Sculpted by the hands of angels.

Mateo, the wise one, the green-eyed.

Leo, the beautiful, the blue-eyed.

Dante, the wild, the honey-eyed.

And back to the front, to the beginning, to Vito, the leader, the black-eyed.

They're waiting for me to do something. To do anything.

I swallow again. It hurts. Christ, everything hurts, from the bottoms of my bleeding feet to the hair on my scalp, the same hair that each of these men has wound their hands through and tugged back on to make me moan and scream and beg in turns.

I didn't expect the end of my life to hurt this badly.

"Well?" I say with a voice cockier than I truly feel. I haven't made this easy on them since the night they took me. I don't plan on starting now. "You found me. Now what?"

"Now," Dante answers with wild, pain-drenched eyes, "we are going to finish what we started."

Click here to keep reading BROKEN SINS.

MAILING LIST

Sign up to my mailing list!
New subscribers receive a FREE steamy bad boy romance novel.

Click the link below to join.
https://readerlinks.com/l/1057996

ALSO BY NICOLE FOX

Kornilov Bratva Duet

Married to the Don (Book 1)

Til Death Do Us Part (Book 2)

Heirs to the Bratva Empire

Can be read in any order

Kostya

Maksim

Andrei

Tsezar Bratva

Nightfall (Book 1)

Daybreak (Book 2)

Russian Crime Brotherhood

Can be read in any order

Owned by the Mob Boss

Unprotected with the Mob Boss

Knocked Up by the Mob Boss

Sold to the Mob Boss

Stolen by the Mob Boss

Trapped with the Mob Boss

Volkov Bratva

Broken Vows (Book 1)

Broken Hope (Book 2)

Broken Sins *(standalone)*

Box Sets

Bratva Mob Bosses

Tsezar Bratva

Other Standalones

Vin: A Mafia Romance

Printed in Great Britain
by Amazon